The Highlander's Improper Wife

Tarah Scott & KyAnn Waters

Published by K.ink

The Highlander's Improper Wife, Copyright © 2014 by Tarah Scott and KyAnn Waters. All rights reserved. No part of this publication may be reproduced, stored in a retrieval system, or transmitted, in any form or by any means without the prior written permission of the authors, nor be otherwise circulated in any form of binding or cover other than that in which it is published and without a similar condition being imposed on the subsequent purchaser.

This is a work of fiction. Names, characters, places, and incidents are either the product of the author's imagination or are used fictitiously, and any resemblance to actual persons living or dead, business establishments, events, or locales, is entirely coincidental.

ISBN-13:978-1502934987

ISBN-10:1502934981

Cover Art: Diana Carlile
Artwork: Period Images

First Trade Paperback Printing by K.ink 2015

The Highlander's Improper Wife

10 9 8 7 6 5 4 3 2

If you purchased this book without a cover, you should be aware that this book is stolen property. It was reposted as "unsold and destroyed" to the publisher, and neither the author nor the publisher has received any payment for this "stripped book."

Trademarks Acknowledgement

The author acknowledges the trademarked status and trademark owners of the following wordmark mentioned in this work of fiction:

The Times: News Corporation

Acknowledgments

Many thanks to Diana Carlile for creating the perfect cover.

Chapter One

Newcastle, England, December 1798

Despite the crush of people that pressed into the intimate corner of the crowded ballroom, the din faded into the background when Lady Caroline Wilmont allowed the hooded blue domino to draw his cape close around them. She leaned against the stone pillar and he rested a muscular arm above her head.

His costume wasn't original—few at such masques were—but the piercing blue eyes staring back at her from behind the mask offered the hope she could forget the prison that awaited her tomorrow.

Guilt niggled. If her presence at the soiree was discovered...she commanded her nerves into submission. Responsibility be damned. She would leave before the assigned hour of two a.m. when the masks were to be removed. No one would know the future Viscountess of Blackhall had attended a masque. Tonight, she was simply one of the many masked women bent on seduction—and being seduced.

Caroline ducked her head, allowing the locks of her long blonde wig to fall to the sides of her face. A crescendo of violins rose from the orchestra. The beat of her heart matched the trilling vibrato. She turned her face just enough to be able to study her admirer through her lashes. His gaze boldly met hers, then dropped to the draped bodice of her Aphrodite costume. Warmth spread through her limbs and brought a flush to her cheeks.

The rich purple of the long sash around her neck contrasted with the stark white of the plunging décolletage designed to accentuate full breasts, bared to a hint of nipple pink. Her pulse skipped a beat. If she leaned forward a hair's breadth...

The crowd pressed closer, up the two steps that separated them from the dance floor. The masked gentleman's leg brushed her thigh, revealed by the slit in the costume's long skirt. She could scarcely believe her luck. A second move, and one so bold this early in the evening. The hour was just before midnight and the more prominent guests had yet to appear. If she had captured his imagination to the extent he would forsake other possibilities, this last night of freedom might cost less than the allotted two hours.

"Your beauty makes me forget my manners," the domino murmured.

She gave a low laugh. "I daresay your manners are impeccable—outside of this room."

His gaze locked onto her mouth. "Do you prefer impeccable manners?"

She drew her bottom lip between her teeth. His eyes darkened, and her heart skittered as he leaned into her. Caroline slid around the pillar towards the wall, intending to draw him into a more intimate semblance of privacy. Her hip collided with rounded buttocks. She twisted to the right. A masked joker grinned at her over the head of the lady she had bumped into. He reached out with the hand that was wrapped around the woman's waist and nipped at the skin just below Caroline's breast.

She turned back around and got a mouthful of her domino's hard chest. She snapped her head up, and blue eyes stared down at her in a blaze of desire. She froze as his mouth descended. Soft as velvet, his lips slid languidly over hers. He flicked his tongue against her lips and she breathed in the heavy aroma of cigars, and recognized the pungent taste of brandy. Her uncle smelt of brandy and cigars.

Uncle? She tensed, eyes locked on the domino's shadowed features. His seductive kiss played on her lips. An unpleasant tremor fluttered in her stomach. Damn her uncle. She closed her eyes tight and focused on the warmth of the domino's lips. A low groan rumbled from him. Strong, solid arms banded around her and pulled her closer. Caroline concentrated on the feel of her breasts flattened against the hard muscles of his chest. Why didn't her heart pound, her breath catch, her body yearn for his touch?

Fear surfaced. *No.* She refused to believe what her betrothed, John, had said only two months before his death. Despite the fact he had come from yet another night of drinking, gaming, and carousing, the accusation that she was a passionless husk had cut deep. The cloying scent of perfume and tobacco that clung to him had reminded her that he felt no regret about going from one woman's bed to another. But doubt lingered.

She forced back the memory. It wasn't lack of desire that kept her from enjoying the domino, but the dread of discovery. Once they were alone, she would discover the ecstasy of his lust. Her heart beat faster with the memory of overhearing John speak of how a woman had driven him mad by sucking and licking his cock. She planned to drive this man wild and discover the part of her that ached for a man's touch.

The domino deepened the kiss and Caroline envisioned him braced over her, hands on her bared breasts, his hard length rubbing against her pussy. Darker features and black hair unexpectedly replaced the fair-haired domino in her mind. A flicker of pleasure tightened her nipples and the desire streaked to the heated petals of her pussy.

Caroline clutched the domino's shirt. His grip tightened as his tongue curled around hers, tasting, stroking. She slipped her hands between their bodies and pressed against his sternum. The firm, contoured muscles of his chest quivered beneath her fingertips. She liked this, would gladly take him, and yet, she had expected something more.

He drew back and trailed fingers over the thin material of her costume, grazing the edge of her breast. From the corner of her eye, Caroline caught sight of lush, blonde hair piled atop the head of a woman wearing a Marie Antoinette costume. She froze. Only one woman between Newcastle and London had such luscious hair that she needed no wig to play Marie Antoinette. *Lady Margaret.*

What was Margaret doing here? Earlier that afternoon, when her mama had asked her if she planned to attend the ball, she had claimed to have a headache. She'd told Caroline privately that she found the ton even more tiresome in Newcastle than she did in London. Caroline would never have dared attend the masque in London, where she was sure to be recognized. But her uncle had insisted at nearly the last minute that they oblige her future father-in-law and hold the wedding in the chapel on his estate. So here in Newcastle, she had little fear of getting caught at the party. Her heart sank. Now Margaret had destroyed her last chance for seduction. There was nothing left but to flee.

The blue domino leaned forward and whispered in her ear, "Aphrodite."

His breath, warm and eager, brushed the tiny hairs on her skin. A shiver raced along her spine and made her scalp tingle. Yes. This she craved. *Damn. Too late, all too late.*

The domino withdrew enough to be able to look upon her face. "Perhaps we should find somewhere more private?"

If he had suggested that but five minutes ago! She would throttle Margaret. Caroline lifted a corner of her mouth in a half-smile. "Pray, sir, fetch me a punch. This room is a veritable sweatbox." She ran fingers over the swell of her breasts, wiping a trail in the sheen of perspiration beaded across her skin.

His gaze followed the action, eyes darkening before he returned his gaze to her face and gave a slight bow. "At your service."

He turned and took the two steps down to the dance floor, then began shouldering his way through the crowd towards the buffet table at the opposite side of the room. Caroline hesitated, the lost hope of feeling that muscled chest beneath her palms and his hard thighs heavy against her, suddenly bitter. She had planned intimate kisses, clandestine caresses, and the memory of a man's hard cock between her fingers. She planned to give all, save proof of her innocence. On the morrow, she would do her duty as the promised virgin. Now nothing. If Margaret caught her at the ball, there would be hell to pay.

Caroline swallowed the panic bubbling in her throat, and turned to the left, intending to skirt the wall to the French doors that lay a few feet away. She met the joker's gaze. He grinned. The woman with him faced Caroline and gave her a sultry look. Caroline turned to the right and glanced in the direction she'd seen Margaret. Where had she gone? Nerves sizzled with apprehension and tension in her neck promised a headache in the morning.

She looked back in the direction of her companion. He halted to the left of the masked dancers and turned to stare at her. A small smile curved one side of his mouth. Her stomach fluttered, then soured. The ball was the event of the season. He would be another ten minutes making his way through the crowd. By then, she would be on her way home. Caroline turned and hugged close to the column as she headed for the balcony doors. She slipped past couples in intimate conversation. Under her breath, she cursed again, and scanned the crowd as she sidestepped a woman dressed as Autumn. Once outside, she would make her way through the gardens to the servants' entrance, then to the front of the mansion where a hackney waited.

She was out the door, across the stone balcony and down the last of the four steps when behind her a voice said, "Have you gone mad?"

Caroline froze, skirt held above her ankles. It had been too easy. She released the dress and slowly turned. Lady Margaret stood at the top of the stairs, the ridiculous pannier she wore spanning half the width of the steps. Caroline started to speak, then paused when another masked domino and sultana emerged from the ballroom. He pulled the sultana closer and she responded with a giggle. They rushed down the stairs, headed for the seclusion of the gardens. Longing stabbed at Caroline. She was a fool to have thought she belonged here.

Margaret's gaze followed their retreat, then shifted back to Caroline. "Looking for a bit of privacy?"

Caroline ignored the cold—she had left her wrap inside and had not intended on retrieving it—and leaned against the stone pillar. "I am alone, as you can see."

"Yes, I can see you are...now." Margaret took two of the steps, stopping so that she towered over Caroline. "Perhaps you have a lover waiting in the garden?"

Caroline sighed. "How did you know it was me?"

Margaret snorted. "We have known one another since the nursery. I would know you in any disguise. Just as you recognized me—and do not deny that is the reason you fled." She descended to the fourth step so that they were eye level with each other and said in a voice barely audible over the music filtering from the ballroom, "You are to marry on the morrow. What in God's name are you thinking?"

"As you say, tomorrow I marry. I go from grieving betrothed to wife." *Unwanted wife*, she mentally corrected. So much so that her future husband's business had taken precedence over their marriage and he refused to come to England until the very day of their wedding. "Surely, I can have this," she added, "my last night of freedom."

Margaret arched a brow. "Do not expect the privileges of rank then flout the responsibilities."

Caroline snorted. "Responsibilities be damned. I have worn black a full year and will wed the Viscount tomorrow, as my rank dictates. Tonight, I am not Lady Caroline, heiress to twenty thousand pounds a year, soon to be Viscountess. Tonight, I am Aphrodite, the goddess of love and beauty, who indulges her whims as she wills."

A couple appeared from the garden shadows beyond the light cast by the open balcony doors. The dark wig on the woman dressed as Curiosity was askew and leaves clung to the cape on the gentleman dressed as Death.

Margaret frowned and waited until they'd ascended the stairs and entered the ballroom before saying, "If word of your escapade reaches his lordship, you may well not become Viscountess."

"By God, I shall rip off my mask now!" Caroline declared.

Margaret rolled her eyes. "Pray, forego the dramatics."

Caroline narrowed her eyes. "Where is your sense of adventure? What is this spell that has turned you into a prig?"

"Good sense and age," Margaret replied. "The same spell you should have fallen under long ago."

Caroline gave an unladylike snort. "A year of mourning has soured me. As if being betrothed to that indifferent man hadn't been enough," she added under her breath.

Margaret's face softened. "Perhaps his brother will be better."

Better? She'd heard rumors. Lord Taran Robertson demanded obedience. As apathetic as John had been, Taran was forceful in his cravings—his sexual cravings. She'd even heard he'd used a paddle on a mistress when she'd been disobedient. A thrill streaked along her spine. Controlling and dominant, yet virile and passionate. She remembered the new Viscount of Blackhall. Eyes the color of copper laced with amber strands had darkened to a rich brown when he'd met her gaze in the instant before bending over her hand. She'd been sixteen, too young to recognize the tremor of awareness in her stomach as desire.

When John died, Taran had become Viscount of Blackhall. A prickle skimmed her arms. Odd, that the same twist of fate that had taken her father had repeated itself and saved her from John. Both had died in riding accidents. Despite her lack of feeling for John, his death had come as a shock. Finding herself betrothed to the brother ere the body was cold had been an even greater shock. She'd had her uncle to thank for that. No. Her father. Had he not left his brother-in-law in charge of her fortune, her future might have looked very different.

Loneliness closed around her heart. She missed her father. He had been a good man, who couldn't accept that his wife's brother, privateer Phillip Etherton, was the infamous pirate Peiter Everston. The fortune Phillip Etherton had amassed came as a result of blurred lines between protecting the seas for the Crown, and murder. But wealth wasn't enough. Uncle wanted to join the elite circles of society, and her marriage to the Viscount of Blackhall was the price.

"John cared nothing for me," she said, more to herself than Margaret. "He was cold and unfeeling." As would be his brother. A lifetime of cold nights and dreary, lonely days stretched out before her.

Margaret placed a hand on her shoulder. "I have heard otherwise."

"From his mistresses, no doubt."

"A man may have as many mistresses as he likes," Margaret replied. "It is no shame to the wife."

"I shall provide the required heir," Caroline replied with an aplomb she was far from feeling. "I am going." She turned and continued down the stairs.

"Car—Aphrodite," Margaret called, but Caroline didn't turn back.

Chapter Two

"By God," Caroline cursed ten minutes later.

Lord Forbes had not been boasting when he'd said his garden maze was unmatched in all of northern England. She blew out a frustrated breath. Of all the nights to become lost in one of the damned labyrinths. She turned down another bend and a white stone statue became visible ahead on the left. Caroline groaned. Already, she'd seen half a dozen replicas of Greek and Roman goddesses. This statue, she realized upon approach, was a large cherubim. The half-moon peeked through a hole in the veil of clouds, illuminating an alcove just ahead.

"Thank God."

Caroline hurried forward. As expected, a stone bench lay nestled between the bushes. She hiked up her skirt and stepped onto the bench. Wind rustled across the hedge tops, setting her nerves more on edge. She scanned the acres of perfectly manicured shrubs that cut and curved in all directions.

"Bloody hell," she cursed.

In the distance, the rear of the maze gave way to trees that stretched heavenward, but she stood no chance of navigating through the twists and turns that led to them. She faced the mansion and studied the path leading back in that direction.

"Left, right, second right, third—no—second left," she said, while reciting a silent vow never to have a stupid maze on any of her properties.

Caroline turned to jump from the bench and shrieked. A masked, kilted god stood nearly eye-to-eye with her. She stumbled back. He seized her waist and yanked her forward. She instinctively threw her arms around his neck to keep from falling and her cheek met the warm, damp flesh of his shoulder. Her heart raced at a gallop.

"Careful, my lady." The deep, cultured English accent didn't quite disguise the hint of Scottish burr.

Gooseflesh chilled her arms. Yet, her body warmed. Her nipples hardened to erect peaks against the thin fabric of her costume.

"My lady," he prodded.

Fear that he would feel the heat of her arousal immobilized her.

"I can stand here all night, if it pleases you," he murmured.

The erotic vision of him doing just that while she rubbed her nipples against his hard body snapped her head up. Dark eyes indistinguishable from the shadow stared at her through a black eye mask.

A flurry of butterflies swirled in her tummy. "I am lost." She cursed the breathless note in her voice.

"Nay, I found you." He shifted. A dusting of hair at the nape of his neck tickled her fingertips. He slowly slid her body against his as he lowered her to the ground.

The scent of leather and cloves clung to him. She inhaled, heart fluttering, then tilted her head up. "You have my gratitude, sir. I would be even more grateful if you could direct me out of this…this…labyrinth."

"Even *more* grateful?" he repeated.

Caroline became aware of the rough wool of his kilt against the sensitive skin of her thigh. She willed her racing heart to slow. Here was the warm flush that had been missing with the domino in the ballroom. Cruel fate. *Far too late has come my redemption.*

"Would you like to return to the masque?" His hands dropped from her waist.

A strange sense of loss washed over her. She steeled her resolve to go home and stepped away from him. "I am leaving."

"Through the gardens?" The harshness in his tone startled her. "It is more likely you fled the festivities to meet someone. The blue domino, perhaps?"

Caroline stiffened. "Anyone attending the masque is well aware of the frolicking taking place in these gardens."

"Frolicking?" he repeated.

"You are here, sir. Need I feel recrimination because I am a woman? Bah," she added in a mutter. "I have no time for this foolishness."

She meant to head towards the mansion, but he blocked the way, so she turned deeper into the maze.

"My lady." He grasped her arm.

She dropped her gaze to his long, dark fingers. His hold, though light, held her firm. An unexpected vision of those strong fingers gripping her hips while he pumped into her from behind caused her to snap her head up.

"No time for *this foolishness?*" He lifted his free hand and drew a thumb along her bottom lip.

Heat coursed through her veins. There was no misreading the invitation. Had he read her mind? He offered what she so desperately desired, a night of passion in the arms of a man who hungered for her. This man would demand more than she could afford—but suddenly wanted with every fiber of her being to give.

He pulled her an inch closer. She took the step haltingly. Amusement showed in the upturn of his mouth and he tugged her so near that her nipples came into contact with his warm chest. A tremor radiated through her. In all her planning, she hadn't considered a man might steal her breath as well as rational thought. Heat crept into her face. She disengaged her arm from his grasp.

"Forgive me. I—" She faltered, unable to trust her ability to resist should he twitch even a muscle. "I fear I may have grossly misrepresented my position."

He gave a low chuckle. "Most who attend these events misrepresent their position. That is the brilliance of the masque, Aphrodite, the night is ours."

A jolt to her pussy drenched her folds. She took a step back only to find the awareness intensified when he countered by stalking closer. The prickle of the hedge against her back halted her retreat. He stopped a hair's breadth from her. Scents of peony and juniper mingled with the dizzying scent of him, assailing her senses. Caroline tilted her head up. Moonlight glinted in the eye slits of his mask.

She drew a sharp breath when he bent and whispered a kiss on her neck. His lips brushed the shell of her ear. "You are beautiful." He flicked his tongue against her beating pulse point. "I want to steal you away, but I will settle for having you here." He cupped the back of her head, angling her mouth for a kiss. She parted her lips and his tongue glided along hers. A low groan rolled from his chest as he pressed the hard length of his cock against her abdomen.

"Having me?" Clutching fistfuls of his shirt, Caroline allowed her head to fall back.

"Yes," he murmured, and blazed a trail of kisses along her jaw, down her neck, to the curve of her shoulder. He traced the swell of her breast, then found and pinched a beaded nipple.

She cried out. He tugged down her bodice, exposing a taut tip, then plucked the bud between his lips and gently bit.

"So sweet."

"My lord," she breathed.

He threaded his fingers through her wig. The wig shifted. Caroline jerked to shove it back into place, brushing her hip against his erection. He sucked in a breath and yanked up his kilt. She froze at sight of the full erection jutting towards her, as if begging her to take what she wanted. His warm fingers closed over hers and guided her hand downward, where he firmly wrapped her fingers around his shaft.

She startled at the velvety smoothness. He was so…she squeezed. Not rough or calloused—her heart raced—what had she expected? Caroline realized with a horrified start that she had no idea what to expect, and released him as if he were a snake. She flattened her palms on his chest in an effort to distance them and met the warmth of his sculpted torso.

"Good Lord." She snatched her hands back.

He cupped her derriere, lifted her more intimately against his arousal, and rested his forehead against hers, their masks touching. "Let me touch you."

Her pulse jumped. They were alone. Margaret believed she had fled the masque. What could a little touch hurt?

"Yes," she whispered before she could change her mind.

He set her feet back on the ground, then slipped a finger beneath the dress and shoulder. Gooseflesh raced along her arms where his warm fingers touched her. She shivered. His gaze remained on her as he slipped the dress off her arms. The fabric dropped to her elbows, exposing both breasts.

Silence drew out between them. She trembled, but knew her reaction was fear and not the damp air that crept across her flesh. What had happened? Had he changed his mind? Caroline stiffened. Was she not beautiful enough? She lifted her gaze to find obsidian eyes staring from within the slits of the mask. He watched for another long moment, then lifted a hand and cupped a breast. She shuddered.

His mouth curved into a slight smile. "Do I please you, Aphrodite?"

Caroline was unable to utter a sound. He gave a low laugh, then bent and traced a circle around her nipple with his tongue. Cool night air chilled the places his hot mouth and tongue touched. She grasped his shirt. A woman's moan of pleasure abruptly intruded on their solitude.

He straightened. Caroline yanked her bodice over her breasts. He pulled her close, sheltering her from view. Whispered words drifted towards them from the maze entrance.

"Bloody hell," Caroline cursed.

He looked down at her. "Interesting vocabulary, my lady."

She scowled. "Not nearly as interesting as our present position."

"Indeed."

There was no mistaking the laughter in his voice and Caroline narrowed her eyes with the intent to chastise him when the woman giggled.

Caroline jerked her gaze in the direction of the voices. "They are searching for a private nook."

"I shall inform them that this particular nook is occupied."

He started to turn and she seized his arm. "No!" The voices drew closer. "Good God."

Caroline released him, and rearranged the sash. The bodice didn't fit as snugly as it had earlier.

She blew out a frustrated breath. "Do you think we will be discovered?"

"There is always a chance."

More giggles followed, closer this time. Caroline squinted past him into the shadows. His warm fingers grazed her cheek beneath her mask. She lifted her gaze up to his. He stared down at her and her pulse spiked. A woman's low moan sounded nearer. Caroline's masked lord grasped her shoulders and maneuvered them a few inches to the left, then back between the bench and denser foliage. The rustling of fabric drew her attention and she peered around his broad shoulders.

"Shh," he whispered against her ear.

A woman dressed as a chambermaid faced the stone cherubim, gripping the angel's shoulders as a masked bandit stood behind her and bunched her drab, brown dress up around her waist.

The bandit swatted her backside with an open palm. A blush of rose colored her cheek.

"Please, do not hurt me," she begged with feigned acquiescence. "I promise to be good."

He swatted her again and chuckled. "That I know, I believe I have had you before."

The bandit held the maid's dress in place, while loosening the tie on his pantaloons with his free hand, then shoved them down far enough to free his cock. The man took a step forward and plunged his engorged member into the woman. Caroline's mouth fell open. The kilted stranger pressed closer. His breathing grew shallow and fingers tightened on Caroline's hips. Did he want the same pleasure from her?

"Beg for my cock," the bandit said. "Beg me to fuck you."

"Please. Please, fuck me," she pleaded as the man thrust his large, ruddy cock in and out of her. Her cries of pleasure matched the rhythm of his pumping hips.

Another loud smacking sound made Caroline jump.

"Oh yes!" the woman cried.

Caroline couldn't tear her eyes from the sight. "Do you suppose this will take long?"

"If it is done right," the kilted god replied.

She glanced at him and his gaze slowly tracked her face and down her body. He growled and pulled her close. Feral grunts from the man joined the woman's pants. Caroline's would-be lover gripped her derrière and pressed her mound against his shaft. A tingle started between her legs and radiated out. The steady, yet rapid beat of her heart throbbed in her nipples and between her legs. He rolled his erection against her a second time and she answered with a tremulous undulation of her hips against him.

"You surely know how to drive a man to his knees," he said.

Caroline glanced down. His tartan stood at a point, aimed towards her, testament to his arousal. She returned her gaze to his face. "I would like to drive you to your knees, my lord."

He stared as if daring her to test his worthiness, to push him to the edge, then beyond. She wrapped her fingers around his shaft through his tartan. He shuddered and an unexpected sense of power swelled inside her. A loud moan from the woman made Caroline's heart pound harder. *Dare I?*

Caroline glanced up at him. Then she knelt.

"My lady," he rasped.

She lifted his kilt, exposing heavy, muscular thighs, then lifted it higher. She gasped. The sight of him, the smell so close, intoxicated her beyond any wine she'd drunk tonight. Deep red, his cock jutted from a thatch of dark, tight curls. Tentatively she closed her hand around the girth. He sucked in a ragged breath. She instantly released him.

"Does it hurt?"

He gave a strangled laugh. "Aye."

He grasped the base of his shaft with one hand and placed the other on her head. She swatted at the hand grasping her wig. If he knocked the wig from her head, the disguise was worthless.

"Take me in your mouth." His strained voice turned gravelly.

He slid his hand higher along the thick, veined stalk. She breathed in the musky essence as her masked lover stroked the length, pulling back the foreskin to reveal a large, mushroom-shaped head. Clear liquid seeped from the tip. Caroline touched the leaking slit, smoothing the slippery cream over the crown. Sticky, yet the velvety skin felt hot to the touch.

Anxiety surfaced with the memory of overhearing John tell of how women pleasured men in this manner. She had gone to the stables in search of him and stopped short at hearing his voice from within one of the stalls. "I tell you, Matthew, when Clarice took my cock in her mouth, she near did me in with the first stroke."

The flush Caroline had felt evaporated at the raucous laughter that followed. She had determined to find and bed a young stable boy. Instead, she'd found herself awaiting John in the drawing room like a good soon-to-be-Viscountess.

Her tummy tightened. This man seemed to share John's baser desires. His cock pulsed. What if she didn't please him? She steeled her nerves and placed a hand over his. With a breath, she leaned forward and took him into her mouth.

"Sweet Christ," he ground out.

Caroline glanced up and found him staring as she opened wider and took more of the engorged length into her mouth. The taste of the tangy sweet excretion from the tip was pleasant, but what now?

He must have understood her silent question because he whispered in soft, encouraging words, "Do what you will. I am yours."

He released his shaft and, covering her hand with his, helped build a rhythm with her strokes. Caroline sucked on the smooth crown and slid her lips along the shaft. She unexpectedly grazed him with her teeth. He jerked and she released him, tumbling to her backside.

She stared up at him, heart pounding. "I—I am sorry."

He gave a strangled laugh and pulled her back onto her knees. "Take me into your mouth again."

He tucked his kilt into his belt then, legs spread, held his cock to her face and cupped the wrinkled pouch hanging beneath. Caroline adjusted herself on her knees more comfortably. In the years to come, this night would remind her that she was a woman capable of inciting a man's passion. Perhaps he, too, would remember the rustle of wind in the trees and the scent of juniper in the air…and the squeals of lovers in the adjacent area. Caroline grimaced. She could do without the woman's cries.

Steadying her trembling fingers, she worked his shaft between her lips with renewed zest. A hint of saltiness sizzled on her tongue. She swallowed and licked the length, dragging her tongue from base to tip, before sucking him deep into her mouth until the crown touched the back of her throat. Slowly withdrawing, she stroked the taut skin, mouth meeting fist in the center of his shaft.

Warmth infused her. Her masked lover groaned, pumping his hips. He gently cupped the sides of her head, but didn't interfere with her rhythm. In an effort to discern his likes, she listened for the change in breathing and subtle shifts in his body.

With a low feral growl, he ripped his cock from her mouth, angling to the side. Cream spurted from his shaft. Muscles in his thighs tensed, then relaxed. The heavy musk scent of his essence made her mouth water. Why had he pulled away? Gripping the back of his thigh, she spun him towards her and took his rod into her mouth.

"Wait." He clutched her shoulder, but she had already begun sucking the head. "By God—*fuck*."

She lapped until he glistened. Yes, she could see why a man would be driven crazy by a woman's mouth. Disappointment unexpectedly surfaced. As a wife, she wouldn't dare pleasure her husband in this fashion. Lust coiled in her tummy. She wouldn't have the courage to drop to her knees for the Viscount of Blackhall, nor would she beg for the pleasure of her husband.

Caroline lifted her gaze. This man begged for nothing. Tonight's memory must last a lifetime, for she would never witness stark lust on her husband's face like that of her masked lord.

Chapter Three

The woman was a she-devil. Innocent as a girl just out of the schoolroom, she had driven him as wild as any mistress, nonetheless. Innocence and sin. Heaven and sweet hell. What was such a woman doing at a masque—what had she been doing dallying with William Edmonds, Viscount of Thornhaven? What did it matter? She had left the earl in the ballroom. And now, she was here with him, submitting to his needs, offering her treasures to him—if only for the night.

Might he see her again? Tomorrow—curse God—tomorrow he was to wed. Instead of this vixen in his bed, he would plough into the dry channel of a woman who had no more use for him than she'd had his brother.

Guilt stabbed at him. She had been but a child when he'd met her. His brother had died a year ago. Not nearly long enough to prepare a man to bed his brother's betrothed.

She adjusted his plaid and slowly rose. He pulled her close, sealed their lips with a kiss. The taste of his musk combined with her feminine scent nearly undid him. What would she do if he tossed her over his shoulders and fled with her back to Strathmore? What would his family do if he married a Sassenach other than the one intended for him? What would she do once she found herself abducted to Scotland?

Taran had never kept an unwilling woman. Aphrodite muddled his thinking. A tryst in the gardens wasn't enough. He wanted her. More than he'd wanted a woman in…in longer than he could remember. But he wasn't yet at the point of locking his paramours in the dungeons of Strathmore.

Taran pulled back. The blonde wig sat askew on her head. What was her natural color?

He realized they were once again alone.

"I believe it is safe to leave."

Her full lips lifted in a soft smile. Tonight wasn't just about sating his needs, but hers as well. He would milk every drop of pleasure from her body.

She shivered.

Taran wrapped his arm around her shoulders and pulled her flush to his side. "The night is young, my lady. I will warm you in my carriage." Her mouth parted in surprise, and he chuckled. "Did you think my pleasure ended the night?" He brushed her nipple with his thumb. "Rest assured, your pleasure is still to come."

She gasped and the soft sound filled him with the need to plunge his shaft into her warm heat. He envisioned her riding him—hard, and all night. Passion, unbridled and uninhibited. Nothing less than full consummation would slake his need. Once she laid sprawled across his bed—Christ, he couldn't take her to his father's estate. William's home would have to do. Could he wait that long?

She glanced past him.

Taran tensed. She had dallied with William in the ballroom. "Is someone expecting you?"

"Do not be ridiculous," she said in an impatient tone.

The milkmaid and bandit were gone. Surely she didn't fear them.

"Something is amiss," he said.

She hesitated.

Taran caressed a cheek with the back of a hand. "We are friends, are we not? Secret lovers for this one night? Tell me anything, my lady, and the secret goes with me to the grave."

"I must—"

"I tell you it is true," a woman's voice interrupted her. "I heard it myself, Lord Blackhall is here."

Taran tensed.

"Here?" a man replied. "At a masque?" He snorted. "That prig would no more deign to lower himself to mingle with English Society than he would—" The man broke off. "Well, he just would not."

Taran mentally laughed. The man was right.

"Well," the woman sniffed, her voice nearer, "Lady Haverly says he *is* here."

Taran offered thanks to his friend. William had prevailed upon him to 'mingle with English Society'. Had he not come, he wouldn't have met the woman at his side. Taran looked down at her. Her face was white.

"My lady," he whispered, realizing the couple would pass them in seconds.

He bit back a laugh. She still feared discovery. He shoved her into the hedge and cut off her surprise, mid-squeak, with a kiss. She arched into him. Her mouth opened and he swept inside with his tongue. She tasted sweeter with each wet, passionate stroke. The heat of arousal surged into his shaft.

"Lady Haverly is a notorious gossip," the man said as they passed. "And a drunk."

"No need to be unkind," the woman said as they turned the next bend.

Taran wrenched his mouth from Aphrodite's and buried his face in her neck. He slid a hand down to her rounded bottom and gently squeezed. His heart thundered. He wouldn't settle for a quick romp in front of the cherubim as had the maid and bandit. He needed time to explore every inch of the goddess' body to learn what brought her to mind-bending pleasure. When she saw the ecstasy he could give, she wouldn't be able to resist taking him as a lover.

"I—I must go," she said into his chest.

He pulled her from within the hedge and headed towards the rear of the maze. He navigated several turns when a woman's soft moans sounded up ahead. Arousal hardened his cock. Aphrodite halted. Taran pulled her into the crook of his arm and gritting his teeth.

The swish of wool rasped against his swelling shaft.

"They care nothing for us," he whispered as he started forward again.

He quickened his pace. Her hold on his arm tightened.

"I am as eager as you to leave," she said breathlessly, "but must we sprint?" Taran slowed.

She fell into step beside him. "Have you a curfew?"

"Not since I was a lad and my father attempted to keep me out of mischief."

"Unlearned lessons, I see."

"You have indulged in your share of mischief," he replied. "I wager the blue domino still searches for you."

Her grip tightened. He liked the feel of her long fingers around his arm.

"In the ballroom," she began, but paused, then said, "I had decided not to remain at the masque."

Taran halted. "What changed your mind?"

She gave a low, throaty laugh that unnerved him. "You did."

He glanced at her profile, unable to tear his gaze from the seductive smile hinted at in the corners of her mouth. "And if I choose not to release you?" Her gaze narrowed.

"A jest," he quickly whispered. "Forgive me. We have tonight."

Taran didn't want to waste another moment when he could have her panting and writhing beneath him.

He led her around three turns, then a left, only to come to a dead end. Taran cursed.

"Lost again," she muttered.

"I will find the exit soon, or beat a path through the damned bush," he growled, and led her forward. "To the left, always to the left," he murmured. "It is inevitable we find the way out of this madness."

"So you say," she replied.

He cast her a glance. "Yes, well I had hoped on luck."

"Perhaps we have exhausted our good fortune for the day."

He had to agree. Finding her was the only stroke of good luck amidst a streak of bad luck that had begun with his brother's death and would continue with his marriage tomorrow. In one fell swoop, Mistress Fortune had saddled him with a lifetime of bad luck. The absurdity of wasting the few precious moments he had with Aphrodite, lost in a labyrinth, was almost comical.

The whinny of horses and the clatter of hooves on cobblestone faintly sounded up ahead. Taran made a quick turn at the next bend, bringing them face-to-face with the rear gate. Aphrodite gave a small cry of surprise. Taran threw back the latch and opened the gate with the intention of fetching his carriage. He stopped, a thought crossing his mind. If he left her, would she disappear? She was certain to balk at the notion of accompanying him to his carriage. She would be right. A tryst at the masque was permissible. Aphrodite leaving the ball with the Scot all recognized as Lord Blackhall would make the morning *Times*. The lady's reputation would be in ruins. A hired carriage would have to do. Away from prying eyes, he could dispense with her clothes—and that damn mask and wig.

They stepped from the alley and he started across the street towards a respectable looking carriage sitting in front of a townhouse. He glanced at her. She wore no cloak. What had the little fool meant, leaving the safety of the gardens for the public streets in that costume?

"I have a coach—" she began.

"Hush," he cut her off as they neared the hackney.

He released her and reached into his shirt pocket for his small purse. Taran opened the door.

The driver's head snapped in their direction. "Hey there, I ain't open for business. I have a customer—"

Taran pulled a coin from the purse and tossed it to him. The man caught the glistening gold piece without hesitation. He cast the lady a glance, clearly taking in her costume, then bent forward to examine the coin in the streetlight as Taran grasped her waist.

"What—" she began, but he cut off the protest by hoisting her into the coach.

Taran grasped the carriage door. "Drive until I say otherwise and there will be another of those for you at the end of the trip." He leapt into the carriage, slamming the door shut behind him.

"At your service," the driver called, and whipped the reins.

Taran settled into the velvet seat across from Aphrodite. The coach lurched into motion, sending the flame in the corner lamp into a momentary dance.

"I must return to my carriage," she said in a quiet voice.

Taran studied her.

"I am at your mercy." The defiant lift of her chin belied the words.

He leaned forward and grasped her chin with two fingers. "No secrets, remember, my lady?"

Light from the lantern, low, but distinct, illuminated the guilt that flashed in her eyes. His heart rate accelerated. What could she possibly be hiding? He brushed her soft skin with his thumb, then leaned back against the cushion.

"Come," he said, "was it not you who said a woman need feel no shame for attending a masque?"

"It is not shame, I feel, but wonder at being kidnapped."

Chapter Four

Taran's body tensed when her gaze turned to steel.

"I am to wed," she said.

"To wed—you mean—" He stared. "What in God's name are you doing at this masque?" But he knew the answer. Innocence and sin. Heaven and sweet hell. When she'd first touched his cock with those delicate, *inexperienced* fingers, he'd nearly exploded.

"Christ," he muttered.

She had purposefully misled him. He should turn her over his knee and paddle her backside. Or her soon-to-be-husband should.

He was a fool. At cards he beat the most skilled player, few dared face him in a dawn appointment, yet this wisp of a woman had brought him to his knees when she'd knelt and taken him into her mouth.

Moonlight seeped through the crack in the window drape and fell across the purple sash that now lay unevenly beneath her breasts. As if reading his mind, she slid the drapery closed.

Taran lifted his eyes to her face, bathed in the soft light of the interior lamp. "Why attend the masque?" he demanded.

Her gaze dropped.

The carriage bumped and rolled along the lane for a long moment before he prompted, "My lady?"

Her eyes rose to meet his. "You know as well as I that a woman has only that which is given her."

Taran thought of the woman who would be his wife tomorrow. Condemned to life with a man she had met once as a girl, her betrothed's brother, a man she didn't know, but must take into her bed on the day they wed.

"I decided—" Aphrodite paused. "I decided to take something for myself."

Taran released the breath he held. This he understood. "Many hours remain before morning. There are ways we may pleasure one another and satisfy your husband in the bargain."

Her expression turned wary.

"Something for yourself?" He extended a hand.

A moment passed, and a vice-like pressure squeezed his chest as an unexpected urge arose to protect her—to claim her for his own. He had no business opening his heart to her. Despite the logic, a fissure in his armor-plated shell cracked. She placed her hand in his and he breathed again.

She moved to his side of the carriage and Taran pulled her close. He kissed her, trailed a hand over her ribs, then cupped a breast, pinching the pebbled nipple until her breath caught and she trembled in his arms.

In his imagination, they lay in a feather bed next to a warm fire while he filled her with his cock and tasted her pleasure in hot, wet kisses. Tonight they had a rented carriage and stolen touches.

He brushed her ear with his lips. "Remove your mask."

She pushed him back so that she could look into his face. "We have left the masque, but the rules prevail."

"Even in the cover of darkness?" He leaned across the seat and blew out the lamp. The compartment plunged into pitch black. He sat back beside her. "My hands shall be my eyes." He removed his mask, set it on the opposite cushion, then reached for hers.

"My lord, no." The fear in her voice reminded him of her innocence and he silently swore constraint.

"I promise, we shall don our disguises before first light."

She tensed, but said nothing when, with careful, delicate movements, he unpinned her wig and laid it onto the opposite bench. He slipped the mask from her face and laid it on the cushion.

Taran cupped her cheek, traced the high arch of her delicate brow, and the length of her nose. Smooth skin, soft as silk, warmed beneath his fingers. Hot breath fanned his thumb as he traced her lips. She flicked her tongue against his skin. Taran stilled. She licked him again, more deliberately this time.

He pushed his thumb past her lips, into her warm, wet mouth. Her tongue curled around his thumb, mimicking the motion from when she'd sucked the head of his rod in the garden. The sensation rushed into his shaft. He felt the tug as acutely in his balls as in the tip of his cock.

He growled and hauled her onto his lap. Taran pulled her bodice down and over her arms, releasing the dress in a bunch around her waist. He kneaded the firm globes, tracing circles with a thumb on the soft skin. Leaning her back, he bent and captured one taut nipple between his lips. Moist and succulent, sweet and intoxicating. Her breath caught and she clutched his shoulders. Shivers travelled over her flesh. The carriage was warm, dark, and her throaty gasp of pleasure swelled his cock to an agonizing length.

She moaned, arching into his mouth. Taran kissed lower. He slid her from his lap, then knelt on the floor. Inching her dress down as he swirled his tongue along her belly and around her navel. Sweat, salty, and musky tasting, beaded on her quivering flesh. He inhaled, deeply drinking in the scent of her arousal as well as the hint of perfumed soap.

"Lift your hips."

She did, and he pulled the dress down her legs and tossed it onto the empty seat. He slipped off the right slipper, gently massaging her instep. He did the same with the left foot.

He sat back on his haunches and lifted her leg.

"Are you ready to discover the pleasure of passion?" He sucked a toe into his mouth.

Her startled cry came in unison with the rocking carriage as it hit a pothole. Taran rained kisses along one leg, then the other. She grasped his forearm. He lifted her hand and one at a time, he slipped each of her fingers into his mouth and sucked them.

"I am on fire," she breathed.

"Wait, my lady, for you are about to learn to fly."

He spread her thighs. The heady aroma of her wet pussy enveloped him. He had to taste her. "You have brought me to my knees."

He slid his palms beneath her rounded buttocks and pulled her to the edge of the seat. He blew against her mound before pressing his lips against her tender, heated folds.

"My lord." Her voice trembled. "I—" She gasped. "I feel as though I will surely die if I do not have your touch," she said as she opened her legs wider, "here."

Taran trailed a finger through the juices that drenched the thin ribbon of downy hair covering her nether lips. Dragging his tongue along the seam, he teased her, drove her to wriggle against him, but he didn't part her folds to ease the ache building within her. She was so eager for pleasure, yet

The Highlander's Improper Wife

he paused at an unwanted thought forming in his mind. What if he were not the first? Jealousy coiled in his gut.

"Have you been touched before?" he whispered.

She gasped and her thighs tightened around his head. "I have told you that I am yet to wed. I am a virgin."

"Aye, a virgin who thrusts against my mouth like a woman accustomed to having a man between her legs."

She seized his hair and yanked—hard.

He growled. The she-devil had returned. "Have I angered you, my lady?"

"You have. Remove yourself from between my legs and return my dress."

Even in the dark, he sensed the daggers aimed from her eyes at his skull. "Nay. You wanted a night of pleasure."

"Brute." She squirmed.

Taran held fast to her hips and once again sank his mouth into her heated mound, sliding his tongue between her folds. She stiffened and cried out. Taran released her and carefully spread the engorged petals of her pussy. He curled his tongue around her erect nub, sucked it between his lips, then lapped the length of her fast and furiously.

She trembled against his mouth. He thrust his tongue into her channel. His nostrils flared and his throat tightened. Aphrodite spread her legs wider. He angled his head, devouring her.

"My lord," she gasped, and pumped her hips against his mouth.

He understood the silent demand, but dared not penetrate her with a finger for fear of breaking the maidenhead. In the confined space of the carriage, he couldn't stretch her opening, worship her body in the manner she deserved. But, by God, he would show her passion. When this night was finished, she would know that she was more than a simple conquest.

Taran licked, nibbled, and sucked her folds until she screamed. Her body jerked and her legs locked to the side of his head. And still she bucked, a wild bird released to soar higher and higher until her body trembled and sweet cream gushed from her channel. "More." She clutched at his shoulders. "My God, more." She panted, thrusting against his mouth.

"Please."

The lady wanted cock and he couldn't give it to her. Nor could he deny her. Taran circled her opening with his finger, then turned his hand palm up and slid his middle finger into her hot, tight passage. She moaned as he pulled out and eased in again.

"Yes. Yes." She clutched his wrist and forced him deep.

She was hot, slick and tight. Slipping into her heat, he curled his finger, rubbing against the secret, sensitive part of her channel wall.

She wildly pumped her hips against his hand as he plunged his finger in and out of her. With his other hand, he reached beneath his kilt and grasped his cock. In a matching rhythm, he worked them both into a frenzy. Taran withdrew his finger from her passage, then slid two fingers inside, slowly stretching the opening. Muscles in his arms bunched as he fucked her with his hand. She seized his cock. He jerked his fingers from inside her. She sat up and slid forward on the seat.

"Fuck," he ground out.

She rubbed her heated flesh against his length. The hairs on her pussy tickled his shaft in agonizing delight. Muscles in his arse clenched with each thrust along her drenched folds. Gripping her hips, he lifted her and sat on the seat with her straddling him. He supported her hips, sliding her along his cock as she rode him without penetration.

"Yes," she cried, and clutched his shoulders, grinding her hips up and down in exquisite torture against him.

"There must be a way," she gasped.

Taran froze. Did she mean— "No," he said in a hoarse voice. "It would mean deceiving your husband."

She leaned so close. Her breath bathed his face. "I *choose* this lie."

Before he could reply, she stole his breath with an open-mouth kiss. She sucked his tongue, swept his mouth with hot, darting strokes, and pressed her breasts into his chest. Taran understood the demand. He pulled back and she trailed kisses along his jaw and down his neck.

"You are so small, so tight. There would be little pleasure for you the first time. Let him take your maidenhead, then I can show you pleasure without recourse."

She reached between them and grasped his shaft. "But there is a way?"

"*No.*"

"Men know these things," she insisted.

Pleasure radiated from his cock and through his body. He thrust into her palm. "Would you have me take your maidenhead, then face a dawn appointment with your enraged husband?"

She kissed him. "Is my innocence any more intact because you have not completed the act? My God, look at me."

"Yes," he replied. "Despite the fact I tasted between your legs, your innocence is intact."

"Liar." She lifted herself up so that she could tease his cock at the opening of her channel.

He sucked in a breath. "There will be pain."

"Life is pain," she replied.

She was right. And he couldn't refuse her.

"Burn into your memory what happens tonight, for you shall have to play the part for your husband."

She covered his face in kisses and positioned herself over his shaft.

"Do not forget the blood on the sheets," Taran said, his mind in half a fog. "Give him wine. If he is in his cups, he will pay less attention and have little care for your pleasure."

Taran tamped down a flicker of guilt. How much care had he planned to take with his future wife's pleasure?

He threaded his fingers though Aphrodite's hair and forced her head back in a vain attempt to discern her face in the dark. "And if the babe that comes this year is not—" He froze. "When are you to wed?"

"What does it matter?"

"I will take care, but there are no guarantees. If you find yourself with child…"

A moment of silence passed before she said, "I have no fear. The wedding is soon. I will not say when."

Or where, he thought, and said, "And if the babe is not your husband's?"

"Only God can know who the father is."

The carriage slowed and rumbled over a several bumps. Propriety be damned, his life be damned. Her fucking husband be damned. Taran savagely claimed her lips. He would burn his memory into her mind. Sear her flesh with his. From this moment forward she would compare her husband to the night she spent in his arms. He would take her to the edge of reason and plunge her into the deepest, darkest places of pleasure. This damned his soul, but he would send her to her husband spoiled.

His heart rate spiked. *Let her husband discover the deception. Then I will claim her.*

Taran yanked his shirt free of the kilt and began unbuttoning it. The carriage turned a corner and her elbow jerked and struck his arm.

He paused. "If you are uncertain…"

Cool fingers groped his arm, found the shirt buttons and finished unbuttoning the last two. He shoved the shirt back from his chest, then yanked his kilt up to his waist. His bare leg touched hers and warmth shot to his cock.

"Come." He reached beside him into the blackness.

She clasped his fingers for support as she straddled his lap.

He kissed her. "You may still turn back."

She pressed a finger to his lips. "Shh. I am not afraid."

"Ah, love. You should be."

She took a deep breath and slowly exhaled. "How much more do I fear the woman I would become without tonight?"

Taran hesitated, stunned by the honest admission. He damned his good intentions to hell, and kissed her. He slipped his tongue into her mouth, pulling forth a moan of pleasure. Pebbled nipples pressed into his chest. She trailed her fingers up his torso, petting the trail of hair, and finally curling over his shoulders. Angling right, then slowly left, he kissed her lips. He fondled a breast with one hand, with the other he detailed each rib, caressed the soft satin flesh of her hips, then parted her damp curls.

Her head fell back and she ground against his arousal. "Please, my lord, do not stop."

Taran sucked her neck, grazing her flesh with his teeth as he struggled for control. He wanted to take her slowly. He slipped a finger into her. She moaned and he plunged harder, deeper, coaxing her cream to flow.

"Sit on me," he rasped.

She rose to her knees, poised her pussy over his throbbing shaft, and slowly lowered herself onto him.

"Careful," he cautioned.

The crown, dripping cream, slipped between her folds and inside the opening.

"Prepare for the pain." He clenched against the compulsion to drive into her, and allowed her heat to slowly envelop him. He groaned in unison with her gasp.

Her form, so slight to his size, stretched to accommodate his girth. Still, she inched down onto his shaft. Nails dug into his shoulders as she panted, taking more of his length inside the tight sheath.

He grasped the base of his cock, leaned his head against the cushion, and endured the sweet agony. She was the most erotic thing he'd ever held. She lifted slightly, then eased down. Her voice caught, and she lifted another fraction. Lowering again, another gasp matched the effort.

"Mayhap we do not fit," she said in a breathless voice.

"We fit too well." The notion struck fear into his heart. He wouldn't think of tomorrow...when she would be lost to him. He didn't steal young ladies' virginities. The only innocent he expected to know was his future wife. But as second born, he had been foolish enough to believe the wife would be one of choice.

His choice. Taran gripped her hips and Aphrodite slid her tight pussy down the length of him. With a hard thrust, he surged upward and buried the full measure of his cock into her.

She gasped. Hot, quivering walls encased him, tightened, and held him deep. He stilled. On the morrow, whatever she left of his heart and body he would pledge to another.

Taran clenched his arse, thrusting deeper.

"Oh!" She cried out and gripped his shoulders. "All lies."

Taran froze. "What lies?"

"That coupling is a burden. Feels so good to have you inside me."

Relief flooded him and he nearly laughed—then she shifted. Pleasure surged through him. Taran let instinct guide her movements. She shifted, rocked, lifted and lowered, looking for the pace and rhythm that brought the most pleasure. That her tight pussy held him in an iron grip was enough to send him over the edge. If not for the need to burn into his memory the feel of her slick passage stroke after stroke, he would already have taken his release. They had only tonight. Every moment counted.

"My lady," he whispered. "This is your night of seduction."

"Yes," she said on a breathy exhale. "I believe you said if done right, this—this—"

"Fucking."

"Yes, fucking. Would you like me to speak crudely, my lord?"

He bit back a laugh that nearly brought pain. "Aye."

"You said, if done correctly, *fucking* can take a long time." Taran groaned.

"Would you like to hear more?" She gyrated her hips, sinking down, taking his erection from tip to base into her channel.

He thrust deep, forcing her hard onto his shaft. "I wish I could see your face when I make you come."

Her breath caught. Satisfaction swelled within him.

"Hear what you do to me." She panted, milking his length in her drenched heat. "Your cock is like an iron sword. First I felt a burn, and now I feel as though I will die from the pleasure."

"The French called it *la petite mort*. The little death."

"How apropos. For surely"—she rolled her hips, faster, her breathing growing shallow—"I have gone to heaven."

And he would spend the rest of his days in hell.

She moaned as vibrations from her inner walls quivered along his shaft, taking him deeper while her hot folds tightened on his rod. His balls tingled, drawing close to his body. His engorged shaft hardened to near discomfort. This time he'd go with her.

Gripping her waist, in frenzied thrusts he plunged his cock into her pussy in rapid strokes.

"Fuck," he groaned.

She creamed around him, heightening the slick friction. Spasms rippled her walls. She screamed. Taran exerted every ounce of strength. Muscles in his arms burned, his thighs trembled, but still he pumped his shaft in and out. Faster, harder. Sweat dripped down his chest. With a primal cry, he erupted. Hot jets of fluid bathed her channel. Each spurt surged with energy yet left him weak. He wrapped his arms around her and locked her close, buried to the hilt in her delicate folds.

Chapter Five

Caroline collapsed against her lover. Her cheek met his bare flesh, damp with sweat. The heavy rise and fall of his chest matched her breathing. Gentle caresses along her spine comforted, but she cared nothing for his concern. His cock, still buried inside her, felt slick, hot and wet with his seed. The heavy musk of their joining scented the air.

Tears stung her eyes. Quick blinks halted the flood that threatened. Gratitude, not sorrow, filled her. This memory would remain in her heart forever.

Caroline straightened and touched his cheek. "Thank you."

He pulled her face to within an inch of his. Warm breath fanned against her skin when he said, "Return home with me."

Her heart wrenched. "I cannot. We are strangers."

"After tonight, we are no longer strangers."

The vehemence in his voice startled her. She lifted off him and his cock slipped from her body as she swung her leg over his hips. Back straight, Caroline settled against the cushion beside him.

"We must say goodbye."

"The damage is done," he said, then added before she could reply, "do not fear, I shall honor our agreement."

Pain twisted her heart, but she couldn't deny the relief. "If we had more time." She trailed a finger across his abdomen.

His muscles quivered and tightened beneath her touch.

"Several hours yet remain before dawn," he said in a hoarse voice.

Caroline let her palm relax on his stomach. She had considered this, but… "We already want more than either of us can give. However, pleasure does not negate responsibility. If I linger even a moment longer…" She lifted his hand and brushed her cheek against his knuckles, then kissed them and set them back at his side.

"This is goodbye, then?"

The formal note in his voice nearly undid her. "Yes."

He groped the opposite seat and, a moment later, fit the mask over her face and secured it into place. Her heart wrenched at the chasm the simple action created between them.

Caroline sat motionless as he collected the dress and slipped the garment over her head. She didn't miss the trembling of his fingers when he straightened the costume on her shoulders. How easily she could lose herself in the arms of this man again tonight, and tomorrow, and the next day. *A man like him, I could want forever,* her heart whispered. He slipped the sash over her head and she forced back a sob.

Her wedding day was tomorrow—no—today. Mabel would already be up and about. Soon, the old housekeeper would come to her room to wake her in preparation for the wedding.

Her lover shifted and Caroline realized he was buttoning his shirt. She remembered her wig and pulled it from the opposite seat, then slipped it over her hair. A moment later, he reached for his own mask. Before he could find it, she touched his cheek for the last time.

"Swear you will think of me"—she bit back tears—"not as a ruined woman, but as a lady without regret." She turned his face towards her and kissed him. Dear God, she must leave before her heart crumbled altogether. "Just think of me," she ended in a whisper.

"How am I to forget?"

His simple reply brought the magnitude of what she'd done crashing down on her. Not her loss of innocence—that she understood and could not regret. "I must go." He banged on the ceiling of the carriage and the driver slowed.

"Please," her lover whispered.

She gave a single shake of her head he couldn't possibly see and he seized her hand and brought it to his lips. The carriage bounced to a stop. Her heart pounded and a lump formed in her throat. She hadn't thought it would be so difficult to say goodbye to a stranger. His words came back, *'After tonight, we are no longer strangers'*.

"You have been"—he paused, and she held her breath as he said—"unexpected."

Tears stung her eyes. She found his face in the dark and put a finger to his lips. "Our destinies are written."

"Heaven can rewrite destiny." He kissed her palm. "He does not deserve you." Her heart broke.

"And if your husband discovers the truth?"

She snapped to attention. The Viscount of Blackhall would not be pleased—nor would his father. She would see to it they never knew.

Her lover brushed a thumb across her cheek and she realized he felt the tear that had escaped. He pulled her close and buried his face in her neck.

"Do not judge yourself harshly," he whispered. "I do not regret our union. I pray you can say the same. Just remember, if your husband discovers the truth, if he rejects you—"

"Please. Tonight you have claimed a piece of my heart." She slid her lips over his. "What is left I will find a way to give to my husband."

He released her, then grasped the door handle. The click of the latch opening echoed in the hollow silence.

He paused. "Tell me your name. I swear, I only wish to be certain you are well."

Tears dampened her cheeks. "I cannot."

"If your husband does not care for you, find me."

He swung the door open and light spilled into the compartment. He stepped from the carriage. His massive frame filled the door as he faced her.

Familiar eyes, the color of copper, laced with amber strands darkened to a rich brown stared back at her.

Caroline barely stifled a gasp. Heat rushed into her face. "Blackhall," she whispered.

"Aye. Come to me when you can," he said, and shut the door.

Caroline stared at the closed door, numb with disbelief. Lord Blackhall wasn't supposed to—had refused to—come to England until their wedding day.

The carriage rolled forward. She yanked aside the curtain and watched her betrothed step back from the street, then turn. Her gaze remained glued to his receding back. She had feared no lasting repercussions from attending the masque. But if Lord Blackhall should discover her duplicity... The man with a penchant for dominance and *discipline* would not be forgiving.

The carriage rounded the corner and he disappeared from view. Caroline dropped the curtain and slumped against the cushion.

"Dear Lord, what have I done?"

Chapter Six

Caroline carefully closed the wrought iron gate leading to her uncle's rented townhouse, wincing at the distinct grate of metal when it clicked shut. She leaned her head against one of the bars, willing her stomach to unknot long enough for her legs to remain steady until she reached her room. She was a complete fool. The gown she'd worn when she left home probably still lay unmolested on the seat of her rented hackney parked outside Lord Forbes' estate.

Mabel, no doubt, had already risen, and had possibly even woken one or two of the maids. If they caught her wearing the Aphrodite costume, by dawn, all of Newcastle would know she had attended the masque. The servants might be in the kitchen, a blessing if Uncle was still out and the front door unlocked in anticipation of his return—the end for her if he had returned and bolted it behind him.

Had she come straight home instead of staying with Taran... Caroline grimaced. Had she not attended the masque at all, she wouldn't be in this mess. She stopped, an awful truth hitting her like a hammer. She couldn't possibly be in *love* with her future husband, not the man she had wantonly given herself to the night before she was to marry him. In the space of an hour, she had completely lost her mind.

With a steadying breath, Caroline faced the house and hurried up the walkway and the four steps to the door. She grasped the latch and gently pushed. Her heart jolted. Locked. She spun, yanking up her skirt as she flew down the stairs and around the house with a silent prayer that Mabel hadn't woken the maids. Caroline didn't relish facing the housekeeper—the old woman had been with her since the nursery—but better her recriminations than the maids' wagging tongues.

At the end of the house, Caroline halted and peered around the corner into the small garden. Faint light from behind curtained windows illuminated the steps leading to the door that opened into a pantry. She cursed. Her luck hadn't held true. Fortune—good fortune—had departed with her future husband. A flush rippled through her at memory of his warm hands on her breasts. She cursed her body's treacherous tightening and crept to the door, then up the steps. Aromas of pastries and yeast breads hung in the air. Things were worse than she feared. Mabel must have risen by midnight—if she'd slept at all.

Keep your nerve, Caroline ordered. If they had discovered her absence, the house would be ablaze with light and servants would be swarming the house.

No movement shown behind the curtains. She paused, hand on the latch, the roar of blood in her ears so loud she grimaced, and placed her ear against the wood. She detected no sounds beyond the door and inched it open. Silence followed, and she slipped into the empty pantry.

Pies, three baskets of rolls, apples, pears, plums, carrots, potatoes, and two platters of meats filled the counter to the left. She'd been right. Mabel hadn't slept, but had toiled through the night so that her wedding day would be an event talked about from Newcastle to London.

The shuffling of feet sounded to the left. Someone ascended the servant's stairway from the kitchen below. She was an imbecile as well as a fool. Caroline flew up the three steps to the stairs, glanced to the right where the stairs descended into the kitchen, saw no one, and raced up to the first floor. At the top, she hurried across the foyer to the main stairs. She seized the newel post and swung herself around and onto the second step. Her foot caught on her hem and she grabbed the railing just in time to save herself from hitting the carpeted stair, face first. Yanking her skirt to calf level, she propelled herself upward.

At the top of the stairs, she paused. She had come too far to be nabbed by a maid who chose this morning to use the main stairs instead of the servants' or rear stairs. She peeked around the wall to the right and scanned the hallway. Empty. Relief flooded her, then evaporated at a faint scratching sound from the second floor.

Caroline darted forward. A moment later, she reached her room and slipped inside. Facing the room, she cautiously closed the door and slumped against the wood. She rested a hand on her heart and slowed her breathing.

Embers glowed in the fireplace. No one had entered her room. Fate had seen her this far. Now to face the day. Never mind *the day*. How was she to face the night when her husband bedded her? Would he plunge into her as he had in the carriage, or would he be quick, as predicted? The absurdity of his instructions struck her. He had coached her on how to deceive *him*. If another man had taught her such things, Lord Blackhall would call him out for the dawn appointment the kilted god spoke of. That was a duel she would pay to see.

All amusement vanished. She would heed his advice and get him drunk. Perhaps, she could use some added insurance. Uncle kept sleeping powders in his bedchamber. If she could steal enough to slip into Blackhall's wine, he would pass out on the wedding bed and wake believing he'd done his husbandly duties. A tremor rocked her stomach. The prowess of the man in the carriage would not be satisfied until he could remember sealing the pact.

Slipping the sash over her head, she crossed to the bed and slid the sleeves from her shoulders, letting the dress fall to the carpet. She hesitated, her gaze glued to the costume pooled at her feet, Lady Margaret's words playing in her mind. *Do not expect the privileges of rank then flout the responsibilities.* She had done just that and altered her future.

Footsteps echoed in the hallway. She snapped her head in the direction of the door. Her future had just become her present. Caroline snatched the dress from the floor and dived beneath the bedcovers. Cold enveloped her naked body.

She bit back a curse and stuffed dress and sash under her pillow, barely yanking the covers up to her chin as the door opened. Mabel entered with a tray of hot chocolate and bread rolls in hand. Caroline blinked sleepily at her.

Mabel set the tray on the bed beside her, then lit the candle on the night table and turned a critical eye on her. "Chilled, are you? Not to worry, tonight you will have a fine lord to warm you."

Caroline's cheeks heated. She knew exactly what Aphrodite would experience in the arms of her husband. Lady Caroline Wilmont, however, would have Aphrodite's castoffs. Unexpected guilt surfaced. The masked stranger—the man she believed she would never see again—was the one man she shouldn't have dallied with.

Caroline sat up as Mabel served her hot chocolate and bread. Caroline kept the blanket tight beneath her arms as Mabel picked up the tray and set it on her lap.

"I do not feel well."

The housekeeper frowned and tugged the blanket down to reveal Caroline's naked breasts. "What is this? No shift, and this being April?" She glared. "No wonder you feel ill." The old woman tucked the covers beneath Caroline's arms, then stopped midway and gave her an assessing look. "You would not purposefully mean to fall ill on your wedding day?" She straightened before Caroline could reply, and added, "Your uncle will see you to the chapel if he has to carry you there and hold you upright during the ceremony."

"And speak the vows for me," Caroline muttered. He would deliver her in a hearse, if need be, and have the coffin carried to the altar. He intended to be the Viscountess of Blackhall's uncle—the Countess of Blackhall's uncle, once the earl died and Taran took his place.

"Do not complain. He is seeing to your best interests."

"And that of his own."

Mabel tsked as she tucked the blanket a little tighter around Caroline. "You need to eat." She crossed to the hearth. "I will not have you faint during the ceremony." She knelt in front of the dying embers and pulled the ash tin from the corner.

While Mabel shoveled ashes from the fireplace, Caroline surveyed the tray. Her stomach unexpectedly growled and she realized she was famished. She picked up a roll and began buttering it. Mayhap she would choke on the bread and end her misery. She reached for the hot chocolate as she took a bite. Her thigh muscles protested the movement and she froze. She hadn't considered the possibility there would be any lasting effects to lovemaking—other than the loss of her heart and a possible child in her lover's image. She nearly laughed aloud at the ridiculous thought. A broken heart and a son to remind her of the man who had moved her beyond words were two things she could live with. That man despising her would be her undoing. If he suspected she was his Aphrodite...*his* Aphrodite. For one night she *had* been his Aphrodite.

What a fool she had been. Had she not attended the masque, she wouldn't have seen this passionate side of him until it was too late. Like most women married off for a price, she would have learned hate before love, and her hell would be only the smell of brimstone, instead of its heat.

Caroline took a swallow of the chocolate, then stuffed the remaining bread into her mouth before tentatively stretching her legs. Thigh muscles screamed—the grating of the ash tin across brick made her jump. She jerked her gaze onto Mabel and saw a fire burning in the hearth.

The housekeeper rose and faced her. "By now your bathwater—what in the world?"

She scowled and Caroline froze. Had Mabel somehow guessed she wasn't the innocent Lord Blackhall expected in his bed tonight?

Mabel crossed the room to the bed. "You are no child to be stuffing your mouth. Is this how you plan to conduct yourself at the breakfast reception?"

Frustration welled up in Caroline. Uncle had arranged this marriage. He could live with the consequences. She swallowed a large chunk of the bread, forcing the lump down her throat despite the discomfort. Mabel lifted both brows.

Caroline washed down the remainder with the hot chocolate, then reached for a second roll. "I am hungry. Ham and eggs, if you please."

"Before dawn, and with the breakfast you will be expected to partake of after the ceremony?"

"Every condemned man *and* woman is allowed a last meal."

The housekeeper's eyes narrowed. "None of your drama, Miss."

"I will have my breakfast."

"That you will, after the ceremony."

Caroline stuffed half the roll into her mouth, swallowed, and bit back a gag Undaunted, she set the tray aside, then threw back the covers and grabbed her robe from the edge of the bed.

She stood. "I am capable of fetching my own breakfast." Caroline slipped her arms inside the sleeves as she strode to the door.

"What's this?" Mabel said.

Caroline grasped the doorknob as she glanced over her shoulder to see Mabel reaching for the edge of the purple sash sticking out from beneath the pillow. Caroline sucked in breath. Mabel grasped the sash and pulled it and the dress free. The costume fell to full length in front of the housekeeper. She squinted at the dress, clearly confused, then understanding dawned on her features.

She swung her gaze onto Caroline. Caroline stood immobile. The jig was up. Uncle would—Uncle would what? Her fingers tightened on the door handle. Why hadn't she seen it before? Her uncle had never cared for her fortune. He was wealthy and, unlike so many of his contemporaries, managed his wealth well.

He intended to buy his way into the most elite circles of London with her fortune. If the new Lord Blackhall called off the wedding because his bride-to-be had defiled herself by attending the masque, Uncle would be furious, but he would simply find another noble in need of money. The scandal wouldn't be enough to stop a desperate suitor from taking her as wife, and would be forgotten inside a month—just enough time for a quick wedding and honeymoon.

Her heart twisted. A honeymoon without Taran. Was a life with his disdain better than life without him? A tremor rocked her belly. Was she willing to have him at any cost, even trickery? Another thought chilled her.

Betrayal or no, Taran Roberston, Viscount of Blackhall, would satisfy family obligation and marry the woman wealthy enough to restore his family's finances. His father, the old Earl, would see to that.

Caroline ran her gaze across the length of the costume, then looked at Mabel with a raised brow. "What does it look like?"

Mabel's lips thinned. "Looks like a costume intended for a masque."

Caroline shrugged. "'Twas my last night of freedom. What did you expect?"

The housekeeper startled her with a loud snort. "You will not be fooling me *or* your uncle so easily." She strode to the fireplace and threw the dress into the hearth.

Caroline lunged forward. "Mabel!" She reached the maid's side and tried to snatch the dress from the blaze of blue flame.

Mabel seized her arm and yanked Caroline around to face her. "No one will believe you attended that masque any more than I do."

Caroline twisted and looked at the dress. Marred beyond recognition. Another instant, and it would be gone altogether.

Mabel released her.

Caroline stared at her. "Why?"

The housekeeper started for the door. "Your bathwater is ready. The men will bring it up. I will return presently to help with your hair."

Caroline jumped with the light click of the door shutting behind Mabel. She lowered herself onto the bench at the foot of the bed. What had just happened? Her beloved Mabel had just sealed her fate, that's what had just happened. When the bath was filled, perhaps she could drown herself in the water.

Chapter Seven

Taran set his plate of eggs and sausage on the breakfast table, then seated himself opposite his father. "Never fear, Father, unlike John, I shall pay the mortgage on Strathmore and purchase the two Friesian stallions you have your eye on before I break my neck."

His father stopped short in placing a napkin on his lap and met Taran's gaze. "Do not speak ill of the dead."

"Ah, yes." Taran reached for the cup of coffee before him. "*I* will be sure to get my bride with an heir before my untimely death—cannot have her marrying some other hapless viscount before her property is firmly seated in the Blackhall family." He lifted the coffee cup in salute and took a sip.

The earl laid his napkin over his lap. "Foul this up and I will be forced to marry the girl myself."

Taran looked up from setting his cup on the table. "Why did you not marry her?"

"Her uncle felt she would look more favorably upon your suit."

Taran watched his father pick up fork and knife and begin cutting the sausages on his plate. He hadn't hesitated in his answer. The fact he was thirty years the girl's senior meant nothing. She was a commodity, and John Blackhall, Earl of Blackhall, had the price her uncle sought—an earldom. Lady Caroline Whitmore would someday be the Countess of Blackhall. He pitied the girl, though wondered if his brother John would have been any better to her than their father.

Taran picked up his fork. How much better a husband would he be? Today, their wedding day, he could think of nothing, save last night and the woman he'd bedded—no. Being bedded required a four-poster bed and a large feather mattress in front a crackling fire. He had fucked her, though not properly. The private admonition didn't stop his cock from hardening at the memory of how she'd cried out when he'd entered her.

The vixen was made for a man's touch, and touch her again he would. Once the honeymoon was over, he would find her. Surely by then she would be married and have fulfilled her duty to her husband. Tension tightened his gut. She belonged to another man.

No, she was to wed another man. She belonged to him.

The door to the breakfast room opened, and William entered. "My lord," he nodded to the earl, then to Taran.

Taran pointed to the seat to his right with his knife. "Sit. Have some breakfast."

The viscount nodded towards a servant standing near the sideboard as he lowered himself into the chair. "Coffee, if you please." William looked at Taran and grimaced. "How in God's name can you eat? You are to wed in two hours, and the breakfast to follow is sure to be a feast. Lady Caroline's housekeeper is rumored to be a cook fit for a king." William added cream to his coffee. "Where did you get off to last night?"

The earl looked up. "Last night? Taran, if you—"

"If I what, Father? I am here, alive and well, the Viscount you need to acquire a fortune." He forked eggs into his mouth.

"I want a grandson by August."

Taran raised a brow. "At your service, my lord."

The earl buttered a piece of toast. "Once you have fulfilled your obligation, you may do as you choose. With the money your marriage brings into the family, I can see your sisters well married, as well as run Strathmore and all our other affairs."

"All? I am sure my wife will be pleased to learn you will see to her *needs* while I am *doing as I choose.*"

His father gave a mirthless laugh and Taran realized the earl had no compunctions about stepping in should a grandson not be forthcoming. For the thousandth time since learning the title had fallen to him, Taran considered defying his father and not marrying Caroline. The tactic had worked when Taran had insisted the earl close the illegal gaming hall he owned. The earl had refused until Taran had announced he would not wed the needed heiress while the threat of scandal hung over his head. The gaming hall had kept the estate out of the tax collector's hand, but couldn't compare to the twenty thousand pounds a year Caroline Wilmont brought to the marriage.

Sadly, his father's entrepreneurial enterprise drove the final nail into Taran's coffin. If he didn't marry Caroline, his father would reopen the gaming hall. Once the Crown got wind of the illegal operation, it wouldn't matter that Taran had no part in the business, he would end up in Newgate. His two sisters would be destitute, doomed to spinsterhood, or worse, marriage to squires and living in some Godforsaken part of the country where they would breed children who then grew up to become squires themselves.

Caroline Wilmont was destined for a life with him *and* his father—for this she may not forgive him—but the girl was doomed in any case. Wealthy heiresses were to be bought and sold, and if he didn't marry her, another would. Perhaps another man would be a better man than Taran.

* * * *

The rolls Caroline had stuffed into her mouth that morning twisted in her belly with a vengeance, but she surprised herself by giving a calm nod to her uncle as he released her elbow and took his place to her left at the altar. The low hum of chatter in the chapel rose to a slight pitch and she knew the guests were in awe of the corseted bridal gown she wore. Like the Aphrodite costume, the bodice dipped nearly to her nipples. A small tremor radiated through her. Would sight of her breasts remind Taran of last night?

She inhaled a deep breath—as deep as her dress allowed. Despite the low bodice, the muted red of the corseted top and the pale gold skirt said nothing of passion. Lady Caroline Wilmont was a woman who demanded she be in the first order of fashion. A gown like this was not to be abused as the Aphrodite costume had been.

But what if he *did* recognize her? She gave herself a mental shake. *Foolish.* His encounter with Aphrodite had been in thin moonlight, then a dark carriage. Gone was the blonde wig. Her raven hair lay atop her head in a fashionable bun, accented by ringlets framing face and neck.

The minister emerged from a door behind the pulpit and strode towards her. At the pulpit, he set a small hymnal on the stand, then smiled with the benevolence only the clergy owned. Caroline gave him a nod in return. To her relief, her nerves remained steady. The goddess of fortune hadn't favored her this last day, but that good lady held no more sway over Caroline Wilmont. Today would end as best it could, but in disaster. But Taran would be free of her.

The low hum of chatter abruptly ceased. Lord Taran Blackhall had arrived. Caroline kept her gaze straight ahead. She had remained calm, but wouldn't risk losing her nerve in this last hour. Despite her efforts, her heart beat like a drum. If he recognized her immediately, he would refuse to marry her on the spot. At least that would end this farce.

He had no proof she was Aphrodite. Would he openly accuse her? No, not Taran. John would have publicly humiliated her. Whatever Taran Blackhall was, he was not his brother. He appeared beside her. She felt his gaze on her, but kept her attention forward. He couldn't see her eyes. Not yet.

The reverend cleared his throat. "All rise."

A unified shuffle sounded, then silence reigned.

"Dearly beloved," the minister began, "we are gathered together here in the sight of God, and in the face of this congregation, to join together this man and this woman in holy matrimony." He glanced down at his book and Caroline reached inside her bodice and pulled free the black, lace handkerchief she'd stuffed there earlier. Her heart pounded in anticipation of the moment the minister caught sight of the black handkerchief that openly stated the bride still mourned the groom's brother.

His head lifted as he continued. "Which is an honorable estate, instituted of God in the time of man's innocency, signifying unto us the mystical union"—his gaze fastened onto the cloth—"that is betwixt Christ and"—he swallowed hard—"his Church." The last word died on his lips and Caroline felt all three men staring at her.

With a steady hand, she dabbed at her eyes with the handkerchief.

"Er." The minister dropped his attention back to the book. "His—his Church, which holy estate Christ adorned and beautified with his presence, and—" He flicked a glance at Caroline. She clasped the handkerchief to her breast and released a melodramatic sigh. The reverend's eyes widened.

A murmur rose in the chapel behind her. Strong fingers seized her hand and forced her palm face upwards. She snapped her head up. Taran stared at the black cloth, his furrowed brow and dark eyes betraying…amusement? He released her and looked at the reverend who stared open-mouthed at them.

"Please continue, Minister," he instructed.

The man remained motionless.

"Have you not seen a woman in mourning before?" he asked.

The minister looked at him. "I-well, I, of course, but—"

"But what?" Taran demanded.

The minister glanced helplessly about, then his gaze shifted to the hymnal, searching briefly for the words before he continued, "Which holy estate Christ adorned and beautified with his presence, and first miracle that he wrought, in Cana of Galilee—"

Caroline tore her gaze from the reverend who was droning on with the vows, and stared at Taran. He turned his head to reveal a slightly arched brow. The scoundrel was challenging her.

Fool, she mentally telepathed, *this is for your own good.*

The handkerchief was abruptly snatched from her grasp. Caroline jerked her attention to the left. Her uncle stared at the minister, the last of the handkerchief being stuffed neatly into his breast pocket. His hand dropped back to his side.

She had prepared for this. Eyes locked on his profile, Caroline reached into her bodice and pulled free a second black handkerchief. His head shifted and his gaze met hers. She turned towards Taran before her uncle had a chance to snatch the second handkerchief from her and came face to face with her soon-to-be husband. His bland expression didn't disguise the faint twitch at the corner of his mouth. Her tummy flipped. What would he do when she displayed the remaining black she wore? With her free hand, she grasped her skirt and lifted the hem an inch.

A collective gasp went up and a woman's low wail sounded in the front pew.

"Silence," her uncle hissed.

A tremor passed through Caroline. *Courage.* It didn't mattered what her uncle thought. Taran's gaze dropped and both brows shot up. Satisfaction surged through her. This is what mattered. The dear viscount couldn't ignore the black, quilted underskirt accented with black, silk stockings. What man would want a woman who publicly announced she preferred his dead brother? Caroline abruptly realized the chapel— including the minister—had gone silent.

Taran seemed to notice it as well, for he looked at the minister. "What did you say?"

The minister's eyes were glued to Caroline's ankles, where the edge of the underskirt and stockings were still visible.

"Minister," Taran said in a firmer tone.

The reverend's head jerked up.

"What did you say?" Taran repeated.

The man cast Caroline an uncertain glance, then straightened and said in a clear voice, "Wilt thou have this woman to thy wedded wife, to live together after God's ordinance in the holy state of matrimony? Wilt thou love her, comfort her, honor, and keep her in sickness and in health; and, forsaking all others, keep thee only unto her, so long as ye both shall live?"

Caroline's breath caught when Taran looked at her and said with conviction, "I will."

The reverend shifted his attention to her. "Wilt thou have this man to thy wedded husband, to live together after God's ordinance in the holy estate of matrimony? Wilt thou obey him, and serve him, love, honor, and keep him in sickness and in health; and, forsaking all other, keep thee only unto him, so long as ye both shall live?"

Love, honor, care for him, yes. Obey and serve? Caroline wadded the handkerchief in her fist. "I am uncer—"

Viscount Blackhall yanked her against him, forcing the last of her sentence into an indistinguishable squeak.

"She does," he growled.

"Who giveth this woman to be married to this man?" the reverend asked.

Her uncle seized her wrist and extended her hand—handkerchief and all—towards the reverend. He blinked, then an unexpected gleam of determination lit his eyes and she realized the good reverend intended to bring her to heel. He gripped her hand and extended it towards Taran. His warm fingers closed around hers with a firm but gentle touch. Her heart jolted. He was supposed to have stormed from the chapel, not taken her hand in his as if he meant to honor the damned vows.

"Repeat after me. I, Taran Robertson."

Taran began, "I, Taran Robertson."

"Viscount of Blackhall," the minister went on, "take thee, Lady Caroline Wilmont to my wedded wife."

Taran repeated the words.

Caroline cursed the tremble in her hand when Taran said, "To love and to cherish, till death us do part."

The minister addressed her, "Repeat after me. I, Caroline Wilmont, take thee, Lord

Taran Robertson, to my wedded husband."

Voice level, Caroline repeated the vows, ending with, "according to God's holy ordinance; and thereto I plight thee my troth."

The reverend laid a hand on their joined hands and said, "Those whom God hath joined together let no man put asunder."

Caroline stiffened. God had taken no more part in their union today than he had last night. Her husband had yet to see her full wedding trousseau. He would demand an annulment before the wedding night ended.

Taran released her hand and reached into his pocket to produce a gold band. He grasped her left hand and said, "With this ring I thee wed, with my body I thee worship, and with all my worldly goods I thee endow. In the name of the Father, and of the Son, and of the Holy Ghost. Amen."

He started to kneel. Caroline didn't move, and he yanked her down so hard he was forced to grab her waist to keep her from tumbling onto her rear. She scowled. He lifted a brow and she fisted her hands with the full intention of landing a blow to his belly before thinking better of it.

"Let us pray," the minister began. Yes, Caroline needed a prayer because in another moment she would be wed.

Chapter Eight

Taran hauled his wife to her feet, placed his hands on her shoulders, and bent to kiss her. Her brow creased in confusion, then her green eyes narrowed. She slapped his chest and jerked back as if he had sprouted horns. He forced back a laugh. The lass had grit.

He pulled her against him, stopping an inch from her face. "I have grit as well," he murmured, and kissed her.

Her lips weren't pliant like the she-devil last night, but they were soft and warm. He touched his tongue to the seam. She gasped and he slipped inside for a taste. Caroline held her posture rigid and her mouth unyielding. He wrapped an arm around her back, then with the barest of whimpers, she relaxed.

She wasn't his Aphrodite, but he sensed passion simmering in her kiss. Her full breasts nearly spilled from her dress. He imagined her hardened nipples prodding into his chest. Tonight he would touch and taste them. He groaned low in his throat, tantalized by the way her belly cradled his stiffening cock. At least he could feel desire for his wife.

Taran released her and caught sight of the black handkerchief peeking out from her fisted hand. If the tenacity she'd shown with her inconsequential, but amusing, rebellions were any indication, their children wouldn't be the mewling creatures he'd feared they might be. He'd underestimated Caroline Wilmont. She wasn't the quiet schoolgirl he remembered. Amusement vanished. John had been a fool. Taran would bed his wife and bring her the pleasure she deserved. Caroline would want for nothing. He would provide husband, home, and children. However, when the time was right, he would seek Aphrodite. And, like all wives of society, Caroline would seek her interests elsewhere.

Taran linked his wife's arm in his and glanced at her face. Her eyes narrowed and her lips remained set in a thin line. Everyone rose. Caroline stiffened, her stare straight ahead. Taran tensed. Had he misjudged her? He hadn't mistaken the passion hidden in her kiss. Tonight would tell him if she was a bitch or just a woman protesting the only way she could. He started down the aisle. For better or worse, they were wed, though he would prefer a woman he could respect to one he hated.

Guests tossed shoes and slippers after them as he hurried them down the aisle and out the chapel doors to his waiting carriage. Taran opened the door and helped her inside, then leapt up and slammed the door shut as he dropped onto the seat opposite her. The carriage lurched into motion.

Her glare turned to him and he read fury in her eyes. "What kind of fool are you?" she demanded.

Despite her clipped tones in the chapel when she'd repeated her vows, the husky note in her voice incited a sense of desire that he found oddly comforting. Her raven hair contrasted with the emerald green eyes with startling clarity far more than he remembered. But he remembered a child, and wagered the woman was having none of his admiration, at least not yet.

"Not the insipid fool you take me for, madam."

Her lips pursed and he couldn't help wondering if she were going to punch him. She had clearly intended to do just that in the chapel. He deserved a good right to the gut. He was little better than his brother—or father. He fully intended on producing the needed heir, then leaving his wife to her own devices. As long as she was discreet, he wouldn't take her to task. He convinced himself that she too would prefer to do as she pleased. Clearly, she would have chosen not marry him at all.

She leaned forward. "I had no desire to marry your brother, and I have even less desire to marry you."

This time, Taran couldn't prevent a laugh. A mind reader for a wife was the last thing a man needed. She threw herself back against the cushion and a black stockinged ankle showed beneath the hem of the black underskirt.

"If I am not mistaken, that was Mrs. Henderland who wailed at sight of your black undergarments," he said. "I believe our good minister is certain a demon possesses you."

His wife eyed him. "Something far worse than a demon possesses me."

Taran blinked, then realized he shouldn't be surprised. In fact, he should be surprised if she stopped at such paltry attempts to dissuade him as wearing mourning black to their wedding. He had underestimated her a second time. He would not do so again.

"Then our minister has a great deal of work ahead of him."

She shot him a disparaging look that said *he* had a great deal of work ahead of him.

He forced the twitch at the corner of his mouth into a frown. "I had not realized you grieved so deeply for my brother. I only hope he does not become a barrier between us." Taran shifted on the seat. "I shall do my best to rise to his stature."

She gave an abrupt laugh and clamped a hand over her mouth, her eyes wide. Taran snapped to attention. What was this? She had a sense of humor? His gaze caught on the long, slim fingers still covering her mouth. Memory of last night and Aphrodite returned with a sharpness that bordered on pain. Her warm fingers wrapped around his cock, the pebbled peaks of her nipples, hard, yet pliant beneath his tongue, the tight sheath that surrounded him when he entered her. Taran shifted his attention to the window and onto the townhouses as the carriage rolled past. He'd been a fool to allow Aphrodite to persuade him to take her maidenhead. He couldn't regret having her, but if she bore her husband a son anytime soon, she would live the pregnancy—and years beyond—wondering if the boy would in some way resemble another man. Would that pain and guilt rob her of happiness?

Despite the fear, he couldn't help wondering how many women would have risked scandal, or worse, to attend a masque before they were wed. Aphrodite had been as brave as she was foolish. He returned his attention to his wife. She sat, hands folded in her lap, lips set in a thin line. She hadn't the courage Aphrodite had, but he thanked God for the backbone she had shown. They would get on well enough, once she accepted she hadn't made as bad a bargain as she might have, had his brother or father been the alternative.

They rode in silence until arriving at her uncle's townhouse. The carriage came to a rolling stop. "I would like a moment alone." She brushed non-existent lint from her dress. "I will see you at breakfast."

He placed his hand over hers, stilling her movement.

Small hairs on her arms quivered when he raked his thumb over her knuckle. "Perhaps I would prefer to join you." She snatched her hand away, and he chuckled.

"Not to worry, wife, we will spend many moments alone. I can be patient."

"I will take some comfort in knowing you have at least one virtue." The door opened. Grasping the layers of her dress, she gave her hand to the waiting footman. Taran couldn't take his gaze away from the rounded fullness of her backside as she bent and, in a flounce, ascended the porch steps.

* * * *

Caroline sat in the drawing room of her uncle's townhouse, spooning a second teaspoon of sugar into a teacup as she released a temporary sigh of relief that the last of the wedding guests had departed. She glanced up to see her uncle in the doorway, a shoulder leaning against the doorjamb.

Apprehension tensed her shoulders when he straightened and strode towards her. His anger at her attempts to ruin the wedding had been plain throughout the meal, but she had managed to avoid being alone with him. Time to pay the piper.

She stirred the tea with remarkably steady fingers considering the clamoring within her. She set the spoon on the tray. He lowered himself onto the opposite end of the divan and stretched a hand out across the back of it. Caroline leaned against the cushion and met his gaze while blowing across the surface of the tea. He had the same raven hair and dark green eyes her mother had…the same coloring as Caroline.

At forty-five, his broad shoulders and muscled thighs still made him a match for even the younger bucks who vied for female attention. Caroline understood why women were attracted to him. The mystique of the privateer turned pirate proved a powerful aphrodisiac and opened more doors—bedchamber doors—within the ton than even his wealth had.

"Your trifling attempts to fend off Lord Blackhall will cost you," he said.

"You mistake me for your former ward," Caroline replied. "I am no longer under your rule."

"Do not be a fool. I still have a great deal of power. Your husband might find your actions amusing. I do not."

She sipped her tea. Oddly, her husband *had* found her actions amusing. She steadied the tremble in her hand. The gold band on the third finger of her right hand weighed her down like lead. How had she managed to lose her innocence to the one man she wanted to avoid?

Another thought struck. Perhaps the light of day had brought Lord Taran Blackhall to his senses and he'd realized the passion he felt for Aphrodite was nothing more than lust. Lust incited by the debauched atmosphere of the masque. That would make his anger all the worse.

Taran appeared in the doorway. Caroline jerked. Tea sloshed over the cup's rim, onto the saucer and her dress. She cried out.

He uncle straightened. *"Caroline."*

Taran was at her side in an instant. He snatched a napkin from the table, dropped to one knee, and dabbed at the spot on her thigh. Fire shot to her core.

"My lord."

She leaned forward in order to set the cup on the table, realizing too late her breast would brush his arm, and tried to dodge him. Cup and saucer hit the table with a clatter. Taran paused in dabbing at her dress. "Something wrong, my lady?" She snatched the napkin from him and glared.

"No need to be embarrassed. The guests have all gone," he said.

"Clumsy girl," her uncle muttered.

Taran shot him a hard glance, then returned his attention to Caroline. "Forgive me for startling you." He rose.

Despite knowing the spot on her skirt was no longer wet, Caroline wiped at it.

"I also ask forgiveness for forcing you to travel on your wedding day," he said.

She jerked her gaze onto him. "What?"

"I am sorry you must face the journey back to Scotland so soon, but I—"

"Scotland?"

Taran frowned. "Yes, that is why I asked that the wedding be held here in Newcastle." She started to reply, but he shifted his gaze to her uncle. "You did not tell her?"

"I thought it best she not be given more reason to balk."

Taran's lips thinned. He looked back at her. "Forgive me. *I* should have told you. We leave straightaway."

"Surely, I need not go with you. I am content to await you here."

He shook his head. "I have business that cannot wait an extra day."

Her stomach knotted. He couldn't wait the night it would take to consummate the marriage. If he were anyone but the kilted god she had met last night, she would lead him to her bedchamber and be done with the consummation.

"My lord, such a trip will require packing and a maid. Surely you would not demand I go without a maid."

"Bring anyone you like."

"But, I have not arranged with anyone among the staff to leave."

"Your personal maid?"

Caroline shook her head. "I employ no personal maid."

"You may employ one when we reach Strathmore." She started to argue, but he added, "I am sorry. Your bags can follow. They will reach us within a day of our arrival. Anything you need between now and then may be purchased."

Anger bubbled to the surface. He spoke easily enough of making purchases with *her* money. "Mabel cannot know what to send. How long will we stay?"

"We will live at Strathmore."

Caroline stared. "Live? But—"

"You will do as your husband says," her uncle cut in.

Caroline took care to keep her attention on her husb—Taran—he was not yet fully her husband, at least not until they consummated the marriage. The fact that the wedding night had taken place before the wedding would be of no consequence, so long as no one knew.

"John and I were to reside in London," she continued.

"Caroline—" her uncle began.

She swung her gaze onto him. "You have married me off, sir. As I said earlier, your right to command me is lost."

His mouth tightened. "Careful, my dear."

She didn't flinch from his gaze. "Will you lock me in my room, or perhaps a dawn appointment will teach me a final lesson I shall not soon forget?"

His eyes darkened. "Do not press me, Niece."

Strong fingers closed around her arm. She found herself pulled to her feet and face-to-face with Taran. "Go on," he said in a low voice. His warm breath fluttered her eyelashes. "See to your things. One hour should suffice."

"One hour?"

"Caroline," her uncle's voice turned hard.

Taran gently pushed her towards the door, then faced her uncle. "Which will it be, Etherton, being locked in her room or a dawn appointment?"

Caroline froze, her stare on her husband's back. She couldn't see his face, didn't need to see his expression. The near whisper with which he'd spoken the words left no room for question that Lord Taran Blackhall had threatened her uncle.

A glint appeared in her uncle's eyes that said he understood full well Taran's willingness to miss his all-important business in Scotland and remain in England through dawn tomorrow. A chill snaked down Caroline's spine. Phillip Etherton climbed the social ladder just as he had plundered the South Seas as Peiter Everston. Dawn appointments were one prize among many.

"The earl asked that I see to it my niece complies."

Taran didn't twitch a muscle. "I have married your niece. Your obligation—and mine—have been fulfilled."

"She intends to force your hand, as you witnessed during the ceremony," her uncle replied in smooth tones. "I am well acquainted with her tactics and can ensure she does no lasting damage."

"Lasting damage?" Taran repeated with a condescension Caroline feared would push her uncle to immediate violence. His reputation kept all but the most foolish youngsters and the occasional enraged husband at bay. "Her amusing attempts to discomfit me," Taran went on, "are no more damaging than that tea she spilt on her dress."

Her uncle regarded him for a long moment. "The earl would not appreciate his son interfering where he should not."

"Beware *you* do not interfere where you should not." Taran started to turn, then added, "Give my regards to the earl." He turned on his heel and scowled when his gaze met Caroline's. He took two steps towards her, catching her elbow as he propelled her forward. "Madam, if you insist on dallying at every turn, I shall miss this, and every other meeting, for the duration of our marriage."

Caroline tripped and his hold on her tightened as he navigated her out of the study. She stared at the long dark fingers encircling her arm, the same fingers that had gently caressed her breasts. How much more steel would she feel from those fingers if he discovered the honor of the woman he defended had been lost to him only the night before? Taran released her at the stairs, inclined his head in a slight bow, then pivoted and headed towards the kitchen.

She gaped at his retreating back. If Uncle discovered the truth and Taran called off the marriage, the dawn appointment would become a reality.

Chapter Nine

Taran cast a glance at Phillip Etherton's front door, saw his wife had yet to appear, then pulled William aside from the waiting carriage.

"Where have you been?" he demanded. "The breakfast is finished and we are about to depart."

The viscount flashed a wicked grin. "A certain young lady at the chapel was in need of consoling. Seems her husband is spending far too much time with his mistress and ignoring her altogether."

Taran gave him a deprecating look. "An angry husband will prove your undoing."

William's grin widened. "If I am fortunate, it will be the lady who proves my undoing."

"Never mind that," Taran snapped. "I need to know the identity of the Aphrodite you were dabbling with last night."

"Aphrodite?" he repeated.

"You and she were behind the column early into the masque."

"Ah, yes. She was a dainty piece. Sent me for punch, then disappeared." William gave him an appraising look. "I wondered who had stolen her away from me."

"I did not steal her away. She fled your company."

William's brow furrowed. "I will have you know no young lady has ever *fled my company*."

"This one did." William opened his mouth to reply, but Taran cut off the reply. "Who is she?"

"I have no idea."

"None?"

"Not the slightest."

"These masques are a jest," Taran said. "Everyone knows who everyone is."

"Generally, that is true. But I do not know her." William smiled. "Made the game all the more intriguing, if you know what I mean."

"She was talking on the balcony with another woman, Marie Antoinette," Taran said. "Any idea who she is?"

"I believe there were at least four Marie Antoinettes at the masque."

"They should not be difficult to locate. Find out who they are, and which one of them knows the Aphrodite."

The viscount eyed him. "I understand you plan on carrying out your life as always, but you might at least wait until the marriage is consummated."

"I do not plan on bedding her tonight," Taran said peevishly, though he wondered if he wouldn't do just that if she allowed it.

William looked past him. His brow shot up. "Your bride is approaching." He nodded towards the house.

"Send word once you have found her," Taran whispered, and turned.

He stopped short at sight of Caroline taking the last stair onto the walkway. The corset she wore narrowed her waist to the point he marveled she could walk, much less breathe. The bow on the back of the dress stuck out on each side of her small waist like wings in flight. But it was the hat she wore that made him stare. The straw brim dipped nearly to her nose and, at the back, reached to her shoulder blades. A bright red feather pointed skyward, then plunged downward almost to her elbow.

She stopped beside Taran. "Sir."

He couldn't take his eyes off the hideous hat. How in God's name was she going to get into the carriage, much less sit on the seat comfortably?

"My lady," William said.

Something flickered in her eyes and concern stabbed at Taran. Surely she couldn't have overheard their conversation?

William lightly grasped her fingers and bowed over her hand. "Lord Edmonds, at your service."

She inclined her head. "My lord." She pulled her hand free and turned to Taran. He ignored the quizzical look William shot him as she said, "If you are ready, sir."

"I am off," William said.

Taran cast him a meaningful glance. "I expect to hear news from you immediately."

"I shall not fail. My lady." He gave another small bow and turned on his heel.

"You are sure I cannot remain here?" Caroline asked.

Taran faced her. "Is that what this is about?"

"What?"

"This." He looked pointedly at the hat, then let his gaze drop, wincing at sight of the narrow waist.

"You insist we travel," she replied. "I hardly see why you should be concerned with my attire."

She stepped forward and he grasped her all-too-narrow-waist, lifting her into the carriage. It was she who should be concerned about her *attire*. If she passed out from lack of air, he would be inclined to paddle her pretty bottom.

* * * *

Taran released a slow breath, at last giving in to the relaxing gait of his mount as he rode alongside the horses drawing the carriage. He could feel his wife's eyes on the back of his head. He didn't have to look back to know the feather still stuck out the window, fluttering in the wind like a war flag.

Two hours into the trip, and she still wore that damned hat. He couldn't prevent a laugh. She sat rigid in her seat, unwilling or unable to relax against the cushions. Their wedding night would begin with him carrying her up the inn stairs and putting her into a hot tub to work the kinks from her back.

An unexpected picture arose of her naked in his arms, of him lowering her into a tub of steaming water. Then joining her. He could almost feel the velvety water as he ringed her nipple with his tongue, the rosy peak puckering, springing upward into a hardened point.

Taran shifted in the saddle to accommodate his growing arousal as the image shifted in his mind. She positioned herself between his legs, her back pillowed against his chest. He cupped her breasts, felt the heavy weight in his palm. By God, in his mind he had her stripped bare. He gulped in dusty air as he imagined flattening his palm against her stomach, then sliding lower, until he brushed the thatch of dark curls between her legs and parting her fleshy slit.

She would arch into his hand—no. He forcibly shook off the fantasy. Lady Caroline Blackhall was his wife, a lady of genteel birth, who expected to be bedded with respect, not passion, as Aphrodite had demanded.

The feel of her, warm in his arms, arose with startling intensity. Despite the pledge, he wouldn't regret their joining, although he couldn't deny the bitterness he felt at having had only a small part of her. Bedding Caroline would not be a hardship. She was beautiful, desirable, but she was a wife, a woman to respect—he thanked God for that much—but she wasn't a woman interested in sharing his passion.

Taran glanced back. As expected, the feather still billowed in the wind, but—he squinted—the feather listed heavily towards the opposite end of the window from which Caroline sat. Had she switched to the opposite cushion? Impossible. The curve of the feather faced forward as it had when she'd stepped into the carriage, only now it touched the far side of the window as if she leaned far forward—or had *fallen forward*.

Taran jerked hard on the reins, wheeling his horse around. "Stop the carriage!" The stallion whinnied and tossed his head.

The driver yanked back on the four horses, and the man riding guard ahead of them came to a grinding halt as Taran reached the door. He leapt to the ground, seized the door handle, and threw it back. Caroline's limp form tumbled through the opening, the feather slapping his nose as he caught her in his arms.

"A knife," he shouted.

"My lord?" Davis, the second man riding atop the carriage repeated.

"A knife, man, have you got a knife?"

"Aye."

"Give it to me!"

Taran hoisted Caroline onto the seat and leapt up beside her. The carriage rocked as Davis dropped to the ground. He propped his boot on the rim of the carriage and lifted the hem of his breeches. He pulled a knife from a sheath strapped to his ankle and extended it towards Taran.

He grabbed the hilt, flipped Caroline onto her belly, and slit the back of her dress in one long cut. Fabric parted with a loud ripping sound and exposed the creamy flesh of her back. Caroline gasped, drawing in a long, harsh breath, and began coughing.

Taran handed the knife back to Davis. "Tether my horse to the rear of the carriage and move on."

"Aye, my lord." He closed the door behind Taran.

Taran grabbed Caroline by the waist and sat her upright. She pitched forward in the throes of a coughing spasm. He caught her, pulling her to his chest.

"Take shallow breaths," he instructed while rubbing circulation into her back.

The carriage listed as Davis hoisted himself up onto the seat. An instant later, the vehicle lurched into motion. Taran braced one hand on the roof of the carriage and pinned Caroline against the cushion with the other. He held her firm while they rumbled over a hole that made them bounce in their seats.

"Of all the foolishness," he muttered. "If you die before we even reach the inn, your uncle will call me out for that dawn appointment—and rightfully so, this time." Beneath the brim of her hat, he saw the downturn of her mouth.

"I should"—another cough took her—"I should have let him kill you," she choked.

The carriage settled into an even sway and Taran released her. "You are certain it would be me who died?"

Caroline drew a deep breath, this one more controlled. "Do not be a fool," she half wheezed. "He is fifteen years your senior, and twice the shot."

"Twice the shot?" Taran repeated. "I think not."

The hat shifted upward and he caught sight of a single eye glowering at him. "There is still time for a match. Turn this carriage around and you can test your skill against my uncle at first light."

Taran leaned against the cushion and crossed his arms over his chest. "I have no desire to test my skill against Peiter Everston, though it would doubtless prove far less taxing than dealing with his niece."

Caroline straightened. "That was your choice."

He snorted. "Not so, my lass. You did not want me—do not want me," he corrected, "but we both know our duty."

"Duty be damned," she snapped.

He closed his eyes. At the masque, he had wished Aphrodite would ignore duty and run away with him. His wife didn't share the same sentiment towards duty. Apparently she didn't plan to face her obligations head on. Rather she intended to make him pay for his effort.

He opened his eyes and looked at her. "What did you hope to accomplish with this idiotic stunt?"

"It is not idiotic. And you ruined my dress."

"When we arrive at the inn, I will have every one of your cases opened and searched. Any other such deathtraps shall meet the same fate as this." He waved, indicating the dress and corset.

Her head jerked in his direction, the feather slapping his eye. "You will do no such thing."

He seized the hat. She cried out as he shoved open the door and tossed it to the ground. Caroline lunged for the opening. Taran grabbed her arm, yanked her back into the seat, and slammed shut the door. He twisted in his seat and forced her back onto the cushion.

"Get off." She squirmed, but only served to remind him of her lush curves and full breasts. The arousal that had vanished when he'd opened the door to find her unconscious returned with a hard throbbing in his cock. He grasped her waist, yanking her onto her back and lay on top of her. In her struggles, her thighs spread and he settled his hips between them. Desire flashed and twisted in his gut.

"Seems to me that you prefer death to being my wife," he said. "Mayhap it is my fault for not showing you the benefits of becoming Viscountess

Blackhall."

He kissed her. After her response to his kiss at the altar—and she had responded—he expected more than the cold thin lips that now pressed limply against his. She squeaked and pummeled small fists against his shoulders. His heart fell. Surely that backbone wasn't cold at the core. She gripped his arms and satisfaction shot through him. He would accept the burn of ire evident in her grip—for now.

He feathered his tongue against her lips. Her fingers tightened around his forearms. Taran slipped a hand beneath her. Velvety smooth skin met his fingertips where her dress lay open at the back. Her mouth parted in a small gasp. Relief flooded him. She was not completely immune to him. He glided his tongue along hers.

She tasted of sweet scones and innocence. Taran deepened the kiss, tasting the smooth inner flesh of her cheek. Her lips softened. Her grip on his arms remained firm, her fingers contoured against his muscles. She pulled him tighter. A low moan rumbled from her chest and her hips arched into him.

He lifted his mouth, dragging in a deep inhalation. By God, he wanted to take her here on the carriage seat, thrust his cock into her, and ravage that sweet body. He kissed her again, gently, tasting her lips and tongue. Memory of Aphrodite's warmth blurred with the desire for his wife and he rocked against the soft woman beneath him. Her full breasts pressed against his chest.

He broke the kiss and buried his face in her neck as he gyrated his hips, rubbing his erection against her. His cock ached, hard, demanding release. Last night, Aphrodite had taken him in hand. He couldn't expect the same of an innocent wife, but he needed some passion. If he closed the window, the interior of the carriage would be plunged into darkness. Part of him knew it wrong to substitute his wife for the woman locked in his thoughts. Yet, as he'd done last night, he could have Caroline straddle him, ride him hard as *she* had—

"Aphrodite," he whispered.

Caroline's nails bit into the muscles of his arms. Taran froze. Had he just called his wife by another woman's name? The carriage hit a bump, rocking them. His cock dug into her belly and she gasped as he bounced on top of her. Taran seized the door handle to keep them from falling to the floor. The carriage levelled out and Caroline shoved at him until he sat up.

She scrambled to the far end of the seat, dress clutched to her breasts.

"What did you say?"

"Caroline," he began in a hoarse voice.

"You toy with me," she snapped.

He started to answer, but paused. Blood roared in his ears and his shaft throbbed as if it had a mind of its own. God help him, he wasn't sure that wasn't the case. How had he confused his wife with the woman he'd met last night? The two glasses of wine he'd had at the wedding breakfast were no excuse. William had been right. A man's cock ruled his will. Taran met Caroline's steady stare. She was beautiful. Raven hair, green eyes that deepened when lit with the fire of indignation, and creamy flesh any man would hunger to touch. Yet, he longed to feel Aphrodite tremble in his arms again. His thoughts and emotions jumbled in confusion.

He drew a deep breath. "Nay, love, I do not toy with you. It was an honest mistake." There was some truth to that. "What wife can fault a husband for likening her to the goddess of love?"

Guilt stabbed deep. She could and would fault him if she knew the truth, but he wouldn't hurt her with the truth. He couldn't prevent a silent, morbid laugh. His sense of chivalry knew no bounds. As if reading his mind, she broke her gaze from his and stared out of the window.

He hesitated, then turned his attention to the countryside visible from his side of the carriage. What had so captured his attention about the woman last night that he was willing to jeopardize the harmony he craved in his home? He had shared passion with other women far more skilled than Aphrodite. The way she moved between angel and devil drew him like a moth to the flame. But why? Damn it. He didn't know why, but he had to find out.

Taran glanced at his wife. She still stared out of the window. He wouldn't again confuse her with the phantasm he'd touched last night.

Chapter Ten

Caroline pulled her cloak more tightly around her and, elbows tucked to her sides to keep her dress from falling from her shoulders, offered her hand to Taran. He lightly gripped her fingers as she stepped from the carriage. She glanced at the sun setting against milky white clouds that hung over the trees in the horizon. The beauty tugged at her mind, but her heart found no solace in the picture.

Taran slipped her hand into the crook of his arm and led her up the walkway of the inn. "A room should await us. I made arrangements a week ago knowing we would have to return right away." She swung her gaze onto his face and he added, "I sent word immediately to your uncle informing him of my plans."

"Informing me would have been more appropriate."

Taran angled his head in acknowledgment. "I will not make that mistake again."

A tall man appeared in the doorway. "My lord."

"Adam," Taran said, then looked at her. "Caroline, may I present the proprietor, Mr.

Adam Main. Adam, my wife, Viscountess Blackhall."

Adam gave a low bow. "My lady. Welcome to the Cross Keys Inn."

"The Cross Keys Inn?" she blurted. "The home to the Society of the Caledonian Hunt?"

Mr. Main shot Taran an inquiring look, then said to her, "You know of the society?"

"I do. My father was a friend of Colonel Thornton's."

Mr. Main's eyes lit. "Colonel Thornton, aye, he is well known to us."

"My father was Ross Wilmont," Caroline said.

"Ross Wilmont," he burst out. "He rode Sir Laurence in the race of ninety-five. He had the race in his pocket—we all knew it—when he—" Mr. Main broke off, a horrified look on his face.

Memory sliced through Caroline like a dull knife, but she smiled gently. "When he was thrown from Sir Laurence and broke his neck, Queen Sheba beat him by a nose." That was an exaggeration, Caroline knew, but not by much. Her father had been riding the most treacherous part of the track when Sir Laurence had thrown him, but everyone said he had such a wide lead, Queen Sheba hadn't a chance to overtake him.

Mr. Main's gaze swung onto Taran.

Taran grasped her arm. "Caroline, I had no idea."

She shifted her gaze to him and startled at sight of his ashen face. "Do not fret. How could you have known?"

His expression darkened. "Why did Etherton not tell me?" Before she could reply, he said, "We will ride on. I know of another inn."

"Nonsense." She returned her attention to Mr. Main. "Sir, my father loved racing."

"That he did, my lady."

"May we come in?" She nodded towards the door, which he still blocked.

He stepped aside. "Forgive me."

"Caroline." Taran's grip on her arm tightened.

She looked up at him. "My father promised to bring me to the Cross Keys Inn." She glanced at Mr. Main. "When racing was out of season, of course." She smiled, and his expression relaxed. She looked back at Taran. "I always regretted not seeing the place he so loved." Taran hesitated and she placed a hand on the fingers that grasped her arm. "He died three years ago. The grief is past."

His grip loosened and she entered the foyer, careful to keep her elbows still tucked around the sides of her dress.

Mr. Main hurried past her. "Your rooms are ready."

Caroline paused at the open French doors to the right. A couch sat in front of the hearth where a fire blazed. Queen Anne chairs sat on each side of the couch, facing one another. A secretary was located in the far left corner, and a table and chairs sat in front of the window on the wall to the right. A lone man lounged in an overstuffed chair to the left of the fireplace. He nodded, acknowledging her with a smile.

She looked back at Mr. Main. "A quiet evening."

"'Tis early, my lady. Another hour and the drawing room will be filled."

"Will the famed ballroom be in use tonight?"

"Aye, a wedding party."

"Ah," she intoned, and refrained from glancing at Taran, afraid he would read the thought—*another poor girl is to walk the plank.*

"This way," Mr. Main said, and led them down a narrow hallway and up a long flight of stairs.

He stopped at the third room to the right and opened the door, standing aside so they might enter. Caroline stepped into the room. To the right, a fire burned in the hearth. Two chairs sat on each side of a small table in front of the fireplace, with a tub between them and the crackling fire. From the corner of her eye, she caught sight of the large, four poster bed on the opposite side of the room, but she kept her gaze on the tub and strolled towards it.

"Have water for a bath prepared," Taran said, "and send up a bottle of your best brandy."

"Aye, my lord," Mr. Main replied.

Caroline ran a finger along the tub's rim, cursing the unsteadiness in her hand and the spike in her heartbeat when the door clicked shut.

"Caroline."

She faced her husband. "A hot bath will set me to rights, my lord. Very kind of you to think of it."

He crossed the room and halted before her. "I am sorry."

She waved him off. "You could not know."

He caught her hand in his. "Nay."

Caroline stood frozen, unable to feel anything, but the warmth of the fingers clasping hers.

"I am sorry I was fool enough not to have consulted you directly about our travel plans. Sorry you could not spend your wedding night in more familiar surroundings." He paused and she feared he could hear the hammering of her heart. "Sorry you were forced to marry a man you did not know, would not have wanted even if you had."

"You owe me no apology. We are both defined by our positions." She stared up into his dark eyes. Lust coiled in her belly. This man had made her toss out all reason and give her heart to a masked lord. Would he be sorry to learn she did want him?

Taran's expression turned speculative and his grasp on her hand tightened. "A shame Etherton did not allow you more freedom. Worldly experience would have better prepared you for what lies ahead as Lady Blackhall."

Caroline stared. Was he saying what she thought he was saying? Hysterical laughter bubbled up, but she swallowed the compulsion. If he even suspected the extent of her *experience*... He lifted a finger to her cheek. She jumped.

He paused, a tender smile spreading across his face, then slowly traced a line down her cheek. "I will do my best to see that you do not regret the bargain you were forced to make."

She couldn't tear her gaze from his. "What have I to regret, my lord, except perhaps the ruin of my dress?"

Surely not the fact he would trade her for another woman if fate allowed. And would she not trade him for the kilted god in the garden? Would she? This morning, she could think of nothing but the emotion he had stirred deep in her breast during the midnight hours. Yet, only hours later when, as Lord Blackhall, he'd faced her uncle without flinching. A trembling began deep inside her that had intensified at sight of the pain on his face when he'd realized he had brought her to the place where her father died.

His hand dropped from her cheek. "Count yourself fortunate you survived that death contraption you call a dress." He slid his gaze down her body.

The quiver in her belly deepened, but she lifted her chin. He had offered his life for his wife's honor, but last night, he had offered Aphrodite his heart. *She* was his Aphrodite. Today, his touch had ignited fires deep in her center, just as it had last night. Her eyes burned with unshed tears. He hadn't recognized her when he'd touched her as his wife for the first time. She should be grateful, but that didn't lessen the sting.

"I hope before the night is through you will have nothing to regret."

Taran reached for her. A hard knock sounded at the door. He cast an irritated glance at the door. "Who is it?"

"Your bags, my lord," their driver called through the door.

Taran returned his attention to her. "It is time I examine your wardrobe."

"As you wish," she said with a nonchalance she was far from feeling. If he made good on the threat and found the vial tucked away in a corner of the smallest chest, the ruse would be up before it had begun. That morning, when Mabel had finally left her to bathe, Caroline had emptied the sleeping powder from the vial she kept in her armoire and extracted precious drops of blood from her finger. That had been the simple part. Getting the blood onto the sheet would prove the real challenge.

She lifted her chin and met Taran's gaze. "Take yourself off while I bathe."

He laughed, the sound deep and masculine. Caroline checked the leap of her heart. The laugh wasn't meant as the intimate insinuation she yearned for. The man was simply a charming rogue who seduced women.

A second knock on the door broke the spell.

Without breaking his gaze from hers, he called, "Enter."

The door swung open and the driver and guard entered, each with a chest over their shoulders.

Taran eyed the trunks. "You made full use of the hour before we left your uncle's. What could possibly be left to send to Strathmore?"

"I could not leave home to find I'd left behind something important."

His brow shot up. "Important?" He flicked a meaningful glance at her dress. "More of the same, I presume."

She straightened. "This is my most stylish dress. The others are not nearly as fashionable."

"Praise be for one consolation," he said, and faced the men. "Over there." Taran pointed to the far corner of the room.

The men deposited the trunks in the corner, then left. Two more men appeared in the doorway with buckets of steaming water. Taran nearly laughed aloud at the wide-eyed glance his wife flicked in his direction. The men filed out and the door clicked shut behind them.

Taran met her gaze. "You look like the fox about to be eaten by the hound."

Caroline wrapped her free arm around her middle before realizing the action confirmed his assessment, and dropped it back to her side.

He crossed the room and halted in front of her. "You haven't a maid. Allow me." He tugged the cloak string loose.

Her pulse jumped. "I...I can manage. The dress is torn, if you recall."

He pushed the cloak from her arms. The thick fabric pooled at her feet as he trailed his fingers over her shoulders. She stiffened, but he pulled her closer nonetheless. He bent and placed his lips to the fluttering pulse in the column of her neck. She inhaled sharply.

"My lord," Caroline whispered and gripped his forearms, "my bathwater." The weak protest trailed into silence.

Tunneling his fingers into her raven tresses, he angled her head up towards him and pressed his lips to hers. He breathed in her gasp and parted her lips with his tongue. Caroline forced her arms to remain limp at her side. He slid his tongue along hers. Desire jump-started her heart. Pray God he misinterpreted her excitement as fear, and not the lust that demanded she open her thighs for him. She must play the wilting lily.

He deepened the kiss and she imagined herself stripped bare, him parting the delicate petals of her pussy with his rod, then plunging into her. Did his core burn as hers did? He ended the kiss and stroked a thumb across her lower lip. She willed her trembling mouth to still, but without success.

"Your bath is waiting." As he drew his hands away, he tugged the fabric of her dress forward.

"Sir." She clutched the dress to her breast. "A few moments of privacy, if you will." She tried a conciliatory smile. "The trip was long."

He leaned close, grazed his lips along her cheek, then whispered near her ear, "I am well past resisting your charms. A bath is not required, just a bed."

She inhaled sharply. Satisfaction flickered in his eye before he turned and strode towards the door. "I leave you to your bath."

The door closed and she stared at the empty place where he had just been. And once the bath was finished, how would she deal with him?

Chapter Eleven

Caroline exhaled a sigh as she stepped one foot, then the other, into the bathwater. Soothing warmth enveloped her feet and sent a quiver of gooseflesh up her legs. How was she to pretend she didn't want Taran when every inch of her body ached for his touch? A tiny flutter played against the inside of her tummy. He desired Aphrodite, but determination had shown in his gaze when he looked at her—he intended to have her. Tonight.

She lowered herself into the water. If only someone would tell her how to keep her heart from melting when heat sparked in his gaze. She cast a glance at the door. If he returned before she finished her bath or devised a way out of this mess, she might be forced to end this ridiculous marriage by throttling him.

Blessedly, he hadn't yet connected her to Aphrodite. When he'd called her by that name in the carriage, she thought her ruse over. A flash of anger blended with a secret pleasure. The slip of the tongue meant he'd been as affected as she by their encounter—and that he was no better than her. The lout hadn't the good grace to keep his women straight.

Jealousy twisted in her belly. Would he confuse her with his next lover? *Foolish.* She had no right to expect him to bed only her. Even if he learned she was Aphrodite, wanted her to be Aphrodite, over time his passion would wane and he would seek other lovers. No wife expected anything less. Once they produced the required heir, most welcomed being left to their own devices...their own lovers. Caroline closed her eyes. That lover would have been the kilted god. Now, she would have neither husband nor lover.

There had to be a way to keep him from her bed—this night and forever. She tensed against the ache that gripped her at the thought of never again touching him. What choice did she have? Lord Blackhall wasn't a man who would stand for being cuckolded—even if he was the man doing the cuckolding. He would despise her. How would she live with a man who hated her?

Caroline stilled at a thought. Perhaps Taran would accept a settlement in return for an annulment. Why hadn't she thought of it before? Surely a year's salary would be enough to pull the estate from ruin while he sought another, more agreeable, wife. Uncle would balk, but with Taran in control of her fortune—her heart sank. Why settle for twenty-five thousand pounds, when he already controlled a fortune well beyond that if he managed the money well? He had two sisters to care for and a father who had determined long ago nothing short of a rich heiress would do for his son.

The new fear that had plagued her all day surfaced. Lord William Edmonds, Viscount of Thornhaven, was a close friend of her husband, and the domino she had dallied with at the masque. The moment he'd spoken, she'd recognized his voice. Her stomach sickened. Over and over, she had replayed their meeting outside her uncle's townhouse, and had detected no hint of recognition in his manner. Even now, he may have realized who she was. Would he inform Taran of her deception, or demand payment for his silence?

Once the marriage was *officially* consummated, once she bore Taran a child, there would be no turning back. If Lord Edmonds exposed her— The door swung open.

Caroline shrieked, ducking deeper in the tub and sloshing water over the sides. Taran stood in the doorway, the tailored riding coat and breeches he had worn for the journey replaced by a simple shirt and front breeches.

Her gaze caught on the swelling bulge of his groin and she jerked her gaze back to his face. "I—I will be but a moment longer."

Amusement twitched at a corner of his mouth. "You will prune." He stepped into the room, pushing the door closed behind him.

She glanced at the swirling water surrounding her. Her breasts bobbed and a dark triangle of hair shadowed between her legs. Places he'd touched, explored and, as her husband, had a right to touch as often as he pleased.

Fear clawed at the thin layer of her composure.

"Please, my lord," she whispered.

He stepped into the room and crossed to the bed while unbuttoning his shirt. "I promise, that will not be the last time you whisper those words tonight."

"I am not sure this is the right time."

"It is the perfect time. You are here and already undressed."

"Such consideration," she snapped.

"I promise to be a very considerate husband." He paused in unbuttoning the last button and looked at her. "You have nothing to fear, Caroline. I know you have not had a mother's instruct—"

"I am aware of what happens between a man and a woman."

His gaze bore into her for an instant and fear shot to the surface before he finally looked away and undid the last button. He shrugged the shirt from his shoulders and Caroline barely stifled a gasp. In the carriage she had felt him, touched him, but without light, she had been unable to fully grasp his perfection. He stood before her now, his broad chest flexing as he reached for the tie on his breeches.

Her cheeks heated with memory of his powerful arms when he'd anchored her to his lap and his thighs as they'd thrust and flexed, plunging his cock deep into her core. He had been hers for a night. And she must make him believe in her purity.

"Are you not hungry, my lord?"

"Supper can wait." He sat on the bed, grabbed the heel of one boot, and tugged.

"I am famished," Caroline went on. "If you give me moment, I will dress, and meet you downstairs in the dining room. A hearty supper and some claret will do us good after the long day's travel." Plenty of claret, she silently added. She needed him drunk—one way or another.

He paused, a brow raised. "Claret, madam? What would your uncle say?"

She started to reply that she didn't give a damn what her uncle thought, then recognized the amusement in Taran's eyes. He returned his attention to his boots and Caroline jumped with the thud of the first boot dropping onto the carpet beside the bed. He reached for the second one, arms flexing with the effort. Her mouth went dry. She was too eager to have those arms around her again. Dear Lord, what was this power he had over her body? Taran pulled the second boot free and dropped it alongside its mate, then rose. Her heartbeat fluttered when he crossed to her and squatted beside the tub.

"Do you fear our joining so much that you would avoid me altogether?" he asked.

The weight of his stare rolled over her flesh. She drew in a shallow breath in an effort to slow her pounding heart. Never had she felt so exposed, vulnerable, afraid of the truth.

"The fear, my lord, is that once our marriage is consummated there is no undoing what is done."

He dipped a finger into the water and traced a line over the swell of her breast. "A futile concern, Caroline. We have said the vows. There is no retreat." He drew a gentle circle around her puckered nipple.

She shivered. "But...but what if I am not what you expect?" Her heart whispered *what if I am more?*

"You are already unexpected."

"Unexpected—" Caroline stiffened.

His attention remained on the nipple he traced. "While I concede you will more likely than not"—a corner of his mouth turned upward—"vex me during the course of our marriage, I am not displeased."

His gaze slid upward to her face and he stared for a long moment. He threaded his fingers beneath the damp hair at the nape of her neck. Heat from his hand sizzled on her flesh. With a gentle tug, he pulled her close. A puff of breath escaped his lips. Closer. She could scarcely breathe. His breath fluttered against her lips.

"My lord," she whispered as his mouth came down on hers.

Gentle pressure parted her lips and his tongue slipped inside her mouth. Slanting his head, he sealed their mouths. Tongue rubbed against tongue. He tasted of aged brandy, and the intoxication of his kiss seeped into her blood—into her body.

At least in the bath, he couldn't see how wet she was for him. A steady pulse throbbed in her sex and tingles tightened her nipples, chasing into the hidden knot of nerves waiting for his touch, the touch of his mouth. But, tonight, she entered his bed as wife, not lover. Uncertainty dug deeper in her stomach. How differently would he treat her as Lady Blackhall? The courtesan of last night had received the full scope of his desire. As wife, she wanted that and more.

Taran trailed a hand from her neck, along her spine and dipped into the water, downward over the swell of her hip while he cupped her breast with his other hand and grazed her nipple with a thumb.

Caroline pulled away from the kiss. "My lord."

She lifted a hand dripping with water and braced the palm against his chest with the intention of pushing him away, but froze at the feel of the wall of muscle beneath her fingers. Last night in the carriage, she'd learned his body by touch, but seeing what she had touched brought with it a dizzying sensation that compelled her to explore every inch of him. Unlike the soft, plump bodies of most men of privilege, Taran's lean, hard body spoke of a man who asked for nothing, but worked for every gain. She frowned at the sight of a jagged scar on the left side of his abdomen, near the middle ribs.

"What is this?" Caroline touched the scar.

He sucked in breath. She yanked her hand back, her gaze lifting to his face. His copper eyes blazed. He grasped her hand and her attention fixed on the action as he pressed her palm to the scar. His muscles tensed beneath her touch and warmth seeped clear to her bones.

"A slip of the sword," he said.

Her head snapped up. "My lord?"

"The scar."

A slip of the sword? Whose, a disgruntled husband, or some young buck who dared challenge a calmer hand? How many dawn appointments had this man faced? Had she miscalculated when she'd said Uncle would defeat him in a duel?

She startled at the brush of fingers on her breast beneath the water. His stare remained locked with hers as he touched her. She flushed, the water suddenly cold. How was she to endure the agonizing pleasure and not leap from the bathwater and onto him?

He leaned forward and rested his forehead against hers. "Caroline, I am no brute. Sharing a bed can bring us both pleasure."

How could she answer? A wife's place was not to question her husband's past liaisons, but the forbidden knowledge she possessed as Aphrodite confirmed the truth of his words. Determination rose. She wouldn't let a fantasy of a woman who didn't truly exist occupy Taran's thoughts. Not tonight. When he plunged his hard, beautiful cock into her, he would know the woman in his arms was real.

She jammed her eyes shut. *Fool*, such liberties were not hers to take. He could never know her as he had Aphrodite, not now, not ever. A mental picture rose of their lives fifteen years into the future, his sudden recognition and hatred, that loathing reflected in their son's eyes as the father's revulsion seeped into every aspect of their lives.

"Do not fear," he whispered near her mouth.

Caroline jarred from the morbid vision and gave a small cry when he kissed her again. The hand on her hip tightened almost convulsively, then wrapped around her back. He slipped his other arm beneath her knees and lifted her from the water.

Caroline squeaked and threw her arms around his neck. Water streamed onto his chest and arms, soaking his breeches and leaving a trail across the floor as he strode to the bed. She shivered, the chilled room a stark contrast to the warm, contoured torso that pressed into her breasts and hip.

He stopped beside the bed and looked down at her. "Kiss me, sweet."

She blinked in surprise. He stared, the dark eyes intense, but pleading for something, anything, to show she wasn't without feeling...wasn't the cold bitch John had said she was. Understanding hit with the force of a gale wind. This man was nothing like John. John would have given no thought to the fact she despised his touch. He would have bedded her until the required heir was produced, then left her a dry husk, never again to be touched or considered.

But Taran had no taste for life with a woman who hated him. Love was not a requirement, but neither was loathing an option. If she didn't give herself to him, he would believe she hated him. Until last night, she had. He deserved better than she would have given John. Tears stung the corners of her eyes. He must never know the truth. She had to get to the vial hidden beneath the mattress and empty it onto the sheets before he awoke in the morning.

Caroline tightened her arms around his neck and inched forward until her lips brushed his. He opened his mouth opened and his tongue snaked between her lips. His gentle but determined thrusts against her tongue set her heart to pounding. God help her, she wanted him. How many more nights could she have with him before this house of cards fell in on her...before he grew tired of her and sought another woman? Her heart twisted. Better another woman than his hatred. She sank into the kiss, drinking in his essence. Never in her wildest dreams had she conceived this moment possible. Her masked lord held her close, sweeping her into a vortex of carnal cravings.

Arms tight around her, Taran sat on the edge of the bed, settling her on his thighs. She gasped at the feel of his erection against her hip and the pull of awareness travelled from her nipples into the hotness between her legs. He broke the kiss and trailed a finger along her face, feathered his touch along the column of her neck and over her shoulder.

He bent his head and closed his mouth over a nipple. Caroline bit down on her bottom lip in an effort to keep from moaning. Despite the pleasure that slipped through her veins, melting her from the inside, she would give herself to him as the expected virgin. His velvet tongue curled around the nipple. She squeezed her thighs against the burgeoning need that rose between her legs. Wet heat rolled over her breast. Answering warmth slicked her thighs.

He would know how she responded, just as she could feel his arousal, hard and erect in his breeches, prodding into her hip.

He shifted and set her on the bed, then stood and stared down at her, eyes dark with desire. Her breath caught. Here was the man from last night, filled with lust.

Tucking his thumbs into the sides of his breeches, he pushed them past lean hips. His broad shoulders, tapered torso, and strong thighs held her mesmerized. And his cock. Long, thick, and fully erect, thrust towards her. Dark curls circled the base and trailed up over his groin. Silvery liquid leaked from the slit in the rounded knob. Her mouth watered, yet she knew she could never again taste him in that way.

He sat on the mattress and began shoving the breeches from his legs. Caroline scrambled to the center of the bed. With a hard tug, she pulled the coverlet from the pillows and dived beneath the blanket. The crisp sheets chilled her, but did nothing to stop the steady thrum that pulsed in her pussy. She was wet and her internal muscles clenched with the desire to have his cock deep inside. Caroline swallowed, thankful his back was to her. Her only doubt was her ability to hide her response to him.

Taran stood and faced her, giving her full view of all that made him perfectly male. "I cannot promise there will be no pain."

He seemed to stumble over the words. Perhaps because only last night he'd whispered a similar sentiment to another virgin?

"I am strong." She winced inwardly at the schoolgirl words. Even last night, when she had been a true virgin, she'd had no fear of this man.

He braced one knee on the bed and cupped her cheek. "Do I frighten you?" *Yes*, her heart cried, but she only nodded.

He leaned forward and touched his lips to hers. Caroline silently cursed the tremble in her mouth, then realized he would mistake the action for trepidation, not desire. Praise heaven for small favors. Now if she could just keep from grabbing his cock and shoving it inside her, she might yet convince him she hadn't tasted him before this night.

He came down on top of her and she was certain the feel of his hard length through the blanket was enough to bring her instant pleasure. He cupped her face and kissed her. She startled at the gentle thrust of his erection against her stomach. He kissed her cheek, then lower, to her neck. She pushed at his shoulders, unable to stifle a whimper when his tongue flicked at the spot beneath her ear in unison with another thrust onto her stomach.

"So sweet," he whispered into her ear.

Caroline shivered.

Taran shifted to the side and tugged the blanket from between them. Cool air rolled across her body, puckering her nipples and tightening her pussy to near discomfort. He sucked in breath and a blush of heat rose into her cheeks. He had never looked upon Aphrodite, never had his cock harden because she lay naked before him. Whatever she might have lost, this belonged to her, his wife.

He shifted back on top of her. Warmth enveloped her like smooth steel heated before a blazing hearth. He kissed her forehead, eyes, then each temple before finally finding her mouth again. Caroline grasped his shoulders. Muscles bunched beneath her fingers and she envisioned those muscles tightening as he pumped into her.

Her breath caught and he gave a soft chuckle. Unexpected embarrassment warmed her cheeks. This was not a man with his paramour, but the gentle touch of a lord with his lady. While last night his lust had incited her to the heights of ecstasy, this was no less arousing. He kissed her, sliding his mouth from her lips, down past her jaw, neck, then lower to the curve of her breasts.

She tightened her fingers on his shoulders, her nails sinking into his flesh. He latched onto a nipple and she couldn't prevent a moan. She shifted, then realized too late she had opened her thighs for him. He settled against her mound and the weight of him pressed so intimately to her brought a wave of desire that was nearly her undoing. His warm hand covered her other breast. He abruptly stopped. She shifted her gaze onto him, her heart pounding. Had recognition come so soon, so suddenly?

His gaze travelled her length and she instinctively reached for the blanket.

"You are mine to look upon." He smiled gently. "To touch." He traced a line down her leg with a finger. "To kiss."

He slid to the foot of the bed and grasped her foot. A tickle caused her to try and yank from his grasp, but his hold tightened as he brought her foot to his mouth and flicked his tongue against her toe. She shrieked when he sucked the toe into his mouth.

Her pussy throbbed. "Bloody hell."

Taran paused and lifted his eyes to hers. He stared for a long moment, then slid his tongue between her toes. Heat raced into her breasts, stomach, fingertips, and her juices soaked her folds. The scent of her arousal intensified, need boiling within her. She stretched her toe and he sucked it the way she'd sucked his cock in the maze, working it in and out of his mouth. She balled her hands into fists against the sudden desire to touch herself and work her fingers between the dewy folds and ease the ache.

Her toe popped from his mouth and her hips dropped onto the bed. Caroline dragged in a breath. Good lord, she had bowed off the mattress like a catapult pulled back to full extension. She had no idea her feet were connected to her pussy. So he had not given *every* intimate secret to Aphrodite? What more would he teach her?

As if reading her mind, he rained kisses up one leg, then the other, rubbing, touching as he drove her beyond thinking. When he parted her legs, her pulse jumped with the hope he would put his mouth on her as he had last night. Instead, he placed soft kisses to her hips, across her pelvis, even tasting her navel before he positioned himself over her. Gaze locked with hers, he settled his hips between her thighs. His cock rode the wet slit of her sex.

"When I enter you, it will not be pleasant." He braced on his arms, keeping most of his weight from her.

Caroline resisted the urge to wrap a leg around his calf. "I understand," she replied in a small voice she prayed didn't reveal how much she wanted his hardness slamming in and out of her passage.

Remember the first time, he'd said as he slid his rod between her legs. Could she recall the pain? The intense, but brief discomfort was a distant memory, drowned within the pool of pleasure that had followed.

Taran laced the fingers of one hand with hers and, leveraging higher, aligned the crown of his stalk with her drenched opening.

"You are so wet." He pushed in an inch and spread her juices over his cock.

Caroline bit back a whimper. The torture of his patience was killing her. *Hold strong,* she commanded herself. *He must believe you are innocent.*

He pushed a fraction deeper, gyrating his hips to stretch her opening. He wrapped an arm under her back and unexpectedly thrust deep. Caroline cried out. Her back arched off the bed at the burn of intrusion. No longer a virgin, but Taran still had the length and thickness to stretch her taut channel. Tears seeped from the corner of her eyes.

He hugged her close, keeping their bodies still. "Forgive me." He kissed her closed eyes. "It is better to get the first thrust over with quickly."

Caroline clung to his shoulders. "I am well, my lord." She shifted beneath him.

"Fuck," he groaned, and pulled back before easing into her again.

His slow, steady strokes built momentum. Cream slicked her channel. Last night, having his cock thrusting into her had been divine. There were no words to describe tonight. He completed her.

Caroline lifted and rolled her hips. The pressure of his erection nudged the very deepest part of her body. He penetrated fully, then reared back slowly. Tremors rippled her internal walls. Sweat beaded on her brow and the weight of his body pressed her into the bed. She reveled in the sensations crashing through her. She gasped for breath, but Taran increased his speed. Sliding into her wet, heated sheath, pulling out, then sliding into her again. Cabled muscles in his arms bunched as he braced above her. A tick flinched in his clenched jaw. He rode her, wringing pleasure from her body.

"My lord." Her heart leapt. Had he detected the fear lacing her voice? She was going to come.

Harder thrusts inched her up the bed. She would not have thought it possible, but his rod felt harder, thicker, and plunged unbelievably deeper.

"*La petite mort.*"

"The little death," she repeated in a whisper.

Caroline jammed her eyes shut. Tiny sparks flashed behind her eyelids. Her tummy tightened and her mind numbed. Convulsions started deep in her core and radiated out through her body. She gripped his shoulders and locked her legs around his hips. Spasms jerked her entire being. Taran's arms tightened then, and with a shout, he erupted. Warm seed pulsed within her, slicking her channel as he continued to pump her full of his cream until he at last went limp on top of her, his chest heaving from exertion.

A moment passed, his breathing slowed, and he pressed a soft kiss to her lips, then rolled to the side. Caroline lay still as a mouse. She didn't dare glance at him. What thoughts weaved through his mind? Had she been convincing as the blushing bride? Her heart still pounded. She hadn't been able to completely stifle her response to his touch.

He stirred beside her, his gentle fingers tracing her arm.

"The tenderness and blood are expected," he said.

She gritted her teeth. Why in God's name wasn't the man already snoring in deep sleep? Damn his eagerness. If he chose now to verify her virginity he would find only a slippery combination of their completion.

He startled her by rising and starting across the room. Caroline stared, mesmerized by the sight of his tight buttocks flexing with each powerful step. Taran reached the sideboard and she jarred from the morbid trance.

He reached for the pitcher and she scrambled to the right side of the bed. The sound of water sloshing into the bowl filled the silence as Caroline stuffed a hand beneath the mattress. Her fingers touched then closed around the silver vial. She pulled it free just as he set the pitcher back on the table. She yanked the cover up over herself with the intention of opening the top when Taran turned, bowl and washcloth in hand.

Caroline froze, the vial gripped in one hand as he strode towards the bed. "Wh-what are you doing, my lord?"

Taran stopped beside the bed and set the bowl on the nightstand. He paused, clearly taking in the blanket clutched to chin level. "There is no reason to be embarrassed." He sat next to her. "Allow me to wash you."

Her heart pounded against her ribs. To have come so far, risked so much, only to be undone by the man's kindness.

"My lord, I..." She choked back the words. How could she ask him to leave the room so she could deceive him further?

He dipped the washcloth in the water. His gaze shifted to the cloth as he wrung water from it and Caroline glanced at the edge of the bed. She could never slip the vial back beneath the mattress without being caught. Tears rose perilously close to the surface. It was enough that he would discover she wasn't the promised virgin, but to catch her trying to deceive him would incur his wrath, maybe even recall his instructions to Aphrodite last night. Recognition would be instantaneous.

He shifted and Caroline stuffed the vial beneath her pillow. Taran faced her, his expression gentle. He leaned forward and breathed a kiss to her neck, caressed the edge of her breast with a feathering touch. Gently, he urged her back onto the pillow, then pried the covers from her fingers. He pulled the blanket down to her feet. Caroline shut her eyes and steeled herself for his wrath.

With pressure to the insides of her knees, he opened her legs. Cool fabric pressed against her mound. Gentle swipes of the cloth wiped away the blending of their cream.

Caroline startled at feel of firm lips pressed to her inner thigh.

"Forgive me," he murmured.

She opened her eyes and looked at him. Back rigid and his mouth a tight thin line, his ministrations were centered on her thighs. She shifted her gaze to her legs. Her breath caught. Streaks of blood stained the sheets. More blood—but how? In a flood, tears filled her eyes and the weight of her secret crashed around her. *More blood.* She hadn't known it was possible. Apparently neither had Taran. She wouldn't need the vial after all.

Taran traced a finger along her thigh. "Our first time—" He shook his head.

Relief washed over her and she couldn't refrain from covering his hand with hers. His head lifted and their gazes met.

Caroline offered a tremulous smile. "We are no longer strangers." Gratitude shone in his eyes and her heart broke.

* * * *

Tentative fingers slid across his stomach. Lower, across his groin. His breath grew thready and blood surged into his shaft. He was dreaming. Lying in a soft bed with a soft woman stretched out next to him. Silky hair draped over his shoulder and warm breath fanned against his chest. She shifted and her fingers brushed his cock. He groaned, reached over, and covered her hip with a palm. Her thighs parted. Soft, damp curls ground into his thigh. The woman moaned. A seductive, sweet sound he recognized. *Aphrodite.* So vivid and real beneath his hands. Smooth, naked curves. Heat from her pussy scorching his flesh. Clamping his eyes shut, he refused to wake. No. He wanted to be encased in her tight, slippery sheath.

Wrapping his hand over her thigh, he slid her onto his lap, a leg straddling each of his hips. Centered over his shaft, her slit parted and her folds surrounded his length. Rubbing, grinding, thrusting against her mound, he braced her hips, then moved his hands higher, over each rib. Finally, he cupped each perfect, full breast in his palms. He pinched the taut nipples and she gasped. Her hips rocked against him, emulating a lover's intimate dance.

Bracing a hand on his chest, she rose onto her knees and grasped his shaft. Taran clenched his jaw and angled his head back. Intense pleasure surged through him. Blood roared through his ears and his heart pounded. Her fingers were tight, yet her stroke was delicate. When she reached lower and fondled his scrotum, Taran thought he would go mad.

With precise movements, she positioned his rod at the entrance of her channel and, in one slow slide, took him in.

"Fuck me, my lord." Her voice was whisper quiet.

Caroline? His eyes snapped open. "Ah, fuck." The sound of his own voice broke the trance. This was no dream. A willing, wild woman sat astride him.

She rocked in a natural rhythm, raven tresses shifting forward then back with each tortuous movement. Embers from the hearth cast soft light, and Taran discerned unfocused, green eyes, heavy with desire. By God, his wife was asleep.

Lifting and lowering, she joined their bodies. Beautiful, ethereal, she was his wife. He tightened his grip on her hips and bucked harder into her heated, quivering sheath. Pulsing contractions gloved his cock, sucking him deeper.

Her thighs tightened to his hips and her eyes seemed to focus on his face. Understanding curled the corners of her mouth. "Tis a pleasant experience to wake to." Her voice, rough from sleep, nearly sent him over the edge.

"If done right, it is," he replied.

She paused, her smile faltered, then she moved again. Faster, quickly building to a frenzy. Her head fell back and convulsed along his shaft. He reached between her legs and carefully grazed his thumb across her swollen button of nerves. Caroline cried out and collapsed onto his chest. Wrapping arms around her back, he anchored her tight to his sternum and sought his own release. The force of his thrust lifted her from his lap and had her plunging down hard onto his cock. Again. And again. He gripped her tighter. Fucked her harder. Penetrated deeper. Finally he exploded, shooting hot ribbons of cream deep into her passage.

Her breathing came hard and fast. She turned her head and placed whispered kisses on his sweat-dampened chest. Taran cradled her head and lifted her mouth to his. He tasted her acceptance and her pleasure. Yes, they would make a fine match. He broke the kiss and she slid onto the mattress. After adjusting the blanket over her shoulder, she curled into his side.

His last coherent thought was of Caroline.

Chapter Twelve

The following morning, Caroline shoved the hood of her cloak back from her head as she slipped into the stables. Three years had passed since her father had died in the racing accident. She didn't expect anything to be the same. How would she know if it were? But to be in the place where he had died sent a wave or sorrow over her. Early morning light streamed into the stable from the cracked door behind her. She halted and gazed down the center of the darkened stable. Familiar scents of leather, horse manure and straw hung in the air. Tears stung her eyes. Riding together had been her and her father's greatest joy.

"Pull yourself together," she instructed. "You have come to put your father to rest, not to grow dewy-eyed."

She had always known she would eventually come to the Cross Keys Inn. How strange that fate had chosen her wedding day to bring her here. A chestnut stuck his head out of the nearest stall to her left and nickered.

"Oh." Caroline approached the stall.

The beast tossed his head and sniffed at the fingers she extended. "You're a tame one." she murmured, and stroked his neck. "You would do perfectly. I wonder—"

"Can I help you, my lady?"

Caroline jerked her head in the direction of the male voice emanating from further within the stables. A form slid towards her from the murky shadows. As he neared, she distinguished a tall, muscular man with greying hair and a long stride that spoke of powerful thighs.

"Yes," she replied. "I was hoping for a morning ride."

The man stopped in front of her. "A morning ride? 'Tis not fully light yet. You should return in an hour and bring your husband with you."

The word *husband* made her stomach swoop. That she would require his permission pricked her pride. She shook her head. "I travelled all day yesterday in a carriage, and am to have more of the same immediately after my husband rises. I will have a little exercise before being confined for another day in that insufferable coach."

To her surprise, the man grinned. "Aye. A carriage is an abominable prison."

"Indeed. Sir, is there a horse I might ride? Twenty minutes is all I ask."

He nodded towards the chestnut beside them. "This fellow is a fine horse, but he has spirit."

"Spirit?" she repeated. "That is exactly what I need."

His brows lifted. "Ye sure you do not want a gelding?"

She grimaced. "I rode before I walked. Such animals are for the weak-kneed."

He grinned again. "I thought you might say that."

He strode back into the shadowed stables and returned a moment later, lantern in hand.

He hung the lantern on the wall beside the stall, then started back the way he had come.

Caroline hurried to catch up. "I can saddle him. You need not bother."

He gave her an appraising look. "Aye, I see you can, but I cannot allow that."

They turned into the tack room and he grabbed brush, saddle, and bridle. He nodded towards something behind her and Caroline turned to see the bucket of apples beside the door.

She beamed at the man, then scooped up two apples. "One for later," she said, "just in case."

The stable master nodded approval and she fell into step alongside him as he strode back to the chestnut. They reached the stall and he tossed everything but the brush on the ground, and reached for the latch.

"Sir," Caroline said, "I would be pleased if you let me brush him down."

He hesitated, then handed her the brush and lifted the latch on the door. The stall door swung open and he stood aside. Caroline smiled a thank you and entered.

"Easy," she cooed to the horse, and laid a firm hand on his neck as she extended the apple.

The chestnut sniffed at the fruit, then opened his lips. Caroline pushed the apple into his mouth, and the horse sucked it in. He crunched as she began brushing his lean back.

A few minutes later, the stable master returned and saddled the horse. He handed her the reins and she led the beast out of the stall. A mare stood tethered beside them.

Caroline gave the stable master a quizzical look.

"I cannot let ye go riding alone. If your husband is still sleeping…" He gave her a penetrating look.

"He is a late sleeper."

"Liam Rose at your service, my lady." He gave a slight bow, looking at her from the corner of his eye. "If your husband doesna' see my good deed as altruistic, I beg you to tell my wife I loved her."

Caroline gave a whoop of laughter, then clamped a hand over her mouth. She bit her lip and removed her hand from her mouth. "I promise you, sir, you have nothing to fear from my husband." She leaned closer and added in a whisper, "Particularly, if we return in the next hour."

Ten minutes later, they were on the hard dirt road headed east out of Kelso. Sunlight streaked through thick clouds in wide beams as sharp as knives.

"Looks like rain," Liam commented.

"Yes." She inhaled air that already smelt and felt heavy with water. Caroline pulled back on the horse's reins. "Is this the road where the Caledonian Hunt is held?"

"Caledonian Hunt?"

She jerked her attention onto him at the edge in his voice. Intense brown eyes studied her.

"Yes," she replied. "Caledonian Hunt. My father—" She broke off and took a slow breath as she slid her gaze along the wide open field before them. Why, after so long, was she suddenly at a loss for words? Caroline returned her gaze to Liam. "My father used to attend the hunt."

Liam studied her. "The Caledonian Hunt is a sight to behold. 'Tis a shame a horse lover like yourself could not attend."

"How long have you been stable master, Liam?"

He glanced heavenward. "We had better start back, my lady. Rain is sure."

"Wait." She slowed and he followed suit. "Please, tell me, where are the markers?"

His gaze bore into hers for an instant, then he nodded to the right of the massive field surrounded by trees on three sides. "That is the starting line." His gaze moved left. "They race across the field and through those trees for half a mile." He pointed to an opening on the left side in the middle of the trees.

"Half a mile through the forest?" She looked at him. "That must be dangerous."

"Aye. That is what makes the race exciting."

Her heartbeat accelerated. Exciting? How could anyone call a race that risked a man's life exciting?

"We must return," he said, and started to wheel his horse around.

Caroline grabbed his arm. "You did not answer my question, Liam. How long have you been stable master here?"

"Twelve years, my lady."

"Twelve!" She snatched her hand back as if singed. "Then you knew my father."

"Many men attend the hunt, my lady."

She stiffened. "How many die?"

"Die?"

She nodded and a chill crept across her flesh at sight of the knowing look that glinted in his eyes.

"Only one, my lady. And he did not simply die."

* * * *

Taran woke to drowsy awareness. Filmy images of creamy skin, full breasts, and dark curls between slim thighs flitted through the fog that shrouded his brain. His cock hardened. A firm mouth took in his length. Green eyes stared up at him as she worked his shaft in and out. Taran groaned, pumping slowly into the mouth. *Sweet innocence. Heaven and Hell. She devil and*—he snapped open his eyes—*wife!*

Morning sun streamed through the window, scorching his eyes. He squinted against the blinding light. As the fog of sleep burned away, memories of Caroline pounded like a hammer. Her taking him into her mouth in the garden, begging him to fuck her in the carriage, her gasp when he'd entered her, her cry of pleasure, and the way she had ridden him last night until they were both exhausted.

He turned his head to the right to discover the spot beside him on the bed empty. He scanned the room. Empty. Fury shot to the surface. Her reticence last night hadn't been a maiden's fear of the wedding bed, but fear of discovery. She had tricked him. But why? What reason could a woman have for seducing her future husband the night before their wedding?

How had she known he would attend the masque? He hadn't planned on attending. William had nearly twisted his arm to get him to go. Taran clenched his fist at memory of her in the corner with William, the upper edges of her nipples only inches from his friend's mouth.

Had she wanted him to become so angry that he called off the marriage? The black handkerchiefs, underdress, and stockings were intended to force him to cry off. Why give him her maidenhead and not reveal her identity? Would he have called off the wedding if she had confessed? By God, he wouldn't have, and she knew it.

He gave his head a hard shake. What the bloody hell was she up to? What woman went to the extreme of giving herself to a man in order to avoid marriage? Did she hate him that much? Impossible. She had wanted him, had reveled in the intense desire in their mating. No woman, no matter how accomplished an actress, could feign responses such as Aphrodite's.

Taran threw back the covers and leapt to his feet. He raked a hand through his hair. His gaze caught on the blood on the sheet. How? He recalled instructing her in how to fool her husband. The blood hadn't been necessary. Unable to control his lust for his wife, he'd torn into her afresh when he'd ravished her body, thrusting his cock into her. How she must have felt relief that she'd bled again.

Recalling the conversation with Aphrodite, he now understood her intention last night. *A little claret will do us both good.* The wench had wanted him drunk to conceal her treachery.

Taran stared at the sheets. He had given great care to her pleasure, yet hadn't suspected a thing. Nay, that wasn't true. There had been clues. He gave a harsh laugh. The wedding itself should have told him, those ridiculous black mourning clothes, but he had been so consumed with memories of Aphrodite.

"I have no fear," she had said. *"The wedding is soon. I will not say when."*

He had asked what she would do if a babe came, and it wasn't her husband's.

"Only God can know who the father is."

"God and you, my sweet," he ground out.

Why would she do this?

"I choose this lie," she had said.

He refocused on the blood and began to laugh.

* * * *

Caroline broke from her thoughts at sight of her husband standing in the doorway of the drawing room. *Husband.* A tremor rocked her stomach. He hadn't discovered she was Aphrodite. Might he never know? If she felt secure he wouldn't figure it out, she could live with this man for the rest of her life and be content. Or could she? He wanted another woman. Did it matter that woman was her?

He strode towards her. Given enough time, perhaps she could make him forget the fantasy, and love her, the real woman. Did that mean she must remain the *chaste* wife? Last night had been wonderful, but she hadn't given herself to him as she had the night before. Was she willing to never again experience his full passion in order to keep him? Would withholding Aphrodite send him into the arms of other women who would be willing to give him lustful passion?

Taran stopped at the table and angled his head. "Madam." He seated himself at the chair across from her. A maid appeared and set a tea cup in front of him. "Thank you." He looked at Caroline. "Have you had breakfast?"

She shook her head. "I eat little in the morning."

He glanced at the untouched platter of rolls in front of her. "So I see." He looked at the waiting maid. "Eggs and bacon for me."

She dropped a curtsy and hurried from the room.

Taran lifted the teapot and began pouring tea. "No hat today?"

Caroline resisted the urge to touch the edges of the simple curls that hung around her ears. "You threw my hat out of the door."

He grimaced. "That was no hat, madam."

Laughter threatened. The look on his face when he had seized the hat and tossed it out of the carriage had been worth nearly suffocating.

She forced a frown. "That hat is the height of Paris fashion."

"Then I am glad we are travelling to the Highlands, rather than France." He set the pot on the table. "And the corset?"

She no more mourned the loss of the corset than the hat, but lifted her chin, nonetheless. "You are aware of women's fashion, sir."

"I am aware of women's foolishness." She started to retort, but he said,

"You rose early.

I had expected to find you beside me when I woke."

Her cheeks flushed. "I thought you wished to get an early start this morning."

"Indeed." He dropped his gaze to her breasts.

Caroline shot a glance at the corner chair where sat the only other occupant of the room, who seemed overly absorbed in *The Times*. He was close enough for her to discern the deep blue eyes that were glued to his paper, and she couldn't help but believe he must have overheard Taran's comment. He glanced up and their gazes met. She flushed, now certain he had overheard them, and jerked her gaze back onto Taran.

He took a sip of tea and set the cup back on its saucer. "You slept well, I hope." He picked up a roll and began buttering it. "I worried I was overly *hard* on you last night."

"My lord," she hissed in a whisper.

His eyes lifted to meet hers. "I am only concerned for your welfare."

"We are not alone." She resisted the urge to look at the man again. She could feel his eyes on her.

Taran waved a hand dismissively, then took a bite of his roll. "This is a private corner."

Caroline glowered. "Do you make a habit of talking so openly?"

He paused in chewing and said as if injured, "I am a happy man."

She snorted. "Satisfied with yourself, is what you are."

His gaze darkened. "You are well satisfied, my lady. I saw to that."

She gasped, then clamped a hand over her mouth. He lifted a brow as if to challenge her to deny the statement and she seized her napkin from off her lap and threw it on the table.

"I will await you in our chambers." She started to rise, but he grabbed her wrist and shook his head.

"Nay. I have sent someone to pack your trunk. By now, it will be loaded onto the carriage. You will finish your tea while I have my breakfast, then we shall be on our way."

Caroline considered arguing, but lowered herself back into the chair. He released her and took another sip of tea.

"What business is so important we had to run pell-mell to Scotland?" she asked.

"Nothing you need concern yourself with."

She narrowed her eyes. "You intend on spending my money the day after our wedding."

The maid appeared with his breakfast. She set two plates before him. "Anything else, my lord?"

He shook his head. She left and Taran picked up knife and fork. "*My* money, love, and I paid creditors before we left Newcastle."

Caroline stared. "How dare you?"

He forked eggs into his mouth. "How dare I what?"

"Did you pay Beetleton and Hoffman?"

Taran halted in grasping a piece of bacon from his plate and looked at her. "What have you to do with attorneys at law?"

"A great deal, when the man I am to marry is in debt to them to the tune of twenty thousand pounds."

"You have been hard at work, I see."

"I am no idiot, sir."

He regarded her for a long moment before murmuring, "No, you are not." He took a big bite of the bacon and dropped the remaining piece on his plate. "Reckless, yes."

"I will not stand for your father taking charge of my inheritance," she said.

Taran laughed. "You just said you were not an idiot. Do not make the same mistake your uncle did in thinking my father runs my affairs."

Embarrassment warmed her cheeks. He was right. "As you say, but you must admit paying creditors the day of our wedding is improper."

"Are you suggesting our creditors wait even a day longer than necessary?"

She stiffened. "Your creditors, sir."

He grinned. "Never fear, madam. I paid your debts as well."

Chapter Thirteen

Taran grinned wider, knowing full well his wife wanted nothing more than to throttle him—a thought he found intriguing.

"Caroline Wilmont?"

Taran twisted and looked over his shoulder at the well-dressed man standing in the doorway.

The older man strode to their table and halted. "Why, it is you."

Caroline inclined her head. "Lord Cambrooke."

He gave a small bow. His attention centered on her ring, then jerked back to her face.

"You—" His eyes flicked to Taran. "My apologies, sir. I had no idea Caroline had married."

"Just yesterday," Taran said.

The older man's eyes widened. "You jest?"

From the corner of his eye, Taran caught sight of the slight grimace that twisted his wife's mouth. He smiled and shook his head. "No jest, sir. She is now Viscountess Blackhall."

Cambrooke's mouth dropped open. "You are the Earl of Blackhall's son?" Before Taran could answer, he flicked a glance at Caroline, then gave Taran a formal bow. "Lord Aldwin Cambrooke, at your service. I am an old friend of the family." His gaze shifted to Caroline. "I wondered how long before you guessed—" He broke off. Something flickered in his eyes. He shook his head. "Forgive an old man."

"No apologies are required." Caroline extended a hand.

He grasped her fingers, bending over them. "Most kind." He released her.

Guilt stabbed at Taran at the reminder he was at fault for the fact that their wedding night had been spent at the place where her father had died. "It is my doing."

"You know I always wanted to come to the Cross Keys Inn," Caroline interrupted. "I insisted we stay." She smiled. "You know I will have my way when I truly desire it."

Lord Cambrooke laughed. "Indeed, she is persuasive." He leaned towards her and said in a conspiratorial tone, "I hope you have satisfied this particular desire."

In a placid tone, Taran said, "The strange thing about desire is that it tends to ignite at the most inopportune moment." Caroline snapped her head in his direction. He smiled as if not noticing the blush that crept up her cheeks, and added, "Regardless of place or time."

Lord Cambrooke nodded, clearly not catching the byplay. "Indeed. Otherwise, a bride could not choose such a place as this." Her gaze swung back to him.

A soft smile curved the old man's mouth upward. "Put this behind you, my dear. Life is for the living."

Something flickered in her eyes. Taran's mind snapped to attention.

Lord Cambrooke patted her arm. "Where are you off to?"

"Strathmore," Taran answered. "Our home."

Surprise reflected in the man's eyes. "Surely, you do not mean to keep Caroline from London?"

Taran regarded him. "Viscountess Blackhall may visit London whenever she pleases. We will reside at Strathmore."

"But of course," he put in quickly. "No offence intended."

Taran inclined his head. "Of course not."

"What are you doing here?" Caroline asked. "This is not hunting season."

"True. But I seldom take part in the hunt any more. Too old."

Taran thought the man looked fitter than many men his own age, but kept silent.

"I am returning from a week in Melrose." Cambrooke grimaced. "A wasted week. But I must be going, I wish to make Newcastle today. So good to see you, my dear." He faced Taran and gave a slight bow. "Sir."

Taran nodded and took the last bite of eggs. He wiped his mouth with a napkin and tossed it on his plate. "Our carriage awaits." He rose and stepped aside in invitation for Caroline to precede him.

Frustration sparked in her gaze. He forced back a laugh and lifted an enquiring brow.

She rose and started past him, but Taran grasped her elbow and stopped her.

"Is something amiss?" he asked.

She gave an almost imperceptible shake of her head. "Marriage is exactly as I imagined."

He trailed fingers higher on her arm. "Is it too much to hope you refer to last night's activities?"

She drew in a thready breath. Desire skittered down his spine.

"How would I have had any preconceptions on that matter, sir?" she asked in a sweet voice that didn't fool him for an instant. "I refer to your determination to bring me to heel. What say have I in decisions that affect me? Before yesterday, I did as I chose."

He paused, gaze locked with hers. "Indeed? I had no idea your uncle was so indulgent." Taran inclined his head. "Never fear, I will give you choices, my lady, while I have you undressed and in my bed." He lifted a brow. "Unless, you have a preference to my lovemaking?"

Her mouth dropped open, and he steeled himself for a barrage of womanly recriminations, but she clamped her mouth shut.

"No preference and no complaints." He nodded. "Good."

"I have a complaint. I loathe another day spent in a hot carriage."

"Indeed?" He gritted his teeth against the feel of his cock hardening at the thought of *another day in the carriage*. "Then I shall be forced to entertain you. There are many activities, besides travel, that can be done in a carriage." As Aphrodite knew.

* * * *

Caroline sat stiffly in the carriage. They had ridden but an hour. The five hours that still lay ahead stretched out before her like a prison sentence. She shifted her attention out of the window to Taran riding alongside the horses that drew the coach. He swayed with each easy stride of the beast as if they were one. Powerful thighs flanked the mammoth animal. The man was master of all he touched—including a lust-consumed wife.

She shivered. As *her* master, he had already begun spending her money. It was ridiculous that it should bother her. He was right, no creditor should wait a day longer than necessary, but it pricked her because doing so boiled their marriage down to the transaction it was.

She was now Viscountess Blackhall and he was lord of twenty thousand pounds a year. Warmth tinged her cheeks with recollection of the accusation that he would allow his father to rule their finances. She leaned against the cushion. Given a choice, Taran would have married Aphrodite...or would he? He spoke of an affair, but marriage had never been mentioned. And why would it have been? They might desire each other, but both knew duty came before lust.

Memory of his buttocks hard as stone beneath her fingers as he thrust his cock deep inside her last night brought a flush to her skin. As if sensing the illicit thought, he glanced over his shoulder at her. Her breath caught. Had he read her mind or, mayhap, the look on her face? Taran wheeled his horse around and she startled as he urged the animal towards her.

A moment later, he came up alongside the window. "You are well, madam?"

Her heart pounded as she drew in the mid-morning air. "As well as can be expected," she said in a calm voice.

He gave a slow shake of his head. "I have neglected you."

Before she realized it, he seized the door handle and leapt from the horse onto the step.

The carriage rocked.

Caroline grabbed the handle. "My lord!"

He laughed and tossed the reins up front. "Davis, if you please," he called, and yanked the door from her grasp.

Caroline scrambled to the far end of the cushion as Taran stepped inside. He dropped onto the opposite seat, his grin wider than it had been a moment ago. The carriage rocked more violently as Davis climbed to the rear of the box and tethered the horse, then climbed back up front.

Taran stretched his legs out on the seat opposite him. "You haven't spoken a word since we left the inn."

The intensity in his eyes stoked a simmering heat deep in her secret places—places that ached for him again. Heat pooled between her legs and sweat trickled between her breasts.

"I am alone in a carriage," she replied. "Who would you have me converse with?"

His expression sobered, catching her off guard. "I am sorry about stopping at the Cross Keys Inn."

"My father died long ago."

He regarded her and she realized she'd spoken too quickly.

"Not so long. Three years, you said."

Familiar sadness tugged at her heart, but she answered evenly, "Yes."

"What of your mother?"

"She died when I was twelve."

"Your father never remarried?"

Caroline shifted her attention to the gently rolling hills outside her window. Recollection of her mother's cold stare contrasted with the soft eyes immortalized in the portrait hanging over the library hearth. Despite the fact the cold look was reserved primarily for her father, Caroline often found him at his desk, staring at the picture.

"He loved her," she said.

"He was a lucky man."

Caroline broke from the vision and swung her gaze onto Taran. He stared intently.

Heat rushed into her cheeks. "Yes," she replied, unable to tell him that her father wasn't at all lucky. Neither was her mother. How was it possible love could make two people hate each other?

Mother had wanted a man who fought duels in her honor, attended her at every soirée until deep into the night, then left her to sleep until noon the next day while he discreetly slipped off to his mistress' bed. Instead, he'd remained loyal, despite her many indiscretions. Her mother hated him as much for that as the tender heart that always forgave her. She died when Caroline was twelve, her father when she was fifteen, but her mother's hatred and father's sorrow lived on in her heart.

"Perhaps as lucky as me," Taran murmured.

Her heart fluttered. Would he feel that way once he discovered her deception? Or would she would follow in her parent's footsteps, would she hate—and be hated?

He removed his feet from the cushion and she froze when he crossed to her side and sat beside her. Anticipation of his touch had her heart pounding so loudly she feared he would hear. He slid an arm behind her and wrapped four fingers along her nape. Trembles slithered over her flesh. She swallowed, the silence hovering between them deafening. Her pussy clenched with the possibility of having Taran plunging in her depths again. She closed her eyes as the blunt tips of his fingers burned through the fabric of her dress. Her nipples tightened to aching points.

"Sir, it is broad daylight." Her voice sounded husky, sinful, dripping with invitation.

"Mmm hmm." Taran pressed a kiss to the pulse below her ear.

He cupped a breast and she inhaled sharply. Desire rocketed through her.

"We are not alone." She choked out the words.

There were men perched on the box and—panic shot to the surface—she and Taran had already played out this scene. There could be no repeat performance. Caroline commanded her body to break free of his hold but his mouth melted her.

She shifted on the seat, aware of the wetness that slicked her thighs. "My lord."

The carriage rocked and his hold on her tightened. "This is our first day as man and wife."

His moist lips seared a trail down her neck and his deft fingers had her dress buttons undone, revealing the swell of her breasts.

"Such things are to be expected." He stroked his thumb over the exposed skin.

Her nipple strained against her shift's fabric. He bent his head and took the taut, cloth covered tip in his mouth. Wetting the fabric with his tongue made the material cling to her skin. She shivered and arched into his mouth. His tongue teased and nibbled. Soft suction tugged on the raised peak and streaked into her core. Caroline pressed against the cushion as if she could sink into the velvet and escape the exquisite torture.

Taran sucked harder. Her pussy clenched. A moan escaped her mouth and she grasped the sides of his head, holding him tight to her breast. She spread her thighs, needing his heavy weight between them.

"Yes," Taran whispered.

Caroline stilled.

His eyes met hers as he grasped the edge of her skirt and slowly inched it upward. Fear tightened her tummy while desire tightened her clit to torturous pleasure.

"Give yourself to me," he coaxed.

Terror ripped through her. He was too close, too aware of her…of Aphrodite.

Seizing his shoulders, she shoved him away. "We cannot do this." Her ragged breath leached the statement of power.

"Never fear," he said, amusement still evident in his voice, "I will teach you how to please a man in a carriage." He paused. "Or perhaps you will teach me?"

Caroline jerked her chin up in a challenge. "Making love in a carriage is not proper behavior for a lady."

He lifted a brow and she flinched, but didn't break from the stare. A corner of his mouth twitched in obvious amusement as he leaned past her and yanked the window curtain closed. Two nights ago, he had done this very thing on the streets of Newcastle. Her heart raced. She couldn't think. He muddled her thoughts, drove her to irrational behavior.

He settled back beside her, his fingers tracing circles on her exposed thigh. "In my bed—or carriage—there is no need for you to behave as a lady."

"I beg your pardon, sir. I am your wife, not your mistress."

His head snapped up. Even in the dim light of the carriage she discerned the glitter in his eyes.

"Last night—"

"Last night is behind us," she broke in. Tears stung the corners of her eyes. How could she continue to lie to him? "We must forget the past."

"I cannot." He leaned forward and pressed his lips to hers.

His tongue traced the seam of her closed mouth and she breathed in a strangled sob. He wanted more of what she had given him last night, the reassurance their union was not built on hate, that she could—would—accept him. How much would she have to give before he was satisfied? Too little would break her heart. Too much would drain her soul.

He lifted her dress and she whimpered, a soft mewling sound. Strong, calloused fingers grazed the flesh behind her knee. Higher, along the inside of her thigh. A shiver raced up her spine. Heat radiating from her core seemed to draw his fingers like a moth to a flame. Caroline parted her lips and glided her tongue along his, sucking him into her mouth. Taran groaned, deepening the kiss, then abruptly broke away. His breathing heavy, he rested his forehead against hers. Caroline sat frozen, until his fingers touched the damp curls covering her sex.

"You burn as I do," he said. "Why resist?" Tracing the slick seam, he then parted her folds. "Feel how your honey flows…" He slipped a finger into her clenching passage. "For me." He plunged deeper, stroking her internally, then easing out.

Cream coated his fingers. She couldn't hide her response to his touch. Anywhere but here in this carriage, if they were anywhere else. "We should stop. This is improper."

He growled, slamming a second finger into her pussy. "Perhaps I do not want a proper wife." A third finger.

Caroline cried out, gripping the edge of the seat as she bucked her hips against his thrusting fingers. Pleasure spiraled through her center. Quivers built in her passage.

Taran jerked his hand from between her legs. Loosening the ties of his breeches, he freed his erect, swollen rod. Juice seeped from the slit, glistening on the ruddy head. Taran grasped the underside of her knees, tugged her to the edge of the seat, and spread her thighs wide.

Positioning his rod at her opening, he looked at her face and thrust his cock into her pussy. Invading, stretching, *oh God*, sending her straight into delirium. His hips pumped, pounding his shaft into her. An orgasm rolled over her. She thrashed, crying his name as her inner walls convulsed around him.

Taran groaned, clenching his jaw as he increased his speed.

Bracing her hands behind her back, she rolled her hips.

"Ah fuck." Taran leveraged over her, plunging hard, rearing back, then slamming deep again. Sweat beaded across his brow. Muscles bunched in his arms. Unlike the sweet love he'd rained over her last night, he ploughed into her channel. Taking, demanding, consuming. Secret pleasure surged within her. He'd lost his control and fucked her like a woman—not his wife.

A shout from above broke into their lust-filled cocoon, and the carriage jerked as it slowed.

Caroline cried out. Tarah ripped from her body and jerked her dress down. He shoved his cock into his breeches and tugged the ties closed. She gasped when he yanked up his trouser leg and pulled a small pistol from within his boot. He shoved the weapon into the waistband at his back, then swung the door open and jumped to the ground.

A male voice she didn't recognize said, "Your sister, my lord."

Taran cursed. "Fiona?"

"Aye," the man said.

Caroline stilled. His sister?

"What has she done?" Taran demanded.

"Run off to Edinburgh, m'laird."

"By God," he muttered. "Where is Ran? The coward should have come himself and faced me with the explanation of how a slip of a girl bested him."

"She administered enough laudanum to put him down for two days," the man said. "A maid discovered him and sent word to Strathmore."

"Leave it to a woman," Taran muttered, then, "You will ride with Davis and the carriage to escort my wife to Strathmore." He glanced at Caroline. "I am sorry." He slammed the door shut.

She slid across the cushion and opened the door. "What has happened?"

Taran untethered his horse from the rear of the carriage, then stepped into the saddle and swung his leg over the horse. He urged the beast up to the door. "Do not choose this moment to try me."

Caroline jumped back when he shoved the door closed again.

He spurred the horse forward. "I expect you at Strathmore by supper," he said, and kicked the horse's belly. The animal lunged forward.

Caroline fell back against the seat when the carriage wobbled into motion.

* * * *

Despite her best effort, Caroline felt the surprise on her face when Fiona's maid told her that Taran's youngest sister had eloped. The maid's eyes widened as if acknowledging she'd overstepped her bounds.

"No need to fret. You have a friend in me," Caroline hurriedly assured her. She patted the place beside her on the couch.

Jennet glanced at the bedchamber door as if expecting the housekeeper to burst in any moment.

Caroline rose and hurried to the door. She slid the lock into place and turned. "There now, no one can interrupt."

The girl cast a nervous glance at the door.

"Never mind." Caroline crossed to where Jennet stood at the foot of the bed and gently grasped her arm while leading her back to the bench that sat near the window. She eased the maid onto the bench and sat beside her. "My husband took off as if chased by the devil himself, and gave no explanation. You can imagine my concern." The girl nodded vigorously.

"That infernal Davis remained silent as a mute." Try as she might, she had been unable to coax more than an 'Aye, my lady', and 'Nay, my lady', from any of the men on the remainder of the trip. "Tell me, why did my sister-in-law elope? Surely, my husband would give her a suitable wedding."

"Indeed, he would," Jennet agreed. "Only, Fiona is but sixteen years old."

"Sixteen?" Caroline gave a slow nod. "Yes, I can see why he would object. But why does Fiona not wait? And the groom." She grimaced. "He cannot want a green girl."

Jennet clucked her tongue. "It doesna' matter. Lord Blackhall has told his sister she cannot wed Lord Huntly."

"She is young," Caroline said.

The maid shook her head. "Nay. She canna' marry him at all."

"Is he a rake, too old perhaps?" Caroline grimaced. "These old men should be ashamed, taking children to wife."

"No," Jennet said. "Lord Blackhall says Lord Huntly only wants to marry her for her money."

Caroline choked.

Jennet shot to her feet. "Are you all right, my lady? Should I fetch help?" She started for the door.

"No," Caroline croaked.

The girl halted and turned. "Are you sure?"

Caroline waved her back. "Sit." Her throat cracked and she coughed.

Jennet wavered.

"I am fine," Caroline said.

"I should return to work." She cast another glance at the door.

"One more question," Caroline said. "Does my husband not plan on dowering his sisters?"

Jennet looked surprised. "Of course. They are his sisters. He would not slight them."

Of course not, Caroline thought. Neither would he allow them to marry a man like himself.

Chapter Fourteen

"He did not simply die."

Caroline jumped at the loud pop of wood that blazed in the drawing room hearth where she stood. A tiny piece of wood shot from the log, bounced off the brick wall, and landed beside the larger pieces that now simmered as red-hot coals.

Despite the warmth, she shivered. The stable master hadn't struck her as a man given to idle gossip. Yet the idea that someone had sabotaged her father's saddle was beyond belief. In the years since his death not so much as a whisper of foul play had reached her ears. Surely, if there were any truth to Liam's claim that the girth on her father's horse hadn't worn loose as was said, but had been cut, word would have filtered down to her. And why would someone want him dead? Her father had no enemies.

She pictured the half dozen horses Liam had described galloping across the field with her father. His stallion drew ahead, the animal's powerful strides outrunning the others' breakneck speed of nearly forty miles an hour. He reached the trees ten seconds ahead of the pack and disappeared into the most dangerous leg of the race. She jerked at the sudden picture of him pitching from the horse. His heart jumped and he had a mere second to comprehend what had happened before his head hit the ground, his neck broken upon impact.

Caroline jarred from the vision of blood pooling around his face, sightless eyes staring heavenward. Her heart knocked against her chest. She grabbed the sherry from the mantle where she'd left it and gulped the remaining contents, then dropped into the wingback chair in front of the fire. At last, her pulse slowed. Liam may not be given to gossip, but neither was she a girl given to theatrics. She would take her time and find out what happened, but without the aid of sherry or schoolgirl emotions.

She knew several men who attended that fateful hunt, Lord Cambrooke, for one. Would he, or the others, keep silent in order to save her feelings? She recalled their encounter at the inn. He was surprised she'd spent her wedding night at the place where her father died, but that was to be expected. Caroline glanced at the empty sherry glass she still held. Damn her nerves. The hour was late—they had pushed well into the night to reach Strathmore—but, Caroline had worked herself into a state of anxiety that even two glasses of sherry hadn't eased.

The front door to the old castle opened and Taran's voice filled the hallway outside the drawing room. "Never mind, Patterson, we will not be needing your services tonight." A quiver radiated through Caroline's stomach.

"Very good, my lord." The old butler's voice echoed from the other end of the hallway nearest the kitchen.

"As for you," Taran said, "go to your room and remain there until I call for you."

"Reverend Gordon will confirm the marriage," a female voice replied.

Caroline tensed. It would seem Taran's sister had made better use of the past few hours than she had.

"He has nothing to say about it," Taran said. "The marriage will be annulled."

"You cannot undo what is done. I may already carry Ross' child."

"What is wrong with you?" Taran burst out. "Once he has spent your dowry, he will blackmail me for more money. He has tricked you, plain and simple."

"He did not trick me," she replied in a tone so reasonable Caroline couldn't deny a trickle of the respect. "*I* tricked him."

"What are you talking about?"

"Ross insisted we wait. He said I was too young to marry." She snorted. "Male foolishness. He did not think I was so young when you were in Edinburgh last week."

"Fiona," Taran said, in a voice that made the hairs on the back of Caroline's neck stand on end, "if what you say is true, I will kill him this very night."

"Kill him?" She snorted. "And deliver the news to your niece or nephew that you are their father's murderer?"

"You are not with child."

"You cannot know that. Besides, you are not *our* father."

"Indeed, I am not. He cares nothing for your future—or your safety. Have you any idea the risk you took riding to Edinburgh alone?"

"I was not alone."

"A single male escort is no security," he shot back. "Not to mention the impropriety. Given what you say, I am surprised Huntly did not wonder at the time you spent alone with your *escort*."

"My God," she snorted, "but you are a fool. Do you think I care what you believe?

Unlike you, I intend to please myself, not my family."

"Do your actions please your husband?" Taran demanded.

"Ross is well satisfied."

"Fiona—"

"Enough of your sermonizing."

Caroline froze at sound of the swish of skirts along the marble floor and Fiona's voice moving towards the drawing room.

"We both know if Ross had money, you would have already betrothed me to him."

"He has a title," Taran retorted. "Let him find an heiress to support him." Caroline's blood went cold.

"I will not see you wed a pauper."

Fiona snorted. "Instead, you would condemn me to a marriage with that fop, Lord Burke. No. One Blackhall sacrificing themself is quite enough." She stepped into the doorway.

Caroline hunched in the chair in an attempt to hide, but Fiona's 'Well, well' told her she'd been unsuccessful.

Caroline twisted and looked around the chair's edge.

Intense eyes the mirror image of her husband's stared back at her. The girl stood at least four inches shorter than Caroline. Honey colored hair piled atop her head. Her full figure explained why her intended victim, Ross, would have been unable to resist her. This was no green girl. This was no girl at all.

Taran appeared behind her. Caroline jerked her eyes up to his face. His gaze seemed to take in the sight of her, heart, mind, and soul in one quick sweep. She cursed the heat that crept into her cheeks, and rose.

"Taran, you did not say she was so beautiful," Fiona said.

"You saw the miniature," he replied, his gaze still locked with Caroline's.

"True, but it did not do justice to that dark hair…and those eyes." She gave an approving nod. "Maybe you are no sacrifice, after all."

"Fiona." Taran grabbed for her elbow but, as if in anticipation of the move, she started forward.

"Your wife heard our conversation," she said.

When Fiona reached her side, she clasped Caroline's hands and held her at arm's length, her gaze sliding down Caroline's frame. Her eyes came back up to Caroline's face as she gave another approving nod.

"Come." Fiona led her around the couch. "Sit."

Caroline lowered herself on one end while Fiona sat at the opposite.

"You must forgive me and my sister for not attending your wedding," she said. "Taran did not think we could withstand the day and a half ride he made, and he was unwilling to send us by coach."

Given the girl's obvious headstrong mind, Caroline wagered she understood his logic.

"'Tis a long ride," she said.

"Indeed, it is," Fiona agreed. "But as Taran knows, I am quite capable of the journey. Our sister Horatia could not have countenanced it. In that, my brother was correct. But then, he could have sent her with a large entourage and allowed a week for the journey."

"Why did he not?"

"Because he believed I would feel obligated to remain here by my sister's side and not elope," Fiona replied.

"I will take you over my knee," Taran said in a low voice.

"You will do no such thing," she said without looking at him. "Do not worry," she said to Caroline, "he is not a man given to beating women...much."

Caroline couldn't resist asking, "What is he given to?"

"He is given to holding a grudge."

The answer came so quickly, Caroline blinked in unison with Taran. "You are mistaken, if you think I will not administer a beating to *your* backside." He gave a harsh laugh. "Perhaps your new husband will ride to your rescue and allow me to be done with killing him."

Fiona turned a hard look on him. "You have salvaged your pride by *saving* me from a night of debauchery. Make good on this ridiculous threat, and I will leave you, dowry, and even my sister, far behind."

His expression turned contemplative. "And if you do carry his child?"

"You care nothing for that."

"But I do," he said. "I cannot save you from a fortune hunter only to have you and your child waste away in poverty."

"But you can," she said, her mouth set in a grim line.

Caroline's pulse jumped. His sister had not exaggerated when she'd said he was unforgiving. "She has made her decision and acted up on it," Caroline said. "What hope have you of undoing the deed?"

His head shifted in her direction. "This is not your concern."

"I believe I like her," Fiona said.

"Why condemn her for taking matters into her own hands?" Caroline asked.

His eyes narrowed. "Taking matters into her own hands?"

His quiet tone sent apprehension coursing through her veins. '*Come to me when you can*', he had told Aphrodite. 'After you have fulfilled your obligation to your husband' had been his meaning.

He had not asked her to abandon her duty, only to return to him after she had satisfied that duty. Lord Taran Blackhall had fulfilled his obligations, expected Aphrodite to do the same, as he expected his wife to do. His response to Fiona couldn't help making her wonder if he didn't already despise Aphrodite for choosing to deceive her husband. How much greater will be his loathing when he learned his wife had cast him in both roles?

"A woman who creates her own destiny risks losing all," she murmured.

"What?" he demanded.

"As you say, what if she carries his child?"

Taran's gaze shifted onto Fiona. "Little did Ross understand the web woven around him."

"Ross knows well enough what he is about," she said.

"Does he? Does he truly understand the woman you are?"

She arched an eyebrow. "So you admit it is I, the woman, who has set the snare."

He gave a slow nod. "You have your part in this disaster. Maybe I should leave you to your fate."

"Leave her to her fate?" Caroline said. "How will you stop her?"

His gaze remained on Fiona. "I will have the marriage annulled and marry her to another."

Fiona snorted. "It would take your entire fortune to induce a man to marry me when he glimpses the shrew he takes to wife." Caroline choked.

"Are you ill?" Fiona demanded.

Caroline shook her head and cleared her throat.

"Taran, fetch her some brandy."

He gave Caroline an odd look, then strode to the sideboard.

"You need not worry," Fiona said. "Scottish law allows me to marry whom I please. Say what he might, my brother cannot annul my marriage, nor can he force me to marry. He may try to browbeat me." She laughed. "That will prove useless."

"You are fortunate," Caroline said.

Taran appeared at her side, brandy snifter in hand. "You do not consider yourself fortunate?" He extended the glass towards her.

Caroline eyed it. She'd had two sherries already. One more drink couldn't hurt. She took the glass and lifted it to her lips.

He continued. "Only last night you gave me the distinct impression you considered yourself most fortunate."

The brandy slid down her windpipe. She sucked in a harsh breath and coughed.

"Taran!" Fiona slid across the couch to her side. She seized the glass and set it on the table. "You will kill her before the night is finished."

"On the contrary," he said smoothly, "I plan on—"

Caroline surged to her feet. "*Sir*," she managed in a hoarse voice.

His expression was all innocence.

"Do not worry." Fiona shot him a deprecating look. "Once you have provided the required heir, you may tell him to go to the devil."

Caroline sucked in another harsh breath and swung her gaze onto the girl.

"Is that your plan, my dear?" Taran drawled.

Caroline jerked her attention back to him. He stared. Was that hope in his voice? He might despise Aphrodite. He might not forgive her, but he would gladly let her spread her legs for him. Taran's words in the garden returned like a clap of thunder—*'It is more likely you fled the festivities to meet someone. The blue domino perhaps?'* Taran had seen her with Lord Edmonds.

'I expect to hear news from you immediately', he had said to William yesterday before they'd left her uncle's home.

Taran had sent Lord Edmonds in search of Aphrodite.

Why hadn't it occurred to her before? When he'd left her in the carriage, he'd told her to come to him when she could, but had planned all along to seek her out. If Taran saw her with Lord Edmonds, then he saw her speaking with Lady Margaret. No one could mistake Margaret for anyone but herself. Margaret would never betray her. But if she didn't realize— Caroline's head whirled.

"I—I—" she croaked. "I would—"

A loud pounding on the door interrupted her.

"Blackhall!" a muffled male voice shouted.

Fiona shot to her feet. "Ross." Her face went ashen. "I told him to wait until tomorrow."

"Blackhall!" Ross shouted again.

Taran started for the door. Fiona hurried around the table after him.

Patterson passed in front of the open doorway. "Coming, sir," he called.

The pounding continued.

Taran reached the doorway. "Never mind, Patterson, I will see to the pup myself."

"As you say, my lord."

Taran disappeared into the hall, Fiona close behind and, an instant later, Patterson passed, heading back the way he had come.

Caroline stood rooted to the spot.

"Black—"

A loud bang of wood against stone reverberated through the hallway and into the drawing room.

"Lord Huntly, I see."

Caroline shuddered at the dark tone in Taran's voice.

He gave a harsh laugh. "Come to face our dawn appointment?"

"Lord Blackhall," another male voice said.

"Reverend Gordon. By God, Huntly, you could not face me man to man? This is the man you would wed, Fiona?"

Caroline started towards the drawing room door.

"Ross," Fiona said, "I instructed you to wait until tomorrow when Reverend Gordon could force Taran to see reason."

Caroline reached the door and peeked into the hallway.

"Blackhall is not capable of seeing reason," a tall, young man replied.

She winced. The lad looked barely nineteen and had to be at least four stone leaner than Taran.

Fiona laid a hand on his arm. "This is not wise."

"Lord Blackhall," the reverend said, "I performed the marriage myself. It is legal."

"Legal?" Taran repeated. "You speak of legalities. Where is your morality? She is not yet out of the schoolroom."

"Perhaps," Reverend Gordon replied. "But the deed is done."

Taran looked at Fiona. "Deed, is it?"

"Do not act as if I hid the truth from you," she replied.

Ross gasped. "You told him." His head snapped in Taran's direction.

"Patterson," Taran called, "my dueling pistols."

Fiona seized his arm. "Brandish those pistols and I will shoot you with one of them myself."

Caroline barely repressed a laugh. That she would like to see. Not to mention, a bullet through Taran's heart would solve all their problems. Well, not through his heart, just a thigh, or shoulder perhaps.

"Never mind," Ross said with a resoluteness that surprised her. "If I must kill him to have you, then so be it."

"Kill me?" Taran looked at Fiona. "The pup thinks well of himself."

"You called, my lord?"

Caroline jumped at the sound of Patterson's voice as everyone's attention shifted to the butler, who stood at the other end of the hallway.

"Caroline," Taran said. She looked back at him. "This does not concern you. Retire to our bedchambers. I will meet you there presently."

She shook her head. "If I am to be made a widow only a day after being wed, I think that concerns me greatly."

He scowled. "You and your family have a habit of underestimating me."

She ignored the flutter in the stomach at the recollection of how Taran had threatened her uncle with a dawn appointment. "What do you expect?" she replied. "What reason have we to believe you can go about engaging in duel after duel and come out the victor?"

"It is not duel after duel," he said, as if injured. "This is but the second."

"In as many days," she reminded him.

"Coincidence," he muttered.

"Good lord," Fiona snapped. "Taran, you are mad. Ross, we are leaving."

Taran seized her hand. "Nay, sister. This whelp and I have unfinished business.

Patterson, those pistols."

"As you wish, my lord."

The butler shuffled to the drawing room and brushed past Caroline.

"Lord Blackhall," Reverend Gordon admonished.

"Taran," Fiona began.

"Fiona," Ross cut in, "you should retire with his lordship's wife. I will see you presently."

She gaped. "You are as mad as he is."

The young man shook his head. "I will not spend the rest of my life looking over my shoulder. We will settle this once and for all."

"The final match," Taran said in a soft voice.

A tremor rippled through Caroline and she knew the others had caught the dangerous note in his voice when they quieted.

"Lord Huntly," the reverend broke the silence. "You are no match for Lord Blackhall.

Let me speak with him."

"Listen to him," Fiona pleaded.

Taran's head dipped in her direction. "What is this? You have set the stage, yet do not wish to finish the play?"

"This is no play," she snapped.

"Indeed."

She levelled a look as dark as his own at him. "You will—"

"Huntly," Taran shoved Fiona into his arms, "take her."

The young man caught her. Taran whirled and Caroline realized his intent even before his eyes met hers. She retreated with the plan of locking the drawing room door against him, but bumped into a body.

A low cry from Patterson was followed by Caroline clutching at the butler's arm as they toppled to the floor, her on top of him. Strong fingers clamped around her arm and yanked her to her feet, face to face with Taran.

"By God, madam, at least have the decency to wait until I am killed before seducing my butler."

Chapter Fifteen

Taran hauled Caroline over his shoulder.

"How dare you!" she howled.

"Patterson, ready those pistols," he commanded, and strode from the room. "Huntly, bring my sister—if you have the stomach for it."

"Ross, do not—" Fiona's words were cut off when Ross threw her over his shoulder and followed.

Taran bounded up the narrow stairs, two at a time and was surprised to hear the young viscount hard on his heels.

"Put me down!" Caroline commanded.

Taran winced at the sound of each word echoing off the stone walls in a staccato that was punctuated by each step he took.

"Ross!" Fiona shouted.

Taran reached the second floor, turned left, and ascended the next flight of stairs. An unexpected elbow to his back sent a sharp pain through him.

"I will have your head for this." Fiona shouted.

Taran couldn't deny a stab of compassion for the boy. He really hadn't grasped what he was getting into with Fiona.

Taran reached the third floor and strode towards the fourth door. He felt Caroline swing to his left and he veered right as he realized she was making a swipe for the claymore hanging on the wall beside his bedchamber door. He couldn't prevent a laugh as he crossed the threshold. If she had managed the claymore, she would have brained him with it. He strode to the bed and tossed her onto the mattress. She bounced twice and started to push to her feet. Taran shoved her back down and straddled her. Light radiating from the low fire in the hearth lit her hair like ebony. He suddenly wished his sister and her hapless husband anywhere but here.

"Good God," Fiona cried as Huntly stumbled into the room.

"This is ridiculous," Caroline snapped. "Get off me."

Taran gave her an appraising look. "Tired of me already, wife?"

Her eyes narrowed. "If your sister does not shoot you, I will."

"But I will," Fiona growled. "Ross, put. Me. Down."

"Now, Fiona," he began, but she cut him off with a scream.

Caroline winced, then her gaze latched onto Taran's. She seized his shoulders and dragged him closer. "You will not kill the boy?" The words, spoken in a whisper that couldn't possibly be overheard above Fiona's command to be released, held a chill that startled him.

"Do not say you are concerned." The edge in his voice sounded dark even to him, but an odd sense of foreboding suddenly rose.

Her mouth thinned. "You go too far with this ruse."

"Ruse?" he repeated.

"You will rue the day you married me!" Fiona shouted.

Taran twisted to see his sister had begun to thrash wildly. Huntly stumbled backwards, barely managing to keep her from slipping from his grasp. Taran jumped to his feet and pulled Fiona from the younger man's shoulder just in time to keep her from being squashed between him and the wall.

Huntly straightened. "Damnation, Fiona, you nearly knocked yourself senseless." From the corner of his eye, Taran saw Caroline slip from the bed.

Fiona swayed. "Release me." She yanked in an effort to free her arm. Taran obliged. She fell to her backside on the rug.

"By God, Taran." Her head snapped in Huntly's direction. "Ross, do something."

His brow creased. "What more would you have me do?" He gave a snort. "Come, Blackhall, I wish to be done with this business." He whirled and disappeared through the door.

Taran started after him. "I believe you have your wish, sister."

Fiona scrambled to her feet. "What are you talking about?"

"You coming, Blackhall?" Ross called from the hallway.

"On my way," Taran shouted back, then said to Fiona as he grasped the door handle,

"Your husband rues the day he married you." Caroline lunged for the door. "Blackhall!" He slammed the door in her face.

* * * *

Caroline crashed into the shut door. Dull pain radiated through her shoulder. She gritted her teeth against the throbbing, seized the handle and yanked in unison with the sound of steel sliding against steel. The door didn't budge.

Fiona appeared at her side. "He's used the claymore to bar the door."

Caroline stepped back and Fiona grabbed the handle and yanked. Wood rattled against a clank of steel, but remained firm. She pounded a fist on the door. "Blackhall! Blackhall!" She placed an ear to the wood for a moment, then straightened. "Damn him."

Caroline stared at the door, still unable to believe it. Taran had bolted the door from the outside with the sword.

"If he kills Ross—"

"He has no intention of shooting your husband," Caroline cut in.

"Did he tell you that?"

"Well, no."

"You said two duels in as many days. What was the other duel about?"

Caroline flushed. "He, well, he…"

"Threatened a duel in your honor, did he?" She faced the window again. "Taran does not make idle threats."

"Surely, he must know you would not forgive him."

"Taran never asks forgiveness."

Caroline felt as if all the air had been sucked from her lungs. "He must know he cannot stop you."

"He knows he can stop me if Ross is dead."

"He would not kill the boy," Caroline said under her breath. The man who made love to her in the carriage was no murderer.

"Ah ha!" Fiona cried. "Your bedchamber."

"What?"

Her sister-in-law raced to a door on the left wall and seized the door handle leading to Caroline's bedchamber and pushed. The door didn't open.

She shoved with her shoulder. Still nothing. Fiona took a step back and looked the door up and down. "He locked this door as well? I did not hear him enter the closet."

Caroline remained rooted to the spot. She knew the door led to the small room that connected her bedchamber with Taran's, for she had locked and unlocked it a dozen times, torn between the notion that a locked door might discourage him from visiting her should he return home late that night. She had decided the idea was nonsense and had left the door unlocked, or so she'd thought.

Fiona blew out a frustrated breath, then whirled in the direction of the curtains of the bay window and hurried to them. With a jerk, she yanked aside the heavy fabric to reveal French doors leading onto a balcony. She threw open the doors and disappeared on the left side of the balcony. Caroline hurried outside and found Fiona, skirts tugged above her thigh as she lifted a leg over the wrought iron railing.

"Fiona!" She lunged for the girl, caught her arm, and dragged her backward.

They tumbled onto the hard stone floor.

Fiona scrambled to her feet and gave her a deprecating look. "What are you doing?"

Caroline grasped the back of a chair sitting at the small table to her right and pulled herself up. "I might ask you the same thing."

"I am going to jump to that balcony." She pointed to the neighboring balcony that opened to the lady's suite.

Caroline scowled. "'Tis five feet, maybe more. You will break your fool neck in the attempt."

Fiona gave a decisive nod. "That would teach Taran a lesson."

Caroline gave her a horrified look. "You are as insane as he is."

Fiona barked a laugh. "It is well known the Blackhalls often skirt reason." Her eyes shifted past Caroline. She gasped and pushed past her.

Caroline turned and startled at sight of three figures marching across the mist shrouded lawn. Young Huntly led, with Taran several feet behind, a lantern in hand, and Reverend Gordon nearly running to catch up.

Fiona grasped the balcony railing and leaned forward. "Stop!" Pale moonlight shadowed Taran's face, but revealed the rigidity in his posture.

He shouted something to Ross. Fiona turned and lunged towards the railing near the lady's balcony. Caroline caught her arm.

Fiona turned a tear stained face towards her. "He will kill my husband."

Caroline glanced at the men, who were still heading deeper into the fog. Taran had nearly caught up with Ross. The dangerous note in Taran's voice when he'd challenged her uncle rose in memory. Fiona was right, the threat hadn't been idle.

"Stand aside." She yanked up her skirts. Cold air rushed across her legs, sending a prickle of gooseflesh racing up her thighs.

Fiona glanced anxiously at the other balcony. "Are you certain you should jump? I am younger and more agile."

Caroline scowled. "I am but two years your senior."

"Yes, but—"

"For God's sake, Fiona, will you stand here and argue while your husband takes a bullet?"

The girl paled.

Regret stabbed at Caroline, but she kept her voice even and said, "Pull yourself together."

Fiona straightened and gave a nod.

Caroline hoisted a leg over the rail and lowered her foot to the outer edge of the balcony. She swung the other foot over. A quick glance at her feet caused a rush of dizziness. The ground disappeared into a dark, airy abyss. She lifted her eyes to Fiona's face. The girl held her gaze for an instant, then her warm hand covered Caroline's white-knuckled fingers gripping the railing. Releasing one hand, Caroline extended a foot towards the other balcony and leaned. Her toe nearly reached. She leaned further.

"Just one…more…inch." She stretched, then cried out when her grasp on the railing loosened.

"Caroline!"

She swung herself back to the railing, insides shaking so badly, she felt as if she would vomit. She met Fiona's wide-eyed gaze. Fiona gave a wordless shake of her head. Caroline blew out a shaky breath, then willed her racing heart to slow and again reached for the other balcony. She stretched until her arm felt as if it would disconnect from her shoulder, before cold iron grazed her fingertips.

"Just a bit more." She gasped, stretching.

"You cannot reach." Fiona tugged on Caroline's fingers.

Caroline took a deep breath and leapt. Her fingers clamped around cold iron as her slippered foot made contact with the tiny ledge on the outside of the balcony—then slipped. Her hip crashed into the stone ledge and her shoulder wrenched with the weight of her body hanging from the railing. She cried out in unison with Fiona's shriek. Pain seared her hip.

"Caroline," Fiona choked.

Caroline grunted against the pain that pulsed with each beat of her heart. By God, if she had a revolver, she would point it at Taran and put a ball through his shoulder. Perhaps his sister had a point. Let him suffer alongside them. Caroline pooled her strength and swung her foot up onto the ledge.

Muffled shouts sounded in the distance. She pulled herself up, then twisted in the direction of the voices. Caroline gave a cry upon seeing Fiona pointing a revolver out across the lawn. The three men were racing towards them.

"Fiona—"

The report of the revolver reverberated back to Caroline as if she were caught between the blast and a roaring ocean. Her eyes instinctively jammed shut, but she snapped them open in time to see Taran stumble and fall to the ground. Her heart jumped into a pounding rhythm.

Reverend Gordon reached Taran's side and dropped to his knees. Caroline's head swam. *He's dead.* She recalled the thought of how a ball through his heart would solve all their problems. Tears streamed down her face. Taran shoved to his feet, throwing the reverend onto his backside.

Caroline gasped. "Taran!"

He sprinted towards the mansion at a dead run. She stared. He wasn't dead. Her husband wasn't dead. He was racing towards her. He had seen them—had seen her jump across the balconies!

"Fiona!"

Caroline jolted at hearing young Huntly's shout. He hadn't realized Taran had fallen and kept running towards the mansion. Caroline cast a glance at Fiona. She stood, revolver still pointed into the night.

"Dear God," she whispered, then crumpled to the floor.

Caroline swung one leg, then the other, over the railing. Heart pounding, she yanked up the hem of her gown, and raced through the door into the lady's chamber, through the anteroom, and into Taran's room. A second later, she was on the balcony, kneeling beside Fiona.

Caroline pulled her into an upright position. Soundless tears streamed down the girl's cheeks. Her eyes slowly parted, heavy with tears, and stared up into Caroline's face.

"What have I done?" She clutched Caroline's neck and buried her face in Caroline's breast.

Caroline stroked her hair until the bedchamber door burst open and the pounding of boots on the carpeted floor sounded behind her. She tried twisting to look back at the men, but Fiona's grasp on her neck tightened. Heavy footfalls pounded on the balcony. Taran gripped her shoulders with strong hands and dragged her to her feet as Ross pulled Fiona into his arms.

"Fiona," he said in a near whisper.

"By God, Caroline." Taran strode into the room, then swung her into his arms.

"Put me down," she ordered.

He lowered her onto the bed. She started to push to her feet. Taran grasped her shoulders, forcing her back against the pillows as he lowered himself onto the bed beside her. "Do not move," he snapped.

She cried out at the sight of a large, blood-stained spot on the britches covering his left thigh. "My lord, you are hit!"

"*I* am hit?" he said, in a tone so dark she riveted her gaze onto his face.

His mouth was set in a grim line. "What of your arm, madam?" His head dipped meaningfully towards her arm and she glanced down.

She gasped. Her sleeve was soaked with as much blood as his trouser leg.

"Huntly—" Taran began.

Reverend Gordon appeared in the doorway, breathing hard.

"Reverend," Taran said, "have Patterson call for Doctor Blakely."

The reverend took the group in with a single glance, then turned on his heel.

"Wait," Taran called.

The reverend faced him.

"*You* fetch the doctor. Patterson will direct you to his residence. Can you ride?"

"I can."

Taran nodded. "Patterson will oblige with a horse."

Reverend Gordon nodded and hurried from the room. Taran seized the fabric on Caroline's dress where sleeve met shoulder and tore it in one hard yank. A deep red gash marred the creamy skin of her upper arm.

Her head swam. She looked up at Taran. "I do not feel a thing."

Chapter Sixteen

Fear coursed through Taran. The wound looked nasty, but wasn't life-threatening. Caroline's near fall from the balcony is what still had his insides shaking. His mind replayed her jump from the balcony and he couldn't halt the vision of her beautiful body, twisted and broken, lying on the cold ground. Blood roared through his ears. He had almost lost her.

Taran grabbed an edge of the linen sheet they sat on and tore a long strip free. Huntly appeared at his side and placed a basin of water on the nightstand beside the bed. Taran gave a curt nod of thanks and dipped the fabric in the water.

"Light the candle," he said. "And that lamp." He nodded towards the lamp sitting on the secretary.

The young man picked up the candle sitting on the nightstand and hurried to the hearth.

"Your leg, my lord," Caroline said.

"My leg will heal," he said through tight lips. "It is but a flesh wound."

"Flesh wound? But I saw you fall."

He swung his gaze onto her. "Did you now?"

"I thought—"

"You thought what?"

"I thought you were dead."

The words spoken in a bare whisper tore a harsh laugh from him. He wrung out the wet strip of linen and gently wiped blood from around the wound. "Then we are even. I have yet to get the picture from my head of you leaping from my balcony."

"Never fear, my lord, I shall live long enough to provide an heir."

He glanced up at her face. Her chin was high, her eyes glittering with indignation. He snorted. "If you keep testing me, I will—"

"You will what?"

"Paddle your lovely backside, then keep you under lock and key."

Her chin rose higher. "Shackled and chained?"

He held her gaze. "At least until I have my *required heir*." *And you understand I will not live without you.* "Huntly," he said, but the younger man was already at his side, holding the candle and decanter of brandy Taran had intended on asking him to bring from the sideboard.

Huntly sat the candle on the table and Taran took the brandy, his gaze catching on his sister standing near the corner of the bed, eyes wide.

"Taran—"

"Not now, Fiona." He took the top off the decanter. "She is yours, Huntly. I will see to it that her dowry is forwarded to your solicitor. Do with her what you will."

The young man paused near the secretary. "Now see here, Blackhall, she is not fully to blame. You did threaten to kill me. You cannot expect a wife to lose her husband the very day she marries him."

"And this but my second day of wedded bliss," Taran replied.

Huntly stiffened. "I will meet you on the dueling field at your convenience."

Taran set the decanter on the nightstand and wrung out the rag. "That is what started this."

"A circumstance which is no one's fault but your own," Caroline said.

He shifted his attention back to her. "I do not think—"

"No, you did not think."

"I will remind you, madam, you nearly got yourself killed."

She gave a short laugh. "Fine talk from a man engaged in a duel."

"I was not."

"We saw you."

Light flared as Huntly lit the lamp.

Taran poured brandy on the rag. "What you saw was me chasing this young fool." He bent to clean the wound.

Caroline seized his wrist. "You called for pistols, then locked your sister and me in your bedchambers."

He blew out a breath. "I did not need two females interfering."

She released him. "That will teach you."

"Indeed," he agreed. "It will teach me to keep my revolvers out of reach." And it would teach him not to underestimate his sister *or* his wife again. Taran dabbed at the wound with the brandy-soaked rag.

Caroline winced.

He paused. "Huntly, one of the tumblers from the sideboard, if you please." The young man fetched the glass and Taran poured a liberal amount of brandy into the glass and handed it to Caroline. "Drink."

She took the glass and gulped the drink in three swallows.

Taran raised a brow. "My wife is an accomplished drinker. Charming." He ignored her scowl and began cleaning the wound.

Patterson entered the room. "My lord."

"The reverend has gone for the doctor?" Taran asked.

"Yes, my lord. Do you need anything?"

"Clean bandages. Bring them when Blakely arrives."

"As you wish." Patterson did an about face and headed out of the room.

Taran tossed the bloody rag on the nightstand and tore another piece of fabric from the sheet. He held it over the basin, soaked it with brandy, then looked at Caroline.

"This will burn."

She gave a snort he could swear was slurred. He dabbed at the wound. Her mouth tightened.

"Are you all right?" he demanded.

"Perfectly fine."

He stared. "What the bloody hell did you think you were doing?"

"Stopping you from killing that poor boy."

"And if he had killed me?"

She snorted again and Taran was certain he discerned a slur. "You assured us it was he who would take the bullet," she said.

"So you decided to take matters into your own hands?" Caroline nodded. "I do not like being locked in a room."

"I do not like being shot at," he retorted.

"But you do," she replied. "Otherwise, you would not go about challenging duels all the time."

Taran suddenly realized his thigh throbbed. He would have a devil of a headache tomorrow. He eyed his wife. She cocked an eyebrow. How in God's name was he to deal with the little baggage? He snatched the glass she still held and filled it halfway with brandy, then swallowed the liquid in two gulps. He grimaced against the burn of alcohol, then sucked in a breath that went down even harsher.

"Thigh beginning to ache, my lord?" she asked.

He set the glass on the nightstand. The woman was too clever. His gaze caught on her arm. There would be a scar. How had she gashed it? He recalled the wrought iron railing on the lady's balcony and the jagged end of a piece of the grill. He winced at thought of the rusty iron digging into her flesh. That deformed section of the grill could have sliced a cheek, or worse, taken an eye. He should have fixed it long ago. The damned thing was a menace. He should have anticipated—he should have anticipated what, that his wife would jump from one balcony to another?

He leaned close to her. "What were you thinking?"

"She was helping me," Fiona said.

Taran twisted his neck and met his sister's gaze. "You have done enough damage for one night."

"Do not bully her," Caroline interjected.

Taran looked at her. "She is my sister. I will do what I please with her."

"She is a married woman. You have nothing to say about her life." Caroline's brow arched. "So you told my uncle." She leaned so close her nose nearly touched his. "When you threatened the duel. You do remember?"

He gave a slow nod. "I do. Huntly, take your wife off."

"Taran," Fiona began.

"Fiona," Huntly said. "He is right. We should go."

"But—"

"They have survived," the younger man interrupted. He led her to the door.

As the door clicked shut behind them, Taran wondered just how long he would survive.

* * * *

Caroline's heart raced. Taran hadn't given his sister so much as a sideways glance. The girl had been right. He didn't ask for forgiveness, nor did he give it. Anger shot to the surface. His sense of justice be damned.

"Your leg, sir."

Caroline forced her voice to remain level. He couldn't be walking around if the wound were serious, but that didn't mean the ball wasn't lodged in his flesh. The way the blood had spread on his breeches worried her.

"My leg will heal," he said. "You, on the other hand, will be lucky to escape infection."

"A ball to a thigh can cause serious infection," she replied.

"The bullet merely grazed me."

His mouth thinned to a grim line as he wrung out the rag in the water and Caroline couldn't help wondering if his anger wasn't due more to the fear of how his father would react if his new heiress died only a day after their wedding. If an accident had befallen her so early in their marriage, her uncle could contest the death. Caroline couldn't help a sense of satisfaction in the irony of the old earl's hard work going for nothing.

Amusement died with the memory that her uncle had sold her so that he could be associated with a noble family. Bastard. Losing that connection would anger him far more than giving up the yearly income. More likely, he would make a deal with the earl to remain part of the inner circle in exchange for not contesting her death. If that happened, Taran would have no need to seek out another heiress until his father had whittled away her fortune.

Caroline recalled Leslie Benton's *accident* two years ago. She had been married but two weeks when her carriage had gone off the road and she broke her neck. Everyone wondered what she had been doing out late in Wanstead with only a driver. She never ventured out of the heart of London, and certainly never went anywhere without proper escort. Her father and mother didn't contest the death and, six months later, were gallivanting about London at all the best parties as relations of their deceased daughter's father-in-law.

Caroline jumped at the sudden sting to the wound in her arm. Her attention snapped back to the present and Taran, who was dabbing at the wound with the rag.

"Must you use that abominable brandy?" she asked.

He didn't look up. "Perhaps that will teach you not to jump from balcony to balcony."

"As I said, my lord, that will teach you not to lock me in another room."

"Caroline—" A sharp rap on the door interrupted him. "Enter," Taran called.

The door opened and Patterson stepped aside for a grey-haired gentleman carrying a doctor's bag and out of breath.

Taran rose. "Blakely." The two men clasped hands. "Thank you for coming."

The older man's gaze flicked to Taran's blood-soaked breeches. "You look worse for the wear, Blackhall."

"'Tis but a flesh wound. It is my wife who needs your attention."

Patterson discreetly set a stack of neatly folded snow-white bandages on the nightstand, then clicked the door shut behind him as the doctor turned in her direction. His gaze dropped to her wound. He put his bag on the floor at his feet as he sat on the bed beside her. He reached into the breast pocket of his jacket, pulled out spectacles, and wrapped the wires around his ears. He leaned close and examined the wound.

"Clean the wound with that brandy?" he asked as he tilted his head to the right and peered more closely at the injury.

"He did," Caroline replied. "And it hurt like the devil."

The old man's eyes lifted to meet hers. "Better the sting of brandy than the pain of infection."

"You might tell my husband that," she replied coolly. "He has yet to apply any treatment to that leg."

Doctor Blakely pulled his bag onto his lap and opened the top. "She has a point.

Remove your breeches. Once I have attended to her, I will see to your thigh."

"Blakely—"

"No arguments," the doctor interrupted, then glanced at the basin filled with bloody water. "We will need clean water."

Caroline didn't miss the limp in Taran's walk to the rope that hung on the wall near the bed. He tugged on it, then crossed the room to the hearth.

The doctor leaned close and looked at Caroline's arm. "Now then, let us be sure this is fully sterilized."

After tossing in another log in the fire, Taran poured a liberal tumbler of brandy and lowered himself into the chair in front of the fire. The doctor pulled a bottle of clear liquid from his bag and unscrewed the top. The pungent odor of alcohol filled the air between them. He picked up a bandage and saturated the cloth with the liquid. Patterson arrived a moment later and Taran ordered fresh water brought up. Caroline endured the doctor's ministrations until the gash had been thoroughly cleaned and bandaged.

Fifteen minutes later, clean water had been delivered and the doctor tied the final knot on the bandage. "Blackhall, a glass of water, please."

Taran rose and crossed to the sideboard. Caroline could see by the stiffness in his walk that the effort cost him. The infuriating man was going to deny to the bitter end his need for medical attention. It would serve him right if an infection got the better of him. He poured water from a jug into another tumbler and brought it to her.

The doctor produced a second bottle from his bag. "This is for the pain."

"I do not need laudanum," she said.

"You will soon enough." He poured a small dose in the water, swished it around and handed it to her. "Drink."

"I—"

"For God's sake, Caroline," Taran snapped. "Drink the damned medicine or I will pour it down your throat."

She opened her mouth to tell him to take himself to the devil, then pictured the doctor recounting the tale of how the Viscount of Blackhall forced laudanum down his new bride's throat. She took the glass, hesitated, then caught sight of the dark look on Taran's face. He would make good on his threat. Caroline drank the mixture.

Doctor Blakely took the glass from her and set it on the nightstand. "Now," he stood, "let us have a look at that leg."

"She will be all right?" Taran asked.

"You did a fine job of sterilizing the wound."

Taran's eyes shifted to her face, before he turned. "I will sit, if you do not mind. It has been a trying day." He sat on the chair and grunted as he tugged off one boot and then the other.

"Indeed," the doctor said, and Caroline glimpsed a twitch at the corner of his mouth before he turned and approached Taran. "Off with the breeches."

Taran stood and shoved the breeches off his hips. His jaw clenched as he pushed the fabric down his legs.

A comfortable sense of drowsiness began to creep across Caroline's limbs. Now that she knew Taran would be treated, she relaxed against the pillow. Firelight blurred in her vision.

She should have called for laudanum the moment she arrived at Strathmore. She might have avoided a great deal of trouble. Maybe—she drew in a sharp breath at sight of Taran's rounded buttocks, his breeches around his knees.

He jerked his head in her direction. "Is something amiss?"

She riveted her eyes onto his face. His gaze intensified in silent demand and she answered with a hurried shake of her head.

He looked uncertain. "Do you wish to retire to your own room?"

She wanted nothing more, but would fall flat on her face in the attempt. Caroline pictured Taran, naked, scooping her off the floor and carrying her to her room. She blushed at the thought of Doctor Blakely witnessing the event and responded to Taran's stare with another vigorous shake of her head. The room around her blurred.

"I am fine," she replied, though it sounded as if she'd said *I am thine*.

What was wrong with her ears? Her muddled thoughts blurred from one memory into another. She couldn't recall what had started this whole mess tonight. Taran's sister had married, but there was something else. Distorted memories of a blue domino searching for Aphrodite flitted through her mind. Caroline grimaced. She was going to have to do something about that domino.

Chapter Seventeen

Taran looked at Blakely. "How much laudanum did you administer?"

The doctor smiled. "Enough to ensure she would not interfere with my doctoring of your leg."

Taran scowled. "I see the good reverend filled you in on the details of tonight's events."

"I understand a duel and jumping from balconies was involved."

"I would appreciate it if you did not repeat that business." He halted. "Where is Reverend Gordon?"

"Downstairs. I doubt he will leave until he learns what has become of you and your wife."

"I will speak with him." Taran finished removing his britches. Pain sliced outward from the wound.

"Turn that chair." The doctor nodded towards the bench behind them at the foot of the bed.

He got the clean basin of water from the table near the window and placed it on the bench as Taran fetched the robe laid out for him on the foot of the bed and put it on. He moved the chair then sat. Blakely retrieved his bag from beside the bed where Caroline slept, and the remaining bandages, then seated himself next to Taran.

"Prop that leg up here."

Taran did as ordered and leaned back against the seat cushion.

"Your sister is a tolerable shot," Blakely commented.

Taran barked a laugh. "It is my fault for teaching her."

"I remember she pestered you until you gave in."

"I should have coddled her more. Seems to have worked for Horatia."

The doctor began cleaning the wound. "Horatia demanded to be coddled. Oh, congratulations."

Taran shifted his attention to Caroline. Asleep, she looked as harmless as a mouse. "I cannot yet say congratulations are in order."

"Huntly is a good man."

"Ah, you refer to my sister's marriage."

"Felicitations on your marriage, as well."

Taran winced at the burn of alcohol on his leg. A shame Caroline had fallen asleep. She would have enjoyed seeing him receive the same treatment he'd given her. She had taken it well, he realized with some pride.

Blakely worked in silence, cleaning the wound for a moment, before saying, "What have you decided about Darby?"

Taran jerked from his concentration on Caroline. Darby was a notorious cattle rustler, who had yet to be caught red-handed. "Darby has been dealt with."

"Are you certain he knows that?"

"What has happened?"

Blakely set the bloody rag on the edge of the water basin and picked up a clean one from the stack. "Unwise of you to ignore this wound for so long."

"Not so long. Only the time it took to fetch you and tend to Caroline."

"An hour," the doctor replied. "You could have at least poured brandy on it as you did her wound."

"I have had worse, as you know. Now, what has happened with Darby? If he has gone back to stealing cattle—"

"Nothing so disreputable as that," Blakely replied. "On the contrary, he now collects, er, insurance, so that cattle are *not* stolen."

Taran stared. "*Not* stolen?"

The doctor lifted Taran's leg, placed a clean rag beneath his thigh, then laid it on the cloth and poured alcohol on the wound.

Stinging pain spiked clear through to the bone. Taran clenched his teeth. "By God, Blakely."

"You have had worse," the doctor replied, and dried the wound.

Taran fell into silence, his thoughts on Randall Darby. The fact the rustler hadn't been caught stealing hadn't stopped the local villagers from nearly hanging him twice. John had intervened both times. Not out of the goodness of his heart, but because their father had threatened recompense if word reached the Lord Advocate that a murder had been committed on their land. Murder didn't bother the old earl. Dealing with the English Crown did. An investigation could lead to the discovery of their illegal gaming hall.

Blakely lifted Taran's thigh and began wrapping the wound. Taran remembered with disgust his father's announcement that they were to become gaming hall owners. John had laughed when Taran had pointed out that they could lose everything—and end up in Newgate—if the Crown got wind of the operation. His father hadn't needed to run a gaming hall, but considered it easier than earning an honest living by working the land. Taran had left the following day and joined the Navy.

He shifted his gaze onto Caroline. She lay, her head tilted to the side on the pillow, the slight rise and fall of her breast a sign she slept peacefully. What would she think of having traded a pirate uncle for a gaming house owner father-in-law? She would never know. The earl's gaming days were over. As for Randall Darby, Taran would see to him first thing in the morning.

"He is not a bad sort," Blakely said as if he'd read Taran's mind.

"He should do as he is told."

"Enough time has not yet passed to give him faith that things will be any better now than they were under your father or John's rule."

The doctor was right. Taran thought for the thousandth time of how the land had been left unused, the people who depended on them for sustenance turning to cattle rustling or thievery to survive.

"May John's soul rot in Hell," he murmured.

The doctor glanced at him.

Taran shrugged. "There is no love lost between my brother and me."

"There is no love lost between John and anyone. Except, perhaps, his mistress." Taran grunted a laugh. "Not even his mistress. Clarice has already found herself another protector."

A corner of the older man's mouth twitched. He tied off the bandage and straightened.

"If any signs of inflammation appear, inform me immediately."

"No matter the time of night or day." Taran stood.

"You might want a dose of laudanum." Blakely strode to the nightstand where he'd left the bottle.

"Nay." Taran glanced at Caroline. "I suspect I will need my wits about me. Is she well?"

The doctor crossed to the bench and placed the bottle inside his bag. "The wound was not as superficial as yours—you were damned lucky on that account, the bullet merely grazed you, but she will be fine."

"Hurt like the devil," Taran muttered.

Blakely's brows rose. "A little higher and—"

"A little higher and I would not be able to sire an heir."

Taran glanced at Caroline. Given her response to him the last two nights, he couldn't bear the thought of not slipping into her heat again. He would be the only man to satisfy her.

Minutes later the doctor departed. Taran had no desire to dress. Despite the ache in his thigh, his *desire* was to climb upon the bed with his wife, kiss her out of her delirium and slide between her lithe thighs. Since their encounter in the carriage—and before Fiona's untimely interruption— his cock throbbed with nearly the same intensity as the wound in his leg.

He turned off the lamp, then crossed to the bed and blew out the candle. Taran grabbed his robe tie, then paused at sight of Caroline. Silken black hair splayed across stark white pillows. Her soft mouth lifted into a ghost of a smile. What sweet visions danced in her mind? He grimaced. Sweet vision? Mischief, more likely.

Taran shrugged from his robe, tossed it to the end of the bed, then slid beneath the covers next to her. She sighed and snuggled against his side. He held his breath when long, delicate fingers tickled across his chest. Quivers tightened his abdomen as blood rushed into his shaft with the same pounding rhythm as his beating heart.

He eased an arm beneath her and wrapped his hand over her shoulder, pulling her closer. His fingers brushed the bandage. Part of him wanted to wring her neck, but he was also thrilled at her gumption. Loyalty was something to admire. In the years to come, he would need her at his side. Yes, he was entitled to her money, now his money, to spend as he saw fit. But he had pride. Together they could return dignity to Strathmore and the people who called his family's land home.

Although his cock lay heavy and erect against his stomach, he closed his eyes and resigned himself to sleep. Until he discovered Caroline's secrets—Aphrodite's secrets—he would bide his time. Then, he thought, as warmth seeped from the hand lying on his chest into his flesh, then he would bed her every night until she couldn't think. He would be much safer if she was too satiated to think of anything but him. His body relaxed. He wanted her to think of nothing but him.

Hairs tickled his sternum. Taran froze when Caroline wedged his good leg between hers and arched her pelvis into his thigh. Damp heat warmed his flesh. His heart raced. She again trailed fingers over his torso.

His gaze caught on the bandage. "Your shoulder," he whispered.

"Hardly hurts." The sound of her gravelly voice startled, then concerned him. She wasn't truly awake.

Her hand dipped below the waist-high sheet.

His cock jerked and Taran grasped her hand. "Caroline, you're not fully awake, and you tempt me beyond thought. I will not want to stop."

"Mm hmm." She propped onto an elbow and bent towards his chest.

Moist lips closed around a nipple. Lust shot to his groin. He groaned at the hardening of his cock to near steel. She flicked the nipple with her tongue, then sucked. His chest tightened against the intense pleasure. The edge of her palm grazed his erection. By God, she had already tasted of his passion. She knew what she did to him. Or did she? Her fingers closed around him and squeezed. Taran braced her ribcage, careful of her shoulder and rolled her onto her back. Her thighs spread and he positioned his hips between them, his erection pressing against her heated mound.

Eyes bright in the dim glow of the embers, she wrapped a hand around his neck and urged him closer. It was the laudanum, and surely only Aphrodite would be so bold, but, damn his soul, he couldn't turn away. Taran closed the space between them, sealing their lips. Her mouth opened and hot flicks of her tongue sent heat racing through his veins.

Her free hand slid around his waist and she sank deeper into the kiss. Taran growled. Tongues, lips, gliding, tasting, sucking. He broke the kiss and tugged down the sleeve of her uninjured arm to reveal a breast. His breath hitched at sight of the rosy nipple that jutted towards him. He latched onto the taut peak. She arched and he sucked more of the supple breast into his mouth, working the tip between his tongue and the roof of his mouth. Softening his kiss, he gently bit the tip, then laved the tightened bud with his tongue and blew against her skin. She shivered. Taran repeated the kiss on the other breast. Her legs shifted beneath him, twisting the garment. She squirmed.

Taran gave a low laugh. "Patience."

He slid a moist kiss from between her breasts, up her neck to her ear and gently took the lobe between his teeth and nibbled. She whimpered. He rose to his knees. She grabbed for him, but he turned her onto her stomach. She struggled to face him.

Taran leaned down and whispered in her ear. "Lie still, sweet."

She complied and he worked the laces from the stays, pulled what was left of the sleeve from the injured arm, then the other arm. He worked the dress down her hips, off her legs, and tossed it aside. She shifted and he stilled her movements by straddling her legs. With a feather-light touch, Taran slid his palms down her back and over her rounded buttocks. Smooth flesh quivered beneath his fingers. His cock jumped.

Careful of her arm, Taran turned her over. Her cheeks were flushed and he placed a hand on her face. Cool flesh met his touch and his shoulders relaxed the tension he hadn't realized was there. Caroline grasped his fingers and brought them to her mouth. Eyes closed, she pressed his palm to her lips and slid a warm kiss along the calloused skin. His heart pounded. By all that was holy, he would never let her go. He needed this—her naked body, writhing beneath him, with her thighs spread as he sank into her silken sheath.

Taran positioned himself over her. Holding his weight with his arms, he spread her legs with his knees. Pain sliced through his leg, but he settled between her thighs and nudged her opening with the blunt head of his cock. Her legs opened wider. With gentle fingers, he parted her drenched folds, breeched her plump pussy lips and slipped his cock in an inch. The hot, wet passage closed around him as if in welcome. With a deep inhalation, she relaxed and he sank to the hilt. Lowering onto her, he took care with her shoulder by staying propped on his elbows, then brushed a kiss across her trembling lips as he pulled out, then thrust. She arched and gasped.

Taran jerked back, his cock slipping from her sheath. "Your shoulder?" She shook her head, but didn't speak.

He hesitated, his rod throbbing, the need to thrust nearly overwhelming, then rolled to his back. "Ride me." He grasped the root of his shaft.

Caroline sat upright and listed a little to the left before he caught her.

"Damn laudanum," he cursed, and started to rise.

She flashed a smile and swung a leg over his hips. Caroline gave a tiny cry and he started to push her off then realized she was staring at his leg. She bent close, then looked at him, brow furrowed in such a dark frown he wanted to laugh.

"My lord, your leg."

He blinked, uncertain he'd truly heard the slur that had made the word *leg* sound like *theg*. She shifted, her curls brushing his shaft, and all amusement vanished.

"True agony is not having my cock buried in your sweet body. Enough talk."

She straightened so quickly he had to stop the momentum that would have toppled her onto the mattress. Before he realized her intent, she grasped his stalk and sank onto him until his cock head pressed against the top of her channel. Pleasure shot through him with agonizing intensity. Caroline gasped, eyes wide.

"Damn it, Caroline," he rasped, but she lifted so that the mushroom-tipped head teased her folds, smearing her juices over his crown. The soft curls covering her mound tickled his cock head and he was certain he would spend himself that instant.

Unable to hold back, he bucked hard, cramming her full of his cock. His thigh burned and pain robbed him of breath, yet he couldn't stop. Caroline arched, crying out as her internal walls gloved his shaft. She rocked on his lap, taking her pleasure as she rode him.

Her cream slicked his easy slide into her slippery passage.

Smooth muscular contractions pulled him deeper into her body. Then she shattered. She slammed hard onto his hips. Pain rippled through his wound. He bolted up and gulped air.

She cried out and scrambled from his lap, falling arse first onto the mattress. "My lord."

He bolted upright. "On your knees."

Caroline stared. Taran pushed to his knees. Pain spiked from his wound, but he grasped her hips and roughly turned her buttocks towards his pelvis. She twisted and looked at him from over her shoulder. He froze at the sight of her wide eyes.

His fingers dug into sweet, feminine flesh. He wanted—needed—to dig deep, fuck her clear to her core, but he forced a slow breath, then leaned forward and gathered her into his arms. He kissed the worry from her brow. Trailing lower, he rained kisses over her cheek, then brushed his lips to hers. When he opened his mouth over her jaw, her head tilted to the side.

He gently bit her neck, then flicked his tongue against her fluttering pulse and whispered, "Trust me."

Caroline relaxed and repositioned on her hands and knees. Taran stroked a hand over the arch in her back as he moved behind her. He caressed her hip, then palmed her arse.

Slipping his fingers lower, he traced the seam of her buttocks until he reached the damp heat of her pussy. He played at her entrance until she whimpered, then he slipped in his finger into her tightened core. Caroline drew a ragged breath and pulsed against his hand. He smiled and inserted a second digit, curling into her passage. Heated honey flowed from her.

There was no doubt this was his Aphrodite. She responded to him without reservation. This wasn't a refined lady of society. She was his lover—now his wife. Pressure squeezed his chest. She may never want to admit to her night of masked seduction, but he vowed he would draw her out, make it safe for her to love him as she had that night. He started at having thought the word love. Aye, she would love him.

In the dim firelight, with her eyes downcast to the bed, he pulled his fingers from her body and slipped them between his lips. He closed his eyes and let the tang of her arousal bring back the memory of the first time he'd tasted Aphrodite.

Raw emotion stole over him. He grasped his cock, slid between her thighs, and fucked his wife the way Aphrodite would demand.

* * * *

Caroline wrapped her arms around herself and stared out over the railing of the lady's bedchamber balcony at the mist cloaked darkness. But for the ache in her arm, nothing—not even her wedding day—seemed real. Perhaps it was the remnants of the laudanum which had been administered a few hours ago. Even the half-moon cast an eerie light that belonged to a nether land, foreign to her world.

She closed her eyes in an effort to recall Taran's voice as it had been in the carriage when she had been Aphrodite, the feel of his arms around her, strong, demanding. Instead, the gentle touch and whispered words of their wedding night filled her mind. She'd glimpsed the passion he shared with Aphrodite, yet his ardent kisses and fierce thrusts had revealed desire for her. *His wife.*

A tear slid from her eye. With every breath she drew and every beat of her heart, she loved him. Leaving would plunge a knife through her chest. But she would survive. Caroline bowed her head. But she wouldn't survive life *with* him once he discovered the truth—and he would. She'd glimpsed that future last night when he sent his sister away. She grasped the railing, glad for the chill of the wrought iron. Had she only known—

"What the bloody hell are you doing?"

Caroline whirled at the sound of Taran's voice. He was halfway across the balcony. Despite the limp in his left leg, he stalked towards her as if he meant to throw her over the railing. She cast an involuntary glance at the other balcony.

"By God, I will redden your lovely bottom if you move even an inch."

She riveted her head back in his direction. A cool breeze caught the edge of his robe, fluttering the silken fabric around his thighs. He stopped in front of her and grasped her wrist.

"My lord, your leg." She shoved at his chest, wincing at the dull pain that throbbed in her shoulder.

"Damn the leg." He scooped her into his arms. "I will not give you another opportunity for mischief tonight." Taran strode across the balcony, through the anteroom, and back into his room. He laid her on the bed, then braced a knee on the mattress and flattened his palms on the bed on both sides of her head. He stared, eyes dark. "Unless of course, your mischief includes me."

Memory of when he'd locked her and Fiona in the room, leapt to mind and she swallowed.

He brought his face to within an inch of hers. "Do not move. Stay here where you belong...in my bed."

"Are you always out of sorts in the morning?"

Taran made a noise deep in his chest like a growl, then shimmied off the bed and limped to the hearth. He grasped the poker leaning against the brick, gingerly bent on his good knee, and pushed aside the screen. He poked the embers until they glowed red-hot, then picked up two split logs from the small pile to his right and laid them on the coals.

"A wife jumping from a balcony is enough to get any man's ire up," he said as if speaking to himself. A moment later, a small fire blazed. Taran looked over his shoulder at her. "Have you not spent enough time on that balcony for one night?"

"I spent little time on *that* balcony, if you recall."

"You are a reckless woman. But that will now end."

A strange calm settled over her. "Reckless, like your sister?"

He faced the fire and gave the coals a vicious stab. "The girl needs a good lesson.

Mayhap Huntly can teach her what I could not."

"You threatened to kill her husband. What did you expect?"

"I expected her to have sense enough to know that marriage at sixteen is a risky business."

"Marriage at any age is risky," Caroline said. "But business, nonetheless."

He paused, but remained facing the fire. "You condemn me for marrying you?"

"You are not at fault for being an astute businessman."

"It was not I who made the bargain," he said in a quiet voice.

A sob leapt to her throat, but she bit it back. So he wouldn't have chosen her as his wife. Did he prefer Aphrodite, or was even Aphrodite unfit to offer her inheritance on the altar of his family estate? Perhaps neither she, nor her alias, were fit to bear his children. Caroline bowed her head.

"Perhaps you regret the bargain." He shoved to his feet. His mouth twisted in pain.

Caroline bolted upright. "Your thigh—"

"Cease worrying about my thigh, Caroline. I have had worse."

"As a result of other duels, no doubt," she snapped.

He gave her a frank look. "That has been one cause."

Despite the pounding of her heart, she didn't drop her gaze. How many of those duels had been fought because of his rigidity? He'd called her reckless. Aphrodite had been exciting, but the goddess wasn't supposed to be his wife.

Chapter Eighteen

Caroline glimpsed Taran turn down the street in the village. Her pulse jumped and she ducked into the tiny lane just before the town hall. Had he seen her? How had he managed to go to the village at the very same time she had? Anger flared. It was no coincidence. He was looking for her. Wasn't she allowed a visit to the village without his permission? She whirled back towards the street, then halted at sound of his voice.

"How much, Darby?"

"Now, laird, you canna' be thinking I would steal more cattle. You warned me."

"Aye," Taran replied. "But apparently I was not explicit enough. I will not have you breaking the law in *any* manner."

"What law have I broken?"

"Extortion," Taran replied.

"Extortion?" the man repeated.

"Extracting money in exchange for *not* stealing cattle is extortion." Caroline clamped a hand over her mouth, barely stifling laughter.

"I wouldna' say extracting," Darby said.

"I would," Taran replied. "You know I am the law here."

"Aye, laird, but surely—"

"Surely what?"

Caroline froze at the edge in Taran's voice.

"Laird Blackhall," a woman said.

Taran's reply to the woman was whisper-quiet. Caroline strained to hear. She inched to the edge of the building and peeked around the side. Taran stood, his back to her, facing a small man she assumed was Darby, and a young woman, belly nearly bursting with the child she carried.

Caroline's breath caught. Long black hair fell across slim shoulders in thick, black waves that reached to full breasts nearly spilling over the woman's bodice. Despite her girth—and the drab grey dress—she was stunning. Even her shy smile exuded a sensuality that would mesmerize a man like a siren's call. Any man would throw himself on the rocks for her. She stared at Taran with an adoration that told Caroline that Taran was one of those men. Was the woman Darby's? A lump lodged in Caroline's throat. Or was the woman acquainted with Taran…intimately acquainted?

The woman turned her dark eyes on Taran and gave him a mischievous look that elicited a surge of jealousy so hard, Caroline's chest tightened. She swung back and collapsed against the building. Taran had insisted on returning to Scotland. She began to tremble. She recalled his concern that Aphrodite had become with child after their night in the carriage. Could he already have children?

Caroline gave her head a shake to clear the muddle. What was wrong with her? She'd completely lost her mind, that's what. Even after Taran had ravaged her as Aphrodite, he'd been honorable, wanting to claim a child if one should result from their union. She placed her hand over her abdomen. What if she had already conceived?

"Where have ye been, laird?" Darby asked.

Caroline hung on the words.

"You know I married," Taran replied.

"Brought the *Sassenach* to Strathmore?"

"She is the Viscountess of Blackhall, Darby. Do not forget that. Even when I am absent."

"Aye."

Caroline peered around the building again.

"Darby, I will have your word."

"Aye," he said. "No cattle rustling, no…donations."

"There is no need now," Taran said. "There will be plenty to go around."

Stubbornness appeared on the man's face. "What you consider plenty may not be the same as me."

"Are you hungry?" Taran asked.

"Nay," Darby answered, his tone that of a belligerent child.

"Have you enough clothing and wood to keep you warm?"

Darby didn't lift his eyes from where he stared at the ground. "Aye."

"Then we are off to a good start. No more extortion. No more breaking the law. If you have need of something, come to me."

The man's head lifted and he studied Taran for a long moment, then nodded. Taran turned so quickly Caroline barely managed to duck back into the lane before he could see her. She hesitated, unsure whether to turn left or right, then hurried down the lane in the opposite direction.

"Caroline."

She froze at sound of Taran's voice echoing off the buildings. This was the second time in less than a week she'd been caught where she shouldn't be. Determined footfalls rang on the stone lane behind her, and she turned as he reached her.

"Good afternoon, my lord."

His brow lifted. "Spying?"

She shrugged. "I just happened to be at the right place at the right time."

"Every spy's defense. What are you doing here?"

"I wanted to see the place I now call home."

"What say you so far?" he asked in a soft voice.

"There is a great deal of disrepair," she answered honestly.

He nodded and grasped her hand, slipping it into the crook of his arm as he started them in the direction she'd been headed. "Aye. My father gave little thought to the upkeep."

"But that will change now that you have my fortune."

He glanced at her. "Would you rather your money go to gambling and mistresses?" No, she had to admit, she wouldn't.

"What plans have you for bringing things up to snuff?"

He laughed, a rich, deep sound that made her want to press an ear to his chest so that she might hear the sound roll through his large frame.

"My plans for bringing things *up to snuff* begin with the supplies that will arrive within the week. Everything cannot be finished before winter, but the worst of the cottages must be made warmer before the first snow."

They reached the end of the lane and broke out onto the street. A stable sat directly across the way with a small tavern to the right. Behind the buildings, on a hill, sat half a dozen thatched cottages, smoke puffing from their chimneys in modest chugs. To the left, an open market buzzed with business.

"How many people live in the village?" Caroline asked, surprised at the market that stretched across two or three hectares.

"Eighty-two," Taran replied. "But this market is the only one within thirty miles."

She looked at him. "A market like this is a huge economic asset. Why hasn't it supported the village?"

"Because my father taxed the merchants into poverty."

The vehemence in his voice startled then warmed her. For all his faults, he was not his father, and he would use her money for a better cause than anyone she could have chosen on her own—certainly better than John, which made her uncle's choice of men nothing more than dumb luck.

"Would you like to see the shops?" Taran asked.

"I would," she replied, then blushed at the delight she had shown.

He smiled, obviously pleased with her reaction, and she couldn't help smiling back.

"You did say you would need to purchase things as a result of being rushed away from England," he said. "You will not find a modiste, but there are some fine fabrics to be had.

Choose anything you like."

Caroline arched a brow. "Giving me permission to spend my own money?"

He grinned. "I am a generous sort. Spend to your heart's content. Fiona can steer you to the best dress designer in the Highlands after you've made your purchases."

Despite her pique, a quiver radiated through her stomach. Unlike so many husbands, he wasn't tight-fisted and showed no signs of setting up a miserly allowance meant to keep her quiet long enough for him to deplete her fortune.

Only yesterday she hadn't been able to imagine a life away from London. She had never been one to attend every party, staying out until dawn only to repeat the process until the season was over. But neither could she have fathomed finding contentment in country life. Yet, looking at Taran, she saw in his eyes their lives as they shared in the building up of the village his father had ruined, their children, then finally grandchildren, playing at their feet.

Reality returned with an adder's bite, and the sting of tears nearly wrenched a sob from her. His warm fingers gently squeezed the hand still entwined in the crook of his arm as he led her across the street towards the market. She moved alongside, legs numb, mind blank, except for the broken picture that had shattered inside her head.

*****

Caroline stood in front of the full-length mirror in the corner of her bedchamber and stared at the deep-blue velvet gown she wore. Despite the carefully coiffured curls pinned atop her head, she looked just as Fiona had intended—*déshabillé*—partially dressed with a careless flair that said the dress had been *thrown on*. Caroline traced a finger along the lighter blue trimmed bodice that dipped to reveal the valley between her breasts. Her sister-in-law was to be the death of her. In the space of a few hours, the girl had planned a ball in honor of her and Taran's marriage—to be held tonight. Then she had sent over this dress. Caroline might have thought the girl meant to amend for shooting her brother last night, but she knew better.

When Caroline had seen her at the breakfast table this morning, she knew Fiona sensed her unease. Caroline's cheeks warmed as they had when she'd entered the room and found Taran dressed as he had been on the night of the masque, in a white linen shirt and belted plaid. His gaze lifted from the morning paper and she couldn't help wondering if he hadn't purposely dressed in that fashion. But, of course, he had. This was the Scottish Highlands, and men didn't all wear breeches or trousers as they did in England. To top it off, seeing his legs when he stood in deference to her as she seated herself had caused her knees to weaken.

She nearly plopped onto the chair.

"Are you well, madam?" He frowned. "I have sent for Blakely."

Her mind was still grappling with the sight of his lean frame, so her only recourse had been to lift her chin and reply, "He may tend to my arm as long as you give him five minutes to look at that leg." Though she had taken great care not to be in the room when the doctor had lifted Taran's plaid to examine the exquisite thigh beneath. The knowing glint in Fiona's eyes hadn't stopped Caroline from adding, "I will not have your father bring me up on charges of murder if you die from infection."

"It was not you who shot me." Taran cast his sister a glance that Caroline could have sworn carried a hint of admiration.

"I feel certain he will not blame his daughter," Caroline had said.

Taran's barked laugh had mingled with Fiona's. "You do not know the earl," he'd said. "But in this case, he would gladly send you to Newgate as murderess in exchange for keeping your money. Unlike me, who will share." He had added the last with obvious relish.

Pain stabbed at her arm. Caroline stirred from the memory to see she'd wrapped her arms about her shoulders and had squeezed the wound. She tugged the sleeve down and found the bandage Blakely had applied an hour ago, still firmly in place, no blood staining the snow white bandages. A shame. If she was bleeding, Taran would be forced to let her remain in her bedchambers for the night. She grimaced. More likely, he would confine her there for the next week, or until the wound was completely healed. Then, no doubt, he would stay with her, day and night, torturing her with all the luscious things he would do to her body.

Caroline shivered. She'd woken this morning with images filtering through her mind. Taran's mouth was on her breasts, fingers dipping inside her warmth and—she swallowed, her throat suddenly dry—her on all fours while warm hands held her hips steady against the firm cock that pounded into her from behind. Warmth spread through her. She'd believed they were fantasies her laudanum-clouded mind had conjured, yet her body was pleasantly sore. Not all had been dreams.

Her reflection in the mirror came into focus, gaze on the exposed cleavage of her breasts. Hesitantly, she covered the mounds with her hands. Her cool hands warmed with contact of flesh on the edges of her palms.

She slipped a hand inside the bodice. The nipples went taut, pebble-like against her palm. She slid her hands down a fraction to cup the full mound. Weight of the soft flesh that overflowed in her fingers sent a thrill through her. Was this what Taran felt when he touched her? She grazed the nipple with her thumb and gasped at the sensitivity that tightened her pussy. Her heart sped up and she cast a glance at the door. Dared she? She took the nipple between finger and thumb and rolled the pink tip. Her clit tightened and moisture wet her channel.

In her mind's eye she saw herself pulling up her skirt and reaching between her legs. Her heart pounded harder. What would it be like to part the folds and trail her finger through up the wet crevice to the sensitive place at the tip? Would her fingers please her as Taran's did? A tremor rocked her stomach. What if he caught her? Would he thrill at the sight? She envisioned herself on the bed, him gently pulling her skirt above her waist, then standing back as she dipped a finger into the wet heat, probing, massaging, flicking the tiny nub until she writhed in pleasure. Would he be so moved by passion he'd join her? The jiggle of the knob on the door between the lady and lord's room jerked her back to the present.

She yanked her hand from within the bodice as the door opened and Taran filled the space. She stood frozen, their gazes locked in the mirror. He wore the same belted plaide and a clean linen shirt, but Caroline didn't dare let her gaze stray from his face for fear the heat in her cheeks would spread down her exposed neck and give away every erotic picture that was now etched into her brain. His keen eyes dropped from her face to the rise and fall of her breasts, then lifted back to her face. He stared for a breathless moment, then strode towards her. Her pulse sprang into action like a too-tightly coiled spring when he stopped beside her, gaze still on her reflection, and wrapped an arm around her waist. He pressed a kiss to her temple. A quiver radiated through Caroline. The kiss had been chaste, but the gleam in his eye was anything but virtuous.

"Lonely, madam?" he asked, lips still pressed against her flesh.

A compulsion to bolt like a frightened rabbit shot to the surface. His arm tightened around her and Caroline attempted to pull away. A corner of his mouth twitched and she wanted to box his ears. He couldn't possibly know what she'd been thinking...*doing*. He breathed deep and exhaled, his warm breath bathing her cheek. She shivered. He lifted his free hand. She jerked and he paused, brow quirked, clearly daring her to explain why the small action unnerved her. With a finger, he traced the edge of her bodice as she had. Warmth pooled between her legs and she fought the urge to fidget.

An unexpected desire surfaced to grasp his hand and guide it downward until his fingers pressed against her pussy. Even with the fabric between them, his touch would be beyond belief. His hand dropped away from the bodice and, arm still around her waist, he slid behind her. Caroline gasped at the feel of his erection pressing into her buttocks and she stood frozen as he shifted, working the hard length between the cheeks of her arse. When he stilled, grasped her skirt, and began inching it upward, her legs weakened. He pulled her more tightly to him.

At last, the skirt was high enough to hint at the curls between her legs and Taran pressed his mouth against her ear and whispered, "Show me what you want." Her eyes widened and she shook her head frantically. "My lord, I—"

"What do you want?" he interrupted.

He released her waist and grasped her hand. She stiffened, but he kissed her ear, then gently took the lobe between his teeth and bit down. Desire exploded through her.

She jammed her eyes shut as he guided her hand downward. "My lord."

Her fingertips brushed her curls and he swirled the tips against the fringes, tickling her mound with the slightest of touches. Her pussy tightened an instant before her fingers grazed the already swollen nub. Caroline jerked back against Taran and jarred with awareness of his cock trapped against her arse. She leaned forward and he plunged the fingers between the warm folds. She gasped at feel of the moist warmth.

"Aye, love," Taran whispered. "Feel yourself as I do."

He undulated his hips so that her clit pulsed against her palm while he guided her fingers into her hot channel.

"Open your eyes," he coaxed.

She gave another frantic shake of her head.

His low masculine laugh sent a shiver through her. "Show me what you like."

"You—you know what I like," she burst out.

His laugh was deeper this time. "Aye, love, but I can make pleasing yourself all the better." He moved suggestively behind her and she swallowed.

He thrust the finger deeper into her channel, then out, then in again. Pleasure radiated through her. She opened her eyes and met his stare in the mirror.

He gave a small nod. "Yes."

In and out, he guided her movement while slowly pulsing his hips so that her clit rubbed against her palm. Pressure mounted and she couldn't resist the urge to make the finger more rigid. Satisfaction lifted a corner of his mouth. He abruptly pulled the digit from within the warmth and began massaging her clit with it in fast strokes. He eased back. The rhythm broke and he cursed, but released her hand. He yanked the skirt higher, crushing it against her abdomen as he yanked up his plaid and stepped close again. Flesh against flesh, his steely length met the soft curves of her rear.

He grasped her hand again and urged her back into the luscious rhythm that mercilessly teased her clit. "Do not stop," he ordered, and released her hand.

She swallowed, but continued as instructed. His gaze dropped to where her fingers worked their magic. His intake of breath startled then thrilled her. Skirt still held firmly at her waist, he grasped her hips and thrust his cock upward through the crack in her arse. Her brain flip-flopped between the pleasure her fingers brought and the feel of his cock tightening as it slid upward, then loosening with the downward slide. Her breath quickened. He abruptly threw an arm around her waist and lowered himself a few inches so that he could slide the hard length between her folds. The tip bumped against her fingers and he sucked in breath. Caroline faltered.

"Do not stop," he commanded again as he bent her forward and, before she realized his intent, he pushed into her channel.

Fingers shaking, she rocked against the digit, her arse bumping against his belly, his cock sliding forward then back. His head fell back and he thrust with the rhythm she created. Pleasure built in her core. His grip tightened. Faster. Harder. Lust coiled tight in her belly. His hold on her hips turned iron. She slicked her fingers through the moist warmth of her folds, fingertips coming in contact with the cock pounding into her.

Memory burst forth of last night in Taran's bed. She sucked in breath. The laudanum had clouded her brain, she hadn't dreamed the encounter. Taran had bedded her as no husband bedded a wife. He had fucked her on all fours. Taken her as hard and savagely as he fucked her now.

"Please yourself," he ground out.

Caroline flicked the swollen nub with a fast motion that brought a sudden flare of pleasure that sizzled along the nerves connecting to her very being. Taran pumped faster. She gulped air, body jarring with the impact of his hips to her buttocks, but he held her, thrusting harder. Pleasure splintered through her. She cried out with her orgasm. Her knees weakened, but Taran held her upright for a final thrust. He erupted, spewing his seed deep inside her. Caroline massaged her clit in another quick motion and a second, more powerful orgasm rolled through her.

"Fuck," he growled, and thrust again, then one last time in unison with the final wave of pleasure that turned her knees to pudding. He caught her to him, breath hard and heavy against her flesh as he buried his head in her neck.

They stood for a long moment, his powerful chest heaving against her back, her body trembling. At last, his breathing slowed and his hold loosened. Mercifully, her legs held her weight. Taran released her and the lush velvet skirt fell down across her legs without so much as a tiny crease. Relief flooded her and she smoothed the fabric at hip length, twisting so that she could see the backside in the mirror.

Taran grinned. "No worse for the wear, madam?"

She paused and looked at his reflection. Male satisfaction was written on his face. "No thanks to you," she retorted, despite the warmth that crept up her cheeks and the trickle of fluids between her thighs.

His brow lifted. "I made good on my promise."

Caroline frowned.

"I said I could make pleasuring yourself all the *more* pleasurable."

She couldn't halt a gasp of surprise or the blush that reddened her cheeks. A knowing gleam entered his eyes and a rush of fear displaced the embarrassment. What they had just done was something no wife did. Such illicit behavior belonged in the world of the demimonde…belonged to Aphrodite.

Chapter Nineteen

Taran scanned the ballroom for his wife. He'd last seen her on the dance floor. Their eyes had met and her expression had said she would murder him at first opportunity. He couldn't prevent a smile. No doubt the wench was remembering another such soirée where the room had been just as stifling and she'd got herself into a pickle by giving her maidenhead to the very man she was trying to cuckold.

For the first time since discovering her identity, he wondered what would have happened had she succeeded. He couldn't halt the vision of her in another man's arms, his mouth on her breasts, finger insider her channel as he brought her to climax before filling her with his cock. Taran recalled the previous night in his bed, her intent to cover her deception. She had tried to avoid his bed, but that was because she feared he would sense the familiarity. She had intended to hide the fact she betrayed him.

"What are you doing to yourself?" he murmured. *"A woman has only that which is given her,"* she had said. *"I decided to take something for myself."* How could he blame her? Any woman of substance would have seen marriage to John as a prison sentence. She couldn't know he was any different and had, in fact, done everything short of running away to get him to cry off.

Taran smiled with memory of how she had accused him of kidnapping her. He nearly had—might have—had she not melted beneath his touch. And she had melted. Her responses hadn't been practiced that night, or the next, or the next. She had intended on experiencing another man's touch before being ruined by the brother she envisioned to be the mirror image of

John. She hadn't bargained for him. Taran laughed. He hadn't bargained for *her.*

"Are you all right?"

Taran turned at the sound of William's voice behind him. He grinned. "Better than I have ever been."

William's brow rose. "Seems married life agrees with you."

"Who would have thought it?"

A shadow crossed William's face. "We need to talk."

Taran motioned him to follow and began threading through the crowd towards the small parlor down the hall on the east side of the ballroom. There was no doubt. William had discovered Caroline was Aphrodite and was certain the news wouldn't bode well for their marriage. Odd, but he couldn't have been more wrong. While Taran wouldn't stand for another man touching her, he was immensely thankful for the woman who wasn't willing to take only that which men allowed her. Yet, in the end, like him, she understood duty. Though, for the life of him, he suddenly couldn't understand why duty dictated she marry a man she loathed. Etherton might threaten poverty, but Taran could see intimidation having little effect.

They reached the edge of the crowd and William came up alongside him as they strode down the hall. Once in the parlor, Taran closed the door and seated himself in the wingback chair across from the small sofa William lowered himself onto.

"Had you not asked me, Blackhall, I would keep my nose out of the whole business."

"You have discovered that Aphrodite is my wife."

Surprise flickered across William's face. "How did you find out?"

Taran laughed. "It would have been hard not to see it."

His friend's expression turned speculative. "You sound as if it is a good thing."

"It is."

"And the fact she was at the masque with another man?"

"She fled your company, if I recall."

William assented with small dip of his head, then said in a neutral tone, "You do not seem perturbed that your wife intended to fuck another man the night before your wedding." His brow creased into a frown. "How is it that you were the man she fucked—er—made love to?"

Taran's cock jerked with memory of Caroline crying out when he'd buried himself deep inside her.

"You two decided to consummate the wedding early."

Taran jarred from the erotic picture and shook his head. "She did not know who I was, nor did I her."

"By God, Taran, that bit of deceit goes too far."

"Beware," Taran said in a low voice.

William regarded him, then shrugged. "As you wish."

"Things are not as they seem," Taran said, regretting the surge of possessiveness that had forced the outburst. By God, he was a besotted fool.

"She is your wife. If you are satisfied with her that is your business." Satisfied was hardly the word Taran would have chosen.

* * * *

The ball was only three hours into swing and already the ballroom was overflowing. Caroline paused at the doors leading to the rear gardens and scanned the dance floor. Anxiety burrowed deep in her stomach. This party was too reminiscent of the masque, and the wanton acts she'd committed with Taran earlier were too close to the things they had done in the gardens that night. How had the truth escaped his notice?

She slipped onto the balcony. Cool air washed over the flushed skin of her face and neck and she wished mightily the elbow length sleeves were shorter. She stepped up to the stone railing and gazed into the darkened garden. Instead of the ridiculously manicured maze of Lord Forbes' garden, tall trees dotted the horizon beyond the expanse of lawn. Branches rose like stick phantoms that beckoned into a dark world where the night creatures' opus rivalled the music drifting from the ballroom.

With a glance through the French doors at the crowd that seemed even larger than it had been a moment ago, Caroline hurried down the steps to the grass and across the lawn. As she entered the cover of trees, she slowed. Insects and frogs went quiet as she crept forward, guided by slivers of moonlight so skimpy it seemed she walked in a dream. She'd had little opportunity to explore such large treed gardens. Her uncle's London townhouse garden was a small patch of land where a solitary elm stood sentinel in the middle of the tiny kingdom.

She had once visited an estate in London renowned for its arboretum, but she'd been there during a day party and had explored but a small section before being waylaid by the Baron of Lochshire. For once, Caroline gave thanks for her uncle. The baron was set on making her his baroness, but Uncle had his sights on nothing less than an Earl for a son-in-law.

Caroline halted beside a large elm. The creatures resumed their song and she relaxed against the hard wood of the tree, eyes closed. So here she was, wed to the earl of her uncle's choosing, the one man she loved, for all the good it would do her.

Taran had given no indication that he found anything about her familiar. Perhaps Aphrodite was nothing more than a distant memory. Hope rippled on a quiver through her stomach. If enough time passed, and he noticed any likeness between her and the woman he had spent the night with in the carriage, he might reason that time had colored the memory. She had never meant to hurt him. How could she have known he was nothing like his brother, that she would fall hopelessly in love with him, and that the crushing need for him made life without him unbearable?

Sounds of a rustle to her left caused Caroline to straighten. She gave a small cry at sight of a large figure approaching.

"Lady Blackhall."

Caroline's blood went cold. *Lord William Edmonds.*

He stopped a few feet in front of her. "Forgive me. I did not mean to startle you."

When had he arrived? Her breath caught. Had he followed her into the gardens? Why? Did he want to confront her, extract money or perhaps her charms in exchange for his silence?

"Quite all right, my lord," she said in a steady voice.

"Gardens like these are a dangerous place," he replied. "Would you not agree?"

Panic pushed her wayward pulse into a gallop. *Did he know what she and Taran had done in Lord Forbes' garden?* Had Taran told him about their tryst? The answer hit with a sick turn of her stomach. He knew because he had been watching when Taran had pulled down her bodice and touched her breasts.

"Is everything all right, my lady?" Lord Edmonds' voice broke the silence she hadn't realized stretched out between them.

"Yes," she replied. "Just tired. I believe I will retire for the evening."

"Retire? Come now, your guests will be disappointed should you disappear so early in the evening. All you need is more fresh air." He grasped her elbow and started deeper into the trees.

"Sir." She pulled free and took a step back. "It is enough we are alone, going deeper into the trees is scandalous."

"Caroline—"

She stiffened. "Lady Blackhall."

Her heart skipped a beat when she thought he hesitated before saying in a low, silky voice, "Lady Blackhall, surely you cannot care what these Scots think."

Caroline gasped. "One of these *Scots* is my husband."

"You need not fear him."

"True enough," she replied. "But you might when he discovers you tried to entice me into the gardens."

"Entice you?" The steel in his voice was unmistakable. "I found you here in the gardens."

"I thought I was alone."

"Alone? That can be even more dangerous than an assignation. A lady never knows what sort of knave she might encounter in the darkness."

"The kind my husband will run through with a sword—even if that man is a friend. He has fought duels over far less things than a man accosting his wife."

William's sudden laughter caught her off guard. "Indeed he has. I have never known a man to challenge so many duels and live."

Fear tightened her chest. Was that a threat? Several heartbeats of silence passed and she had the impression he was studying her in the dark.

"Forgive me, madam. For a moment…never mind. I had better get you back inside before Taran sends a search party."

This time, he placed a hand beneath her elbow and gently guided her in the direction of the mansion. They broke from the trees in time to see Taran standing at the balcony railing, silhouetted by the blazing lights of the ballroom. He had stated to turn back towards the doors, then pivoted back in their direction. He stilled, stared for an instant, then hurried down the steps towards them.

The light behind him kept his face in shadow, but there was no mistaking the determined gait in his stride. Over the course of the evening, Caroline had noticed the almost imperceptible way he favored the injured leg. He made no such consideration now, and she cursed her stupidity for seeking refuge in the trees. He was furious, and if anything could trigger his memory of their night in the gardens, it would be the reversal of roles in this garden.

He reached them, but she kept walking. Caroline caught sight of the downturn of his mouth and steadied the sudden wobble in her knees. No matter what, he wouldn't say anything in front of Lord Edmonds. Or would he? And why not? That was what she wanted, wasn't it, to be free of him and the threat that hung over her like an adder ready to strike? It wasn't a matter of *if* he would remember, but *when*.

"Madam," he growled, and grasped her arm, bringing her to a halt.

She winced at the pain that splintered through her injured arm, but he appeared not to notice.

"What are you up to?" he demanded.

Despite his right to ask and despite good sense, ire flared. "Only the worst kind of chicanery, my lord. Nothing short of exactly what you expected." Her heart broke. Once Lord Edmonds revealed her identity, Taran would never believe Aphrodite had gone into the gardens alone. It would seem Lord Edmonds agreed.

Caroline pulled free of his grasp and marched across the grass towards the mansion.

"Lord Taran," she heard William say from where he and Taran still stood, "but you are a fool."

* * * *

Caroline hunkered down in the saddle, pulled her hood up around her face, and rolled with the cadence of the horse's gait. Damn these Highland nights. They were colder than those in England and even more dismal for a ride. Her head throbbed, and she wanted to change from her gown into the warmer riding habit she'd sneaked from the castle. But she had been gone for only half an hour and needed to put distance between herself and Taran before he discovered her absence. Uncle would threaten death once she told him her plan to annul the marriage, but her promise to marry the first man he chose would ensure his cooperation. He would insist she marry quickly, before paternity could be determined for a child born within the next nine months.

Many a nobleman desperate for an heiress would take a bastard child as their own. She envisioned Taran's dark-eyed child cradled in her arms, soft, warm, cooing. The picture vanished and reality hit. A child born too soon would bring an immediate challenge of paternity from Taran. His testimony of their shared hours in bed—as well as in the carriage the night *before* their wedding—would force an annulment, and give him an unimpeachable claim to her, the child, and her fortune. Unless…would he want a child whose mother was a practiced liar? Why not? An heir would secure her fortune for him. Panic shot to the surface with scalding intensity. The hand grasping the reins trembled.

"Calm yourself," she ordered. The chance she was carrying his child was slight, but she would have to wait until her next monthly flux to be certain. But Uncle—damn his soul—would gladly beat her into submission.

Her stomach churned. If she returned to England, Taran would make good on this threat to meet Etherton for that dawn appointment. Taran was nothing, if not consistent. She hadn't thought through her actions. Lord Edmonds' appearance had frightened her, then Taran's anger brought her to the sudden conclusion there was no choice but to leave. *Now.*

Her heart sank. She was caught between the Devil and the sea. Going meant forcing Taran's hand with her uncle. Staying meant living with his disdain for the rest of her life. After enough time—and women—she would grow to hate him.

Could she ease her pain as he would…take lovers? A mental picture flashed of herself, sprawled naked on a strange bed, a faceless lover over her, muscles bunching with the effort of each thrust of the foreign cock driving inside her. Her heart squeezed and a sob broke the near quiet of hooves on moist ground. Any child conceived by Taran and foisted onto another man would suffer the same fate she had. She'd loved one parent and hated the other.

How could she sentence a child to that life? How could she be that hated parent?

Caroline closed her eyes and forced herself to relax into the easy rhythm of the horse. Cool night air dried her tears. If she tricked another man into marriage while carrying Taran's child, she would be guilty of being the worst sort of scheming female. The exact sort of female he would have a right to hate.

Whether she went or stayed, he would discover the truth—that she was Aphrodite, or that she had raced into marriage in hopes of hiding a possible pregnancy, both were equally damning. Caroline opened her eyes and straightened in the saddle. She had to face her husband and confess the truth.

Her words that night in the carriage rose in memory, "*I decided to take something for myself.*" What man would accept that as good cause for cuckolding him—even if *he* were the lover she had taken? None.

She couldn't look in his eyes every day and see his hatred, nor could she watch him return every night from another woman's bed. But once an heir was born that was exactly what she would have to do, for he would keep her as wife, but in name only. Margaret was right. She had flouted the privileges of rank. Now she would pay.

Caroline gently pulled back on the reins. The stallion slowed and she steered him around back the way they'd come. She glanced at the cloud shrouded moon. By the time she reached Strathmore, little more than an hour would have passed. Even if anyone noticed her absence, she could claim she'd simply taken a ride. Taran would be furious, would likely know the truth, but there would be no scandal, no annulment, no life and death drama.

With a deep breath, she urged the horse into a trot. She'd gone fifty feet when a rider shot from within the trees. Caroline cried out and yanked on the stallion's reins, barely missing the rider as she swerved around him. Her horse gave a high pitched whinny when she pulled him in a hard circle.

"Have you lost your mind?" she shouted, then gasped when the man's horse lunged towards her.

She dug her heels into the stallion's ribs. He flew forward as if born to the wind. They would reach the trees in seconds. She steered him to back towards the road. Hooves pounded behind her. She glanced over her shoulder. The rider had turned on an intercepting course. Her heart leapt into her throat. No matter which direction she turned, he would cut her off. She must head for the trees.

Fear sent her already pounding heart into an erratic beat. She fought dizziness and tugged the reins to the right. The stallion veered as commanded. What was she supposed to do once they left the road? The question had barely formed before they were enveloped by the murky darkness of the forest. The horse slowed, unable to keep up the gallop within the trees. Where could she go? *Nowhere.* Her mind went blank.

"Halt!"

The man's harsh command startled Caroline from the paralysis and she yanked the reins again, ducking in time to miss a low-hanging branch. The crunch of leaves and twigs behind her indicated the rider was close. She fought tears. The stallion moved fast, too fast for safety, not fast enough to elude her pursuer. Hysteria threatened to immobilize her again. *Concentrate.* How to escape? If she jumped from the horse and ran, she might out man oeuvre the man—if she managed the jump. But she could never outrun him on foot.

Caroline leaned forward onto the horse's neck and urged the beast forward. If she put herself between the man and the road, she might be able to get out of the trees and outrun him. The stallion swerved to miss a large tree and Caroline discerned the edge of the woods up ahead. She kicked the horse's ribs and he lunged into a gallop as the trees thinned. She ducked a low branch. He leaped over a rock, then another before they broke into the open.

A second later, a blur shot onto the road almost beside her. Caroline hugged the stallion's neck so tightly she could feel the animal's dense sinew contract with each mighty stride. Tension cramped her muscles, but she forced her body to remain relaxed in the saddle, at one with the beast's fluid gait.

Dear God, she hadn't been gone from Strathmore long enough for anyone to miss her. Her attacker could rape her—or worse, kill her—and no one would know before it was too late.

Chapter Twenty

Taran stepped into the stirrup and swung his leg over the saddle, with a nod to William and Huntly, who waited mounted beside him. He kicked the chestnut's ribs. The massive horse jolted forward, the men close behind. Fiona appeared in the stables door.

"Taran," she called as he neared.

He didn't slow.

"For God's sake," she raised a pistol that had been hidden from view at her side, "you will need this."

As they flew through the doorway, Taran recognized the triple barrel flintlock pistol he'd given her for her thirteenth birthday. He had taken the two pistols from his desk drawer, but the triple barrel pistol fired three shots without needing to be reloaded. If he ran into trouble while fetching his wife home, the pistol would be a strong advantage.

His gut clenched at the thought of Caroline alone on the road, and he pulled back on the reins. William and Huntly slowed. He gave them a nod, turned the stallion back, and stopped alongside where Fiona now stood outside the stables. She extended the pistol towards him, barrel pointing into the empty space of night. Their gazes met as he reached for it.

"Do not give me that dark look, Taran. You bullied her just as you did me, and she is no more willing to put up with it than I was."

"Fiona," he began, then stopped. She had hit too close to the truth. For all his sister's faults, she read him well.

That Caroline was willing to seek refuge with the uncle she loathed made Fiona's accusation all the more gut wrenching. Caroline had left no clue as to her destination, but the moment the stable master reported that his boy had seen her slip from the stables on horseback, Taran knew she was headed back to Newcastle—and her uncle. William had confessed his conversation with her. Taran had been furious, but the truth was, it was his anger at finding her in the gardens with William that had chased her away, not William's ridiculous need to meddle.

Taran should have told her he knew she was Aphrodite and been done with it. He told himself she wouldn't be able to face him if she knew he knew, but the truth was he had derived perverse satisfaction out of watching her grapple with the question of when he would puzzle it out. Taran stuffed the pistol into his belt, having already stowed the other pistols in the saddle holsters.

"Any news," he said to Fiona, ignoring a tightening in his chest. "*Anything.* Send word."

"She has been gone no more than a quarter of an hour," Fiona replied. "Barely enough time to get off Blackhall land. And your wife is no fool." *No,* Taran thought. *I am the fool.*

* * * *

Caroline's horse flew across the road, the silent blur of darkness an eerie contrast to the thunder of hooves that barely drowned out the fierce pounding of her heart. She wasn't far from Strathmore. Surely she would encounter someone before the rider caught her? Her horse's warm breath curled into cool night air. The rider drew closer on the left. Caroline gasped and veered right. A powerful arm shot around her waist and yanked. She grabbed for the pommel, but he swerved away from her horse, dragging her from the saddle.

Pain sliced up her injured arm, but her cry was muffled when he mashed her face against his shoulder. Caroline kicked her dangling legs against the horse's ribs. The beast bellowed in unison with the man's curse. She swung a fist, making painful contact with the hard line of his jaw.

"Little bitch," he cursed.

His grip went slack and she dropped to the ground, the impact ricocheting through every fiber of her body. Knife-like pain pierced bone deep into her wound. Her head thudded against moist ground. She cringed against the pain, tried shoving into an upright position, but her head felt heavy as lead. A large figure appeared over her.

She squinted up at the hulking form. "Have you lost your mind? My husband will have your head for this."

He seized her arm and yanked her to her feet.

"Unhand me," she wrenched hard to free her arm.

Nausea twisted her stomach, her knees weakened and her surroundings spun. The man muttered something indistinguishable and swung her into his arms. Bile filled her throat. She shoved at his chest, but her arms seemed to be made of cotton. He started forward, heading for his horse. Panic tightened her throat. If he intended to rape her, why not do the deed here, or maybe drag her into the woods? Caroline batted ineffectually at him, but he only grunted. They reached the horse.

"Fool," she snapped. "My husband is the Viscount of Blackhall. He will kill you." The man gripped the pommel and, her still in his arms, mounted.

He urged the horse into motion. "You are the fool." His cultured voice startled her. This was no average highwayman. "You could not simply marry Blackhall and leave well enough alone," he added.

Caroline froze. She didn't know this man. But he knew her, knew she was newly married. This wasn't opportunistic malice, but rather planned treachery. He pulled up alongside her stallion, grasped the reins, and snapped his horse's reins. They broke into a trot.

The ground beneath her whirled. Caroline fought dizziness. "What did I not *leave well enough alone?*"

"Do not play innocent." He snorted. "You are just like your father."

Her heart went stone cold. *Her father?* Fear of the unknown morphed into an altogether different sort of terror. "What have you to do with my father?" He gave a nasty laugh, but didn't answer.

Anger roared to life. With a sudden burst of energy, she slapped his face. He yanked back on the reins and seized her shoulders. Her injury felt as if it was on fire. He jerked her face so close to his, her stomach roiled with the sweet stench of his breath.

"You want to end up like your father?"

Her heart thundered and her mind reeled, but she brought her face even closer to his. "What have *you* to do with my father?"

His fingers flexed on her shoulders. She winced at the feel of poker hot pain radiating from her injury, but didn't flinch from his gaze.

"When Etherton is finished with you, I pray he gives you to me." He forced her against his chest and urged the horses forward again.

Confusion swirled in a dense fog around her. *Uncle?*

"He will, you know."

Caroline stiffened at sound of the voice that could have belonged to any nobleman of the *ton*.

"He will give you to me."

"My uncle is no fool," she replied.

"True. But he has no conscience."

* * * *

A rider came into view up ahead on the road. Taran glimpsed the dress-clad legs dangling from the right side of the man's horse and recognized the blue velvet of Caroline's gown. The man was holding her in his arms. Rage shot through Taran and he yanked the pistol from his belt as he kicked the horse's ribs with vicious force. The beast gave a piercing whinny and lunged forward. William and Huntly charged at full speed alongside him.

The man twisted and looked in their direction, then faced forward. His horse lurched into a gallop and Caroline cried out. Taran's heart pounded. By God, when he caught the man he would shoot his fingers off one by one for touching what didn't belong to him.

Caroline was wrong to have lied to him, but come what may, she was his. His to torture, tease, make love to…protect. If the man had already raped her—Taran hunkered down close to the horse's neck and willed the animal to go faster. Stride by mighty stride, the beast began to outrun his companions' mounts.

Taran's heart hammered at the enormity of his mistake. He should have told Caroline that he knew she was his Aphrodite. Had he not received some perverse pleasure out of making her pay for that bit of deceit she would be safe at home, in his bed. But, by God, he would get her back.

And when he again had her in his bed…

* * * *

The horse jolted forward. Caroline cried out and threw her arms around her attacker's neck to keep from falling. He leaned forward, pinning her ribs painfully against the pommel. She shoved at him, but he was a leaden weight. She wheezed in a breath. Tears stung the corners of her eyes, pain and fear, forcing the release, yet rage brought on a renewed sense of strength.

Caroline rammed her knee into the man's ribs, as hard as she could. He stiffened, and she kneed him again. His hold slackened and she raked nails across his cheek. He straightened and, even in the dim light, she discerned the furious glitter of the blue eyes illuminated by a burst of moonlight.

She sucked in a breath. The moon disappeared again behind clouds, but there was no mistaking those deep blue eyes. They belonged to the man who had been reading the newspaper in the corner chair when she and Taran had breakfasted at the Cross Keys Inn. He had followed her from inn? Why?

Her mind raced. What had the stable master at Cross Keys Inn said? *"...He did not simply die."* The girth hadn't broken, but had been cut. This man, her captor, had seen her with Liam, had deduced what they'd spoken of. Another fear slammed against her. Had this man harmed Liam? Her mind muddled. This was too much. There were too many questions—the man twisted to look behind him and she caught sight of three riders hard on their heels.

Her heart beat harder. She hadn't heard the other horses over the sound of her attacker's horse's hooves and the roar of blood rushing through her ears. She gulped in air when the animal's movement jolted her lower spine against the pommel. If the man threw her from the horse, she would face three instead of one. But none of those three were her uncle—she choked back a sob—the man who had killed her father.

The pursuing horses' hooves grew louder. Caroline held herself rigid. Tears streamed down her cheeks. If she didn't escape, Taran would never know the truth. Not about her father, her uncle…or the love of his wife. His Aphrodite.

The horse's breathing grew labored. The pursuers continued to gain ground.

"Release me and save yourself," she said.

"Have you heard nothing I've said?"

The man's head dipped. Caroline tensed, then realized he was looking at her. Shadow hid his expression. Yet, he was hesitating. This was her chance.

"Touch me, even at my uncle's command, and my husband will kill you." His hold tightened.

Gunfire pierced the air.

He twisted in the direction of their pursuers, then faced forward. "We will meet again." Caroline gasped as he flung her from the saddle.

* * * *

Taran's heart stopped. Fear twisted soul deep when the man shoved Caroline from his horse.

"No!" Taran bellowed.

She hit the ground. Blinding rage shoved aside the terror. He levelled his pistol on the man. Caroline shifted. Taran jerked his gaze onto her as she rolled to her knees. He swung his gaze back to the man who was riding as if a demon was on his heels—a demon *was* on his heels—then gritted his teeth against the primal urge to empty his pistol into him and stuffed the weapon back into his waistband.

"Get him!" Taran shouted, and veered in Caroline's direction.

William and Huntly sped past.

She stumbled to her feet and took several sideways steps. She glanced in his direction, then unexpectedly shot towards the trees. Taran blinked in confusion. *She doesn't recognize me.* Unreasonable laughter threatened. His wife was running from *him*. She reached the trees and disappeared into them an instant before he leapt from the saddle. Taran reached her in three heartbeats and seized her arm. She whirled, raking nails across his jaw.

He winced. "Caroline!" He yanked her to his chest.

She shoved at him, pounded with small fists against a shoulder. He hugged her close, forcing her to still. The tremble in her body sent another wave of rage through him. If William and Huntly didn't catch the bastard who had tried to take the Viscountess of Blackhall from her own land, he would. Caroline had chastised him over his dawn appointments. There would be no gentleman's score. The man would see his last sunrise. Taran bent and pressed his mouth to her ear. She stiffened, then pushed hard against his chest and began to struggle.

He tightened his hold. "Caroline, tis' me, Taran."

Her head snapped up. She groped his cheek, then trembling fingers slid across his lips. He closed his eyes and drank in the feel of the soft fingertips he'd feared would never touch him again. She sobbed and threw her arms around his neck.

"Shh," he soothed with gentle strokes to her hair. "All is well." But was it? What damage had the man done?

"No" she said through tears. "It is not all right. He…he…" Taran's heart wrenched when she gulped air. "Cross Keys Inn—he followed us…followed me. He killed my father."

Killed her father? "Who?" The highwayman? She wasn't making sense. Her father had been gone nearly three years. Taran kissed her temple. "You are safe now."

She shook her head stubbornly. "No." Ragged breaths racked her body. "He promised to return for me."

"Promised to return—Caroline, love, no highwayman would be foolish enough to return."

"He said we would meet again."

"He will not escape Huntly and Edmonds," Taran insisted.

Caroline shoved at his chest. "My father—" She struggled to break from his hold.

Taran grasped her shoulders. "Calm yourself and tell me what happened."

"I have told you." The irrational note in her voice frightened him. "He—my uncle—they killed my father."

"Etherton? What has he to do with this?" Taran demanded.

"He said I would end up like my father."

"End up like your father?" Taran repeated. Her father had died in a riding accident. Why would Caroline concoct a story of murder? Dread slammed through him. She wasn't capable of such a lie. Etherton, however, was quite capable of murder. Caroline seized Taran's arms. "My God."

"What is it?" he demanded.

Her nails bit into his biceps. "What if he harms you? Taran." She spoke his name in a whisper. "What is one more murder to my uncle?"

"He cannot harm me."

Hysterical laughter broke from her lips. "No? You risk too much."

Taran's gut twisted. She was right. His desire to be right had put her in danger. His pride had put them both in danger. If anything happened to him, she would again be at Etherton's mercy.

Something rustled to their right. Caroline cried out. Taran grasped the butt of his pistol as he jerked his gaze in the direction of the noise. A tree branch moved as shadow in the murk and wind whistled passed. He released the pistol, hand shaking. Caroline tried to pull away.

"It is just the wind," he assured her.

"I cannot lose you," she choked.

Taran crushed her to him. "Caroline."

Reason warred with need. He needed to get her home, safe in their bed where her mind could settle into the understanding he would never again let harm come to her. But he also needed her. *Now.*

"I cannot lose you," she had said. She wanted him. Was it possible she loved him?

Taran's heart thundered as he cradled her head and claimed her lips. Caroline whimpered, and he plunged his tongue into her mouth. His kiss turned frantic, as desperate as her emotions. By God, he had to show her he could protect her…had to show her he couldn't live without her.

"Kiss me," he whispered against her lips.

Lifting on tiptoes, she tightened her fingers on his neck. She leaned into him, breasts crushing into his chest, sending a lightning bolt to his groin. His cock thickened as he rocked into her. What was he doing? How could he take her now…when she was confused and afraid?

Because she was confused and afraid. After he made love to her, he'd make sense of what had happened. Right now, she needed him.

He kissed her harder and Caroline's mouth opened, demanding more. He sank into her sweet taste. His cock, now hard and throbbing, bordered on painful. He needed to drown in her heat, needed to know she was all right, that she was his. Taran stiffened against the fierce need surging through him and broke from the kiss.

"Caroline, I need you."

"Yes." The word spoken in a breathless voice sent a jolt of desire to his groin. She reached between them and covered his cock with a warm palm.

Desire clouded his brain. He ached to take her...to make love to her. Her fingers closed around his erection. She trembled. Or was the tremble rolling through him? He knotted his fingers in her hair and tipped her head back as he devoured her mouth. He drove his tongue inside and searched out hers, connecting, tasting, driving out all thoughts but the woman in his arms. His woman. Holding her tight, he dropped to his knees and pushed her onto the moss covered ground.

"Hurry," she urged.

Caroline drew up her knees, feet flat on the ground, and spread her thighs. She dragged her skirt above her waist. He pulled the pistol from his waist and set it on the ground beside them, then cupped her mound. Moist heat from her pussy warmed his palm. Cream dampened his finger. Gliding along the plump folds, he slipped a finger into her tightened passage.

"More," she begged.

Caroline tugged down her bodice and pulled his head to a nipple. He latched onto the marbled point. Her hips lifted and Taran inserted a second finger, sawing in and out, stretching her. She gripped his wrist and bucked against his hand. Taran drew hard on the nipple as he fucked her with his fingers.

She cried out, as desperate as he was for a physical connection between them. She didn't want finesse and comfort. Rather a hard fuck, and he was just as primed. He ripped open the ties of his breeches, grasped his pulsing rod and settled between her thighs. Her body opened for him and he shafted his cock deep in one fluid plunge.

Caroline wrapped her legs around his hips and rose to meet his thrust. She whimpered and clung to his shoulders. "I am sorry, Taran."

"Shh." He braced his upper body on outstretched arms and poured his emotions into his movements. "You are safe now."

Her back bowed off the ground as he drilled into her again. "And I am yours."

Taran growled and fucked her the way she needed—to feel alive and safe in his arms. Slow, measured glides spiraled into hard intense thrusts. Momentum built. Faster, all the way in until the head of his cock bumped the top of her core and she clutched at his back.

Hot inner walls gloved tight to his shaft.

"Oh." Her channel quivered with her release. "Taran," she gasped on a hard breath. Her body shattered beneath him. She shivered and exquisite pressure milked his cock.

With a guttural groan, Taran slammed into his orgasm. Hot seed erupted from his rod and filled his wife.

Chapter Twenty-One

Taran lay beside Caroline, head resting against the soft swell of her breast, and drank in her scent. His heart pounded and his body, replete in passion, molded to hers.

"You are mine," he whispered against her flesh.

She combed fingers through his sweat-dampened hair. "Only yours."

He pulled back and stared at her shadowed features. "Did he harm you?" Taran gently stroked her jaw.

Caroline covered his hand with hers. "No." Tears slipped from her eyes. "But my father…" She buried her face in his chest.

Taran's heart pounded. He held her close as more tears fell. "I will deal with him. Trust me."

On owl screeched. Caroline flinched. Taran lifted his head to assure her all was well, but the trees rustled, and her head jerked towards the dense scrub to their left. He squinted at where slivers of moonlight shimmered as if alive.

"Someone is there." She scrambled to a sitting position.

Taran grabbed the pistol and shoved to his feet as a large figure emerged from the trees.

Taran pulled back on the hammer. The soft click broke the quiet like a thunderbolt.

The man halted. "I'd feel more welcome if you would lower your weapon."

Taran pointed the pistol skyward and released the hammer. "Damn it, Edmonds, you nearly got yourself shot."

"So I did," the earl replied in a dry tone.

Taran grasped Caroline's arm and pulled her to her feet. "You picked a fine time to make an appearance," he said.

"My apologies," Edmonds replied. "But I assumed you would want to know we caught him."

Caroline's fingers tightened around his.

Taran pulled her against his side and whispered into her ear, "Trust me to keep my promise." No one—least of all Etherton—would hurt her again.

* * * *

Caroline was thankful for the comfort of Taran's arm around her waist as he guided her through the trees, but she wished Lord Edmonds was anywhere but with them. Their last encounter confirmed that he knew her secret. Taran led her around a fallen branch. She needed to confess the truth about Aphrodite, but Lord Edmonds' presence made that impossible. Would Taran see her silence as yet another deceit? A kaleidoscope of butterflies flitted in her stomach. He hadn't *fucked* her in the forest. He'd made love to her, claimed the last of her heart. How much better was reality than the fantasy she had so desperately wanted...created? Truth and fiction were blurring within her mind. Before another opportunity passed, Taran had to know the truth. Tonight, Aphrodite died.

"We tied the bastard's arms and legs, and threw him over his own horse." Lord Edmonds laugh broke into her thoughts. "Young Huntly will deposit him in the dungeon at Strathmore for safekeeping."

Taran's fingers flexed around her waist. His fury was evident. Caroline repressed a shiver and was glad when they broke from the murk of the trees. The horses stood tethered to a nearby branch. Caroline moved to break from Taran's hold, but gave a small cry when he swept her off her feet. He rounded her horse to his chestnut and hoisted her onto the saddle.

She grabbed for the pommel. "My lord! I am capable of riding my own horse."

He swung up behind her. His arm snaked around her waist as he urged the beast into motion. "After tonight's events, I intend to keep you close." He pulled her flush against him. "Very close."

Caroline glanced to the left at Lord Edmonds. The sight of his slightly upturned mouth caused her cheeks to warm. Taking off for England in the dead of night was the single most stupid thing she'd ever done. No. Going to the masque had been even more stupid. No. Lying to Taran took the prize. As if he'd read her mind, his arm tightened as though it was possible to pull her inside his skin.

"My lord," she gave his hand a slap. "You are holding me too tightly. I cannot breathe."

Taran pressed his mouth against her ear. Warm breath against her ear sent a shiver through her.

"I wish to do more than hold you," he said.

She forced back pain. "You will think differently when we arrive home."

Taran shifted the reins from his right to left hand, and she startled at the unexpected weight of the free hand on her leg. He began inching up her skirt. Caroline froze. What was he doing? She clamped a hand over his, but his stronger fingers continued to draw the fabric upward. She darted a glance at Lord Edmonds, but he seemed oblivious to Taran's shenanigans. He wouldn't be once her skirt was above her waist!

"What are you doing?" she hissed under her breath.

He didn't answer and she gave the top of his hand a hard pinch. The skirt continued its slow upward slide. When the hem reached thigh height on her right leg, he slid his hand beneath the skirt and let it fall over his arm. Caroline bit back a gasp at feel of his fingers sliding down her inner thigh. When he brushed the edge of her mound, she squeaked.

"*Sir.*" She started to grab his arm, then realized that would draw attention to his hand between her legs. A finger brushed her curls, then dipped between her folds. "This is improper," she said through gritted teeth.

He gave a low laugh, the sound rich and dark in her ear. "Mayhap I want an improper wife." The finger slid inside her channel. "Tell me, wife," he whispered as he plunged his finger in and out—out and in, "would you prefer a proper husband?"

No, she wanted Taran. Sudden awareness of the erection digging into her back caused her mouth to go dry. He rubbed against her as his thumb began massaging her clit. She couldn't halt the need and rocked into his hand, then back against his cock. Cream slipped from her passage. Teetering on the edge of euphoria, she bit down on her bottom lip and closed her eyes.

"Why would I want a proper wife when I have you, my..."

She snapped open her eyes. My...? Her heart pounded. His finger increased the pressure on her clit. Her channel convulsed around his probing finger. She whimpered as a shuddering orgasm rolled over her. A few final, gentle flicks to her clit brought a second, soft orgasm, then Taran removed his hand and banded his arm around her, pinning her to his chest. She melted against him.

He kissed her temple. "Will you fault me for pleasuring my wife?"

She drew in a shaky breath and tried to form coherent thoughts. "There is no reasoning with a man's sexual appetite."

"Hungry only for you," he interjected.

Strathmore loomed in the distance, ablaze. Apparently, the guests hadn't noticed the hosts' absence. The soirée would go until the wee hours of the morning, but she was too tired to join the merrymaking. A pleasurable drowsiness clouded her brain. She needed to talk to Taran. Aphrodite—she had to tell him the truth about the masque. Caroline snuggled closer to his warmth. Come what may, she would have this moment. He desired her, his wife, not the fantasy woman he'd known for but a few hours.

Caroline froze. *"Why would I want a proper wife when I have you, my..."* He had been about to call her...*Aphrodite.*

The pieces fell into place with a sickening turn of her stomach. *"Perhaps I do not want a proper wife."*

He had purposely *fucked* her in the carriage after leaving the Cross Keys Inn...just as he had fucked Aphrodite.

"You burn as I do. Why resist?"

He had known *then* that she was Aphrodite.

Their first night at Strathmore, when he'd had her on all fours, then the next night in front of the mirror. What man *bedded* his wife in that fashion? A man who knew that the women in his bed had the same appetite he did. A man who knew he'd married a—she closed her eyes—a spoilt woman.

Why hadn't he told her? Why let her agonies? Why rut with her as if there were no tomorrow? Was he trying to produce an heir while he could still stomach being between her legs? She recalled the way his cock pounded into her while they were in the trees, and his finger pleasuring her on the horse. Those were not actions of a man who couldn't stand to touch a woman. No. Those were the actions of a man taking possession of what was his.

Her head reeled. He knew and still wanted her? How was that possible? It was possible, she realized, because he was enjoying letting her squirm in fear—so long as she squirmed on his cock when he so chose. Her pussy tightened at the thought of his rod rubbing the sensitive folds of her sex, teasing, bringing her to a fevered pitch before finally giving her what she wanted.

And there was no denying, she wanted his hard steel as often as he would give it to her. He had demanded she let him do what he would to her on the ride home. What would he do if she demanded he drive his cock into her this very moment—time, place, *and* onlookers be damned? Would he think her wanton for not being satisfied with having him pleasure her twice already today? He wanted Aphrodite. He would have her. On her—his wife's—terms.

Then she would have his head on a platter. No. His bollocks.

* * * *

Caroline preceded Taran into the foyer, with Lord Edmonds behind him. Her desire to drag Taran upstairs as his head thumped on each step had taken a back seat to reality. Despite the party that was still in full swing, Taran was intent upon dealing with the man who had attacked her. First, she had to make sure Taran understood what the man said to her.

"My lord," she began.

The door opened and the boy who stood outside greeting guests, stepped aside for an older man and woman as they entered.

"Blackhall," the man said. "Giles," Taran said. "Madam."

"Edmonds," Giles said. Lord Edmonds nodded.

"What in God's name happened to your jaw?" Giles burst out.

Taran frowned, then touched the spot on his jaw where Caroline had raked her nails across his flesh. He shifted his gaze to hers as he traced the scratch with a finger. "A run in with a wild cat," he said.

"Too close for comfort," the man said.

"Aye," Taran agreed. He cupped Caroline's elbow. "May I present my wife, Caroline Robertson, Viscountess of Blackhall. Caroline, Baron and Baroness Debrett." Caroline offered her hand to the baron, who bowed over it.

Another couple appeared from the hallway leading to the ballroom.

"Ah, Blackhall," the man said. He and the woman stopped beside them.

"My lord," Taran said.

"Where did you get off to?" The man looked at Caroline. "A stolen moment with your bride, perhaps?"

Taran canted his head. "She is hard to resist."

Caroline shot him a narrow-eyed glance, but he seemed not to notice. Not surprising. He didn't realize she'd figured out the truth, and he was intent upon attending to the *guest* in the dungeon. Her pulse jumped. *Father.* Uncle had murdered her father. She tamped down on the rising tide of emotions that threatened tears.

"If you will excuse me," Taran said.

"My lord." Caroline grasped his arm. "I will walk with you." He gave her a thin lipped look, but said nothing.

Caroline nodded to the others. "Forgive us. I must speak with my husband." Before anyone could protest, she started him towards the stairs. He veered left, and she was forced to follow him into a narrow servants' corridor.

"In here," he said, and opened a door on the right.

Taran shoved her through the opening and she found herself in a storage room filled with towels and linens. She turned as he closed the door. His gaze met hers. All at once, she wanted to throw herself into his arms, shout the question, *Why have you lied to me?*

Instead, she began, "The man who attacked me was taking me to my uncle. He said I should have married you and left well enough alone. He must have mistaken my leaving

Strathmore for the decision to find out what happened to my father. "

"You said you recognized him from the Cross Keys Inn," Taran said.

She nodded.

"He did not harm you? I want the truth."

"I am well, my lord." She flushed. "As you know. He was intent upon delivering me to my uncle."

"How did the bastard think he would ride with you all the way to England and without being caught?" Before she could answer, he added, "Because Etherton is not in England. What else did he say?"

"That is all. But there is no doubt he is the man from the Cross Keys Inn, and he somehow knows of my conversation with Liam."

"Liam?" Taran demanded. "Who is Liam?"

"The stable master at the Cross Keys Inn. That morning, I rode with him too see where the race is run."

Anger flashed across his face. "Caroline, I realize you wished to put to rest your father's death, but I would ask that you cease going off alone—or in the company of strangers."

"If I had not *gone off alone*, I would not have learned that my father was murdered."

"And you would not have nearly gotten yourself killed. For all you know, this Liam is part of this scheme."

"He had no reason to tell me of the strange events surrounding my father's death. Had he kept quiet, I would have remained ignorant." Caroline placed a hand on Taran's arm. "My father was murdered," her voice choked, "by my uncle."

Tears at last crashed through the barrier. Taran pulled her close. Her legs gave way and he swung her into his arms. He crossed to a crate and lowered himself onto it, then settled her across his lap. Caroline clung to his neck, her face buried in his chest as he whispered indistinguishable words into her hair. At last, the tears subsided. Her chest remained tight with sorrow, but she could breathe, could think.

Taran grasped her chin and tilted her face upwards. "Will you be all right while I see to the man?"

She straightened. "I will."

But would she be all right once this business was sorted out and she faced her husband with the question of why he had lied to her?

Chapter Twenty-Two

From the corner of her eye, Caroline scanned the ballroom for Taran, but found no sign of him amongst the still too-crowded room. She nodded without hearing the droning of a doting mother, who chattered loudly enough to be heard over the orchestra about her daughter's first season. An hour had passed since Taran had instructed her to entertain their guests, then disappeared into the dungeon. Why would he take so long with her attacker?

The music ended and the woman's voice sliced into Caroline thoughts. "Your husband has promised to attend our next ball. We expect you to accompany him, of course. Oh, but Sophie has three offers already. None that we can consider them, only a baron and two military men. I do not know what possesses them to think they should offer for the hand of an earl's daughter."

Caroline shifted her attention onto the woman. "My husband was a mere military man, until his brother's unfortunate accident."

The proud mama's eyes widened. "Of—of course, but these men cannot compare to your husband."

Caroline lifted a brow. "No?"

"Oh, no, no, they are very young and have yet to prove their mettle. You understand.

We cannot give our Sophie to a man who has yet to make his way in the world." Unfortunately, Taran would agree with the abominable woman.

The woman's eyes shifted past her. Caroline turned to come face to face with her uncle. She couldn't halt the gasp of breath ripped from her chest. Tremors rolled through her belly.

Comprehension flickered in his eyes. "Caroline," he said in a cultured voice that would have fooled anyone into believing he was anything but the murderer he was.

A scream rose to her throat—along with the demand to know what he was doing there. But she knew the answer. His henchman hadn't appeared at the appointed meeting place, so he had come to investigate. And her reaction had told him more than he could have hoped for.

He gave a slight bow of his head to the woman. "If you will excuse us, madam, I must speak with my niece."

The woman's cheeks reddened in obvious fluster at the sultry note in his voice. "Niece? Oh, of course, sir."

The orchestra began playing a minuet, and couples headed for the dance floor. Etherton's fingers closed around Caroline's elbow and he turned her towards the door.

"I am busy." She yanked her arm in an effort to free herself, but his grip tightened on her flesh as he pushed them through the crowd.

He said under his breath, "Make a scene, Niece, and I will slit your husband from sternum to cock."

Caroline lifted her gaze to his. "Blackhall is not the easy mark my father was."

Etherton steered her around three women oblivious to their presence. "So you have met Phillips. What did the fool do?"

She yanked hard and he released her. Caroline halted and locked gazes with him. "Tried to kidnap me."

Her uncle's mouth tightened. "What did you do to deserve that?" She didn't answer and he added, "You are a fool, Caroline."

"Just like my father?"

"You are your father's daughter."

Before she realized his intent, he snaked his arm around her and the barrel of a pistol dug into her side. She glanced down and he opened his coat wide enough to reveal the double flintlock Blunderbuss pressed against her waist. She recognized the pistol as the one that hung over his mantle. He'd kept the weapon as a souvenir from his days as privateer. He had spoken of how the gun was particularly useful in warding off pirates trying to board a ship. Her heart rate accelerated. What had he loaded it with, shot, nails, glass? The pistol fired anything with the potential to harm the target—and was especially effective in at close range. Even if she survived being shot, the doctor could never retrieve from her body all the pieces of whatever he had loaded into the barrel. She would die of infection, if she didn't bleed to death first.

Caroline looked up at him. "There are two hundred witnesses present."

"The report of the pistol will cause chaos," he answered without hesitation. "You will be dead, and I will be forced to shoot at least two others in order to ensure my escape." She started to say the pistol fired only one shot, but he cut in, "I never carry only one weapon.

Where is your husband?"

Panic shoved forward. If he discovered Taran was in the dungeon, he could dispose of her first, then surprise him and Lord Edmonds, and kill them.

"He has taken your man to the sheriff."

Her uncle cast her a condescending look. "Blackhall owns the sheriff. He will dispense justice, then inform the sheriff of the verdict and sentence after the fact." Etherton glanced around the crowded room. "I imagine there is a tolerable dungeon in this castle. Likely accessed from the kitchen or perhaps beneath one of the towers."

She startled. How many dungeons had the infamous Peiter Everston visited? How many had he been imprisoned in? She had never been in a dungeon, hadn't thought to ask Taran where the dungeon was. How long had he been gone now, one hour and fifteen minutes? Perhaps he was no longer in the dungeon. It would be like him to leave her in the dark while he discussed matters with Lord Edmonds. For once, she would be glad his male mind didn't take into account her female sensibilities.

Etherton started them towards the exit. "Even a peep, Caroline, and I will shoot you, then find your husband and kill him."

"You will do that anyway," she replied.

"I may let you live," he replied.

He skirted the dancers and, a moment later, they reached the door. He led her down the hallway, deeper into the castle's interior. Here was her chance. Caroline whirled. The back of his hand came across her mouth with such intensity stars streaked across her vision. He seized her shoulders. Footsteps sounded in the corridor up ahead. He turned in the direction of the sound. Hope rushed to the surface.

"I will shoot whoever that is," he hissed, and shoved the pistol into his waistband.

Caroline tried to shake the grey fog from her brain. She tripped, and he plastered her to his side, forcing her to walk alongside him. The approaching footsteps were too soft to be Taran's. Patterson appeared from around the bend. Her heart fell. The old butler would be of no help, and Uncle would make good on his threat.

Patterson stopped in front of them and frowned. "Is something wrong, my lady?"

She recalled Etherton's slap to her face. Was her cheek bruising? Her head throbbed with every beat of her heart.

"My niece is overwrought," her uncle said. "She wishes to see her husband."

Patterson's eyes shifted to him. He seemed uncertain, then gave a slight, deferential incline of his head. "His lordship is still indisposed." Etherton's fingers dug into her waist.

"Yes, Patterson," she burst out. He blinked in surprise and she gave a quick smile. "I am growing concerned. Please, where is the, er—" Her mind froze. Did Patterson know what Taran was up to? Yes, he must, for the way he said *indisposed* indicating he hadn't wanted to reveal his master's whereabouts. "The dungeon, Patterson. He told me that was where he was going."

"The west tower, my lady," he replied, his face expressionless. "The entrance is in the alcove directly below the tower. I can show you the way." He started to turn.

"No need," her uncle said. "I saw the tower when I arrived. This corridor will lead there if we keep the left. Am I correct?"

"Indeed, sir."

Etherton nodded. "I will see to my niece. I wish to speak with her husband as well."

"As you wish." Patterson bowed and continued on his way towards the ballroom.

Uncle started forward. She had to stop him, slow him down somehow, anything to buy Taran time. She also had to know…

"Why did you kill my father?"

His head turned in her direction. "Why do you think?"

Her heart pounded. "What did he know?" He faced forward.

"Bastard," she hissed.

Caroline twisted in his grasp. He yanked her feet off the carpet and lengthened his stride. Tears sprang to her eyes with the sudden realization that he didn't intend to kill her and leave her body hidden in some alcove as she'd thought. Instead, he meant to use her against Taran. She began to thrash. Pain ricocheted inside her skull, but she kicked and raked her nails across his cheek.

"God damn you," he cursed, and backhanded her again, this time harder than the last.

Ringing filled her ears. She felt as if she was going to slip from his grasp. But then he slung her over his shoulder like a sack of potatoes. She gasped for air. They turned a bend and, a moment later, he pushed through a door into a stone passageway. He grabbed the sconce hanging on the wall to the right and continued forward. They passed a window facing the inner courtyard. He pushed through another door and she glimpsed an arched entryway to the left.

Nausea pitched her stomach as he made his way down a narrow staircase. At the bottom, he slipped the sconce into a holder, then lowered her to her feet. Her surroundings swam and she clutched at thin air. He grabbed her waist and opened the door to a well-lit stone corridor. Caroline drew in a breath to scream. He clamped his free hand over her mouth and wrenched her head back against his chest. She grabbed his hand out of reflex, then froze when he pressed his mouth against her ear.

"I will empty my handgun into your skull, then fill your husband full of what I have in the Blunderbuss. He will slowly bleed to death. Very painful, I am told."

She still gripped the fingers clamped over her mouth as he crept towards the T at the end of the hallway. Her mind raced. He planned to surprise Taran and threaten him with the fact he held a gun to her head. Etherton had yet to pull the Blunderbuss from his waistband, and he didn't know Lord Edmonds was with Taran. If she screamed, Taran and Lord Edmonds would be alerted that something was wrong. Was that a better advantage than showing up, or would Etherton shoot them when they raced from whatever cell they were in once they heard her scream? What would Uncle do if Taran wasn't in the dungeon?

Indecision mingled with fear. What would give Taran the best chance of survival? They reached the T and Uncle leaned forward. Five feet to the left, another corridor ran parallel with the one where they stood. He turned left, then left again down the hallway. If she bit down on his fingers and yanked with all her might, she had a chance of dislodging the hand. A wrought iron gate barred an empty cell on the right. A faint murmur sounded from another bend up ahead. Her heart sped up. She couldn't tell if Taran or Lord Edmonds was speaking. *Please, Lord Edmonds, keep quiet.*

Uncle crept to the next corridor and peered around the corner. A grated iron door stood open to the middle cell.

"I will ask one more time," Taran's voice was soft, but lethal.

Tears burned Caroline's eyes. Her heart pounded so loudly she wondered that he couldn't hear it.

"Where were you to meet Etherton?"

Her uncle's low laugh sounded in her ear.

A slurred response followed from the man in the room.

Blood roared in Caroline's ears. Had Taran brought a weapon with him? She recalled the pistol he'd pointed at Lord Edmonds when he'd come upon them in the trees. He might have the weapon with him. Would he keep it close? How would she save him? If Lord Edmonds was with Taran, Uncle would have to keep the gun on her in order to manipulate the two men.

Caroline bit down on her uncle's hand—hard. He stiffened. She ground her teeth against the thick finger. Blood spurted across her tongue. She gagged. Then screamed. He yanked his hand from her mouth. A dark curse burst from him in unison with heavy footfalls on stone. Uncle took two steps backwards and stopped, his back against the wall, and lifted the Blunderbuss to her temple.

Taran shot into the corridor, then came to a skidding halt thirty feet from them, a pistol aimed at them. Caroline darted a glance at the open door. Where was Lord Edmonds? A sob lodged in her throat. She had counted on the viscount being there. Etherton would be far more nervous at facing two men, instead of one.

"Drop it," Etherton ordered.

Taran's gaze flicked from the gun at her head to her face, and she read that he was familiar with the weapon.

"Drop it," her uncle again ordered.

Taran tossed the weapon down. It hit the stone with a clatter and skidded several feet towards them.

His eyes shifted behind her. "Come to finish the job yourself, Etherton?"

"If you had taken your wife in hand, she would be safely in your bed, instead of here."

Taran's gaze remained neutral, but Caroline sensed he didn't disagree. Hysteria blurred her vision. She clawed at the hand banded around her waist. Her left elbow bumped something hard at Uncle's waist.

"What do you want?" Taran demanded.

Caroline froze. Was that a second pistol in her uncle's waistband?

"It is no longer a matter of what I want," he replied, "but what I need."

Taran nodded. "And you need me dead. Caroline, as well."

"Caroline can live."

Taran's gaze didn't break from his. "So long as she remains in a laudanum-induced state?"

"She will serve a purpose."

Her mind raced. That was a second pistol stuffed inside the waistband. He surely had a third pistol in his boot. But he would never be able to get to it before Taran was upon him. If she grabbed the pistol from his waistband, he would be forced to fire the weapon at her temple—if she didn't get a round off into his belly first. Either way, Taran would be safe.

"Patterson knows you are here," she blurted. "He will inform the sheriff."

"Good," Etherton replied. "That will aid the story that I fought to save you both from your attacker."

Her heart thundered. He had yet to cock the pistol. How fast was he? Faster than her.

But that was of no consequence. She thrashed. Taran took a step forward.

Etherton dug the pistol into her temple. "Halt."

Caroline yanked the gun from his waistband as she rammed her other fisted hand into the arm holding the gun to her head. The gun jostled away from her. She pulled back the hammer and jammed the barrel against his side.

Taran lunged.

She fired.

The report exploded in her ears. Warm liquid bathed her side. Etherton stretched his hand forward, the pistol pointed at Taran.

"No!" she screamed.

Taran halted.

Time seemed to slow as her uncle's thumb pulled back the hammer and she reached for his arm. Uncle shoved her. She propelled forward and hit the stone, shoulder first. Pain radiated up her arm, blood stained the bandage covering her injury. She dropped to her knees.

Another shot sounded. Confusion rolled over Caroline. Etherton stiffened. The pistol went limp in his hand, then clattered to the stone not far from Taran's gun. Etherton slumped against the wall, then crashed to the floor.

Caroline gasped at sight of Patterson, only the half of his body that pointed the revolver visible around the edge of the wall at the end of the hallway. His arm dropped to his side and he stepped into full view.

His eyes shifted to Taran. "So sorry, my lord, Lady Albrey waylaid me and I had to brandish this revolver in order to get the woman to let me pass."

Caroline burst into tears.

* * * *

Taran pulled Caroline into his arms.

Footsteps pounded around the bend and Edmonds shot into the hallway as Taran started down the corridor.

William came to a sudden halt. "My God."

"Aye," Taran said. "See to our guest. And Patterson," he added as he neared the butler, "call for the sheriff."

Caroline clung to his neck and he held her trembling body close as he kept to the servants' hallways until they'd reached his bedchambers. Taran lowered her feet to the carpet. She stood motionless as he unbuttoned her dress, then stripped her of the shift. Anger twisted his gut at sight of the blood that had seeped through the dress. Etherton would have splattered her brains across the floor if necessary. Taran urged her between the covers, then stripped off his clothes, and slipped in beside her. When he pulled her into his arms, the dam broke, and she cried into his chest. He forced his shaking hands steady and stroked her hair.

He would never be able to wipe from his mind the picture of that pistol pressed against her temple. Taran closed his eyes. He'd almost lost her a second time. Was ever a bigger fool born than him? It hadn't occurred to him Etherton would chance coming to Strathmore. He hugged her tighter. She buried her head in his neck. The quick beat of her heart reminded him she was alive and well, but she had intended to sacrifice herself for him. His chest tightened. How would he ever let her out of his sight again? "You knew all along I was Aphrodite." Taran froze at Caroline's words.

"Do not deny it, Taran."

Emotion flooded him. He wanted to laugh. Leave it to a woman to try and save a man, then take him to task afterwards.

"Aye," he replied.

"You enjoyed watching me twist in the wind."

"Aye."

"This is all your fault."

All amusement vanished. "Aye."

A moment of silence, then, "Is he dead?"

"Aye."

Caroline leaned her head back and levelled her gaze on him. He traced a finger down her tear stained cheek.

"*Aye?*" she said. "Is that all you can say?"

He blinked, then nodded. "Aye. And that I love you."

Her eyes narrowed. "Your Aphrodite?"

He rolled onto her. "Nay. My Caroline."

Her mouth parted in surprise, and he covered her lips with his.

Chapter Twenty-Three

The door to the drawing room opened and Caroline looked up from her needlework.

Taran entered. She smiled as he crossed to the couch and sat beside her.

"What did you learn? Did the captain have any news?"

His brow rose. "Not even a kiss?"

She pressed a quick kiss to his lips. "Well?"

"Married but two months and already you tire of me."

"I will be an attentive wife once you have told me what you learned."

He gave a long suffering sigh. "In June 1787, the British Royal Navy frigate *Lady Victory* gave chase to a Spanish frigate. They boxed the Spaniards into a cove off the coast of Venezuela only to find themselves flanked by another ship."

"A trap," Caroline said.

Taran nodded. "It was foolish on the part of the captain to have chased the Spaniards, for his ship was laden with bounty from three other raids by privateers." Taran paused. "One of them was Phillip Etherton."

Dread began to unfurl through Caroline.

"As always," he went on, "there was an inquiry. But the single witness who survived the attack mysteriously disappeared."

Caroline thought back to the stories she'd grown up hearing. "Pirates fly false colors to lure their victims into security." Taran nodded.

"My God," she breathed. "My uncle was a traitor." She stared at Taran. "He sunk one of his country's own ships."

"There is no proof," Taran replied. "But I wager your father knew something—or Etherton believed he did."

"After all these years?" she asked. "Why wait so long to expose him?" Before Taran could answer, she added, "My father always seemed completely ignorant of the pirate Peiter Everston. I—" She choked back a sob, "I loved him, but, on this score, I thought he was a fool." Not only on this score, she realized, but with her mother as well. He tolerated so much from her. A thought struck. "Oh, Taran, is it possible he knew all along and played the fool?" Taran took her hand in his. "I did not know him."

She nodded, but read the lie in his eyes. Taran didn't know her father, but the truth would have been obvious to a blind man. Her father had known all along who Peiter Everston was, but he'd played the fool to ensure the safety of the women he loved. Had her mother known? How could she have not? Caroline closed her eyes against the pain that suffocated her. She had seen the lengths to which Etherton would go. What threat had he made to guarantee his brother-in-law's compliance? No threat, perhaps her father simply knew.

Caroline released a sigh and looked at Taran. "My father was a good man."

"Aye."

She grimaced. "Is that all you can say?"

He shook his head and took the needlework from her hands. "Such a dutiful and proper wife."

"And you would prefer an improper wife?" She lifted her mouth in a coy smile as she traced a finger across his lips.

"Aye."

"I have yet to forgive you for allowing me to stew."

"Ah, yes," he replied. "It is all my fault."

She nodded. "But I am willing to let you make amends."

His eyes darkened. "How long do you say it will take?"

She shifted her gaze from his mouth. "Forty or fifty years."

###

From the Authors

We loved writing Taran and Caroline's story. Sometimes, love is found in the most obvious places—and sometimes it takes a little urging for a man to recognize the right woman when she's right under his nose. But where would be the fun if he caught on too easily? For your reading enjoyment, we have included a sizzling excerpt from our erotic paranormal *Born Into Fire*.

Enjoy!!

KyAnn and Tarah

BORN INTO FIRE

She's fire…he's air. Together, their power is hot enough to melt steel.

Air Element, Erion, aches to feel the heat of Kenna's emerging fire. However, merging with her while she is on the cusp of transformation risks enslaving her forever. But when a male Fire Element hunts Kenna in order to harness her power, Erion must break his vow not to join with another Element. The only way to protect her is to merge his wind with her fire.

Aspiring glassblower Kenna Lang is on the rise. A chance meeting with Erion ignites an attraction hotter than her glass furnace. Drawn together in an erotic joining she can't prevent, they become more than human, and Kenna is born into fire.

Now her world is going up in flames.

Neither are prepared for the emotions awakened by their union…or the immortal battle waged against their kind. When Kenna disappears, Erion seeks out those he knows are responsible—their race's sworn enemy, the shape-shifting dragons known as Drakaura.

In the Beginning…

Eons ago, a mighty wizard risked the peril of the void that is Ghen and drew forth the primal elements. He merged element and man to create the Ryalda, champions ordained to guard the world of form. But the emptiness beyond battled back. The warrior heroes fought, but in the end, were consumed by the formless Ghen.

Now, Shadows bleed into the world.

And Sentinels watch…to maintain balance…and defend against the Elements.

Chapter One

A breeze, that was him, fluttered the ivory curtains. Moonlight streamed through the open window, outlining the sleeping form beneath the sheet covering the queen-size bed. He hovered. Why had he answered the call of her element? He had no right. Anguish wrenched through him. Long ago, he'd answered the call of another Element, and she'd paid with her life. The memory—the pain—didn't stop the rake of his gaze down the cotton sheet that revealed every lush curve of the sleeping woman's body. Desire streaked through him. The fabric ruffled in response to his command, then slid downward.

He sucked in a harsh breath. Softly molded shoulders gave way to rounded breasts tipped with quarter-size areolas then a flat tummy and trim thighs led to long, toned legs. An unexpected vision surfaced of those legs wrapped tight around his waist while he thrust into her. The swirling vortex that was his core leaped into a furious dance.

Go, his mind commanded.

Fluid veins of amber light erupted beneath her skin. He stood frozen, her fire a drag on his wind that lay open the ache buried deep within.

Leave, came a second panicked admonition.

She inhaled.

Realization hit. *Too late*.

She drew him deep into her lungs. Warmth infused him in a heady rush. He struggled in desperation to escape the current, but each beat of her heart thrummed through him, echoing in his mind in a thunderous rhythm. The flow of blood through her veins washed over him like a thick velvet river.

And he gave in.

As if sensing him, she hesitated, then breathed him out on a shaky exhale. He shuddered, the loss tearing a howl of fury from him.

"*More.*" She wanted more. He needed more.

As wind, he lay beyond tangible comprehension, a cool breeze, nothing more. He could take a small piece and not imprint on her. This woman would be born into fire—without him.

In one decadent breath, he draped himself over her, *touched* all of her. Her heated skin cooled. No mortal man could experience her as he did. No mortal man could touch her as he could. He chilled the air over her nipples, then watched as they peaked, and felt them pucker. Commanding a gentle breeze, he caressed her contours, fitting his shape to hers.

She moaned. Excitement rocketed through him, and the current within him swirled. She shivered. He hesitated. Even a second too long would leave her with a sense of familiarity. He must leave or risk revealing himself—or worse, bonding.

Heat pooled between her legs. Every fiber of his being screamed, *go*. Yet, as if anchored by unseen chains, he remained motionless, unable to tear his eyes from the sight of energy that built in her erogenous points.

Only a moment, his heart urged. A mere whisper of her essence to ease the emptiness. Then he would leave.

He focused hot pressure, the wispy kiss of an Air Element, to her neck. As he trailed the pressure to her nipple, he turned the air icy. She bowed off the bed. He filled the space behind her arched back, curving up toward her neck and down across her rounded buttocks. Her breath came in quick pants, frosting the air—*him*.

Frigid pressure tightened her nipples to erect peaks. He swirled air around the tips. She collapsed, thrashing on the pillow, and covered her breasts as if to ease the aching cold he created. Her hands heated until they glowed. *The fire within her.*

The glow spread up her arms, radiated out from her torso, and emitted a scorching heat that heightened his frequency to a fevered pitch. Fire.

Fiera. His heart constricted. He had no right to name her. He would not be the one to bring her into being. She would seek another. But he would have this memory.

Air spun around her body. Faster, hotter. The friction against her skin hardened him. His core grew heavier. *"Spread your legs."* The unbidden words echoed in his mind, but the unspoken command carried on the current of his breath and caressed her ear. She pulled her legs up and, knees bent, opened wide for him. He glided downward until his breath disturbed the auburn curls covering her mound.

The scent of her arousal penetrated his core. A need to shift into human form and taste her sweet nectar pooled energy into his center. He moved upward, concentrating until he held the gossamer form of a man, and settled vaporous hips between her thighs. In air form, he couldn't slip his tongue into the sweet recesses of her mouth, couldn't spread her damp folds, or plunge his rigid cock into her forbidden depths. But he could feel the heat.

"*Open for me,*" he coaxed.

Fiera moaned and reached between her legs. With a delicate stroke, she traced the seam of her pussy. He vibrated the air over her clit. A soft smile tilted her lips. Satisfaction rippled through him. She wanted more.

In a cyclone of current, he swirled around her. Strands of her flaming red hair danced in the static-filled air. Her peach-hued nipples puckered, her chest rose and fell with each deep breath she took.

More energy. Faster wind. *Yes.* Her hips rose off the bed, and she plunged a finger inside her channel. When she fit a second finger into her drenched opening and thrust deep, energy shot in a jagged pattern from his core to her channel. She cried out. Her eyelids fluttered, but she didn't wake.

With her free hand, she touched her clit and thrust her hips wildly against an unseen force. *Him.* Gyrating her hips, bucking and arching, she fucked him, but used her own fingers. His mind whirled with her energy. It was as if *she* swirled around him.

The other female Air Element, the one who now haunted him, had engulfed him as Fiera did. He forced the anguished recollection into the fury of energy. Fiera convulsed in pleasure. He envisioned thrusting his solid cock into her channel, her sheathing him with breath-stealing strength. He clenched against the intensifying need to shift into human form, centered his energy on the torrential wave of her release, and absorbed the fragrance of her cream as she cried out.

Chapter Two

Kenna Lang jackknifed upright in bed. Wind blasted over her fevered flesh. Her pussy pulsed with sudden emptiness, and she dragged in breath with a final wave of orgasm. Holy shit. *A dream.*

She jammed her eyes shut and mentally clutched at the receding edges of the erotic vision. A barely distinguishable whirlpooling shadow moved against the darkness within her mind, then evaporated. An answering echo of pleasure clenched her pussy.

Wind fluttered over her, cooling the sweat-dampened hair at her temples, soothing her rampant heartbeat. She opened her eyes and stood. The room seemed to shift. She grabbed the edge of her grandmother's armoire and inhaled a steadying breath. Curtains billowed at the window opposite the bed, then stilled. Rain and wooded scents lingered in the air…as did the heavy aroma of sex.

She took two steps, scooped up the robe that had fallen from the bed, and slipped her arms inside the long sleeves as she crossed to the window. Cool air washed over her heated skin when she drew near, and she let the robe fall open. Goose bumps chased across her arms. Despite the chill—needing the chill—she leaned into the brisk air and gazed heavenward. Stars sparkled in the cloudless night sky over Lakewood, Colorado. A hawk screeched in the distance. A storm had blown straight through while she slept.

Kenna faced the bed. The sheet lay in a tangled mess across the mattress. She'd flung her pillow clear to the door. The chaos explained the uneasy feeling in her belly. She'd obviously had a fitful night. But the dream, the sexual energy, had been so real. Given the hard orgasm that woke her, she should be feeling ready to take on the world. Yet sexual tension still hummed through her like a live wire. Another wave of shivers raced across her flesh. She'd come, but the experience had been unlike any she'd ever dreamed—or imagined. She hadn't been that aroused…ever.

She grimaced. The pent-up anxiety over her upcoming show must have channeled into emotional chaos. Just thinking about the show started the gnawing in her stomach that had begun when Michael Laird first contacted her three months ago. This was her first major glass art exhibit—and it was now only two weeks away. Half a dozen crates had been shipped to the gallery. Several in-progress pieces lined a shelf in her workshop, but it was the special not-yet-started project that had her nervous. As a child, she'd envisioned the piece and, good or bad, the dragons she called Drakaura would define her as an artist.

A nervous quiver radiated through her. Marshall Thomas would be attending the show. She hadn't seen her mentor since showing him her first attempt at Drakaura two years ago. He'd accused her of copying William Gudentrath, and she'd walked out without a word.

She understood the risk of blowing dragons in glass. William's dragon glass goblets were world renowned. But he worked in muted copper, dark wine, ivory, and soft green, whereas her Drakaura was vivid greens, reds, and oranges. Still, Marshall's accusation had played into the very fear that her critics fueled: the hidden passion within the glass was missing. What would they think of her dragon theme? What would Marshal think of it?

He had read about her upcoming show. His congratulations had included an offer to fly in from Texas and help out. Sadness tugged at her. She missed him, the way he brought the art to life for her, his patient teaching. But was she ready to see him?

Kenna shrugged off the anxiety, changed into faded jeans and a T-shirt, then started down the stairs of the two-story Colonial that had once been her grandmother's home. The third step creaked. Kenna smiled. The seventh step would grumble next, then the eighth, and lastly, the twelfth.

Many found the groans of an old house creepy, but she knew the sounds began and ended with the wind.

Ten minutes later, a hot cup of coffee in hand, Kenna walked the few feet from the house to her garage turned workshop. She slipped the key in the lock and opened the door. A breeze wafted past as she entered.

Her heart always jump-started at the sight of the three glassblowing furnaces that dominated the workshop. A massive five-by-six freestanding crucible furnace to melt the glass sat near the farthest right-hand corner. To its right, along the garage doors, a six-by-four front-loading annealing oven used to slowly cool the glass sat on steel legs, while a pipe-shaped insulated firebrick glory hole furnace used to reheat the glass lay beside it. Five years of eating alphabet soup, bread, and skim milk had been worth it.

Nearer the middle of the room sat the marver, the steel table where she worked the glass. Two parallel rails held the pipe while she worked with the glass to form the skin. Blown glass filled the shelves lining all four walls.

Kenna closed and locked the door, then crossed to the workbench and set her coffee and keys on the tabletop. After lighting the glory hole furnace, she stood, her gaze on the far shelf where she'd tucked away the piece she'd named *Twilight Glide*: a solid fire-colored base with a translucent yellow half-moon in the middle. A swirling crimson stem rose from the moon, and a sleek dragon, its dark green wings spread, soared above. Not quite Drakaura, but nothing like Gudentrath. This new piece was to follow the others already shipped to the Michael Laird Gallery for the *Emergence of the Dragon* exhibit.

The yet uncreated centerpiece rose in memory as if stepping from the furnace fully formed. A tremor of familiar excitement fluttered her heart. Dreams as a child had conjured feathered dragons that guarded her in the deepest part of the night. Their memory outlived even Santa Claus and the Tooth Fairy and metamorphosed into the *Drakaura*, sensual creatures that flowed in harmony with the glass. A soft breeze skimmed across her arms.

Kenna smiled.

Today was the day.

KyAnn Waters

KyAnn Waters is a multi-published, award winning author. She lives in Utah with her husband, two children, and two dogs. She spends her days writing and her evenings with her family. She enjoys sporting events on the television, thrillers on the big screen, and hot scenes between the pages of her books.

To Wed a Wanton Woman
To Bed a Montana Man
Betrayed Vows
To Serve and Protect

Connect with KyAnn
www.kyannwaters.com
https://www.facebook.com/KyAnnWaters
https://twitter.com/KyAnnWaters

Tarah Scott

Award winning published author Tarah Scott cut her teeth on authors such as, Georgette Heyer, Zane Grey, and Amanda Quick. She writes classical romance, suspense, horror, and mainstream. Tarah grew up in Texas, and currently resides in Westchester County, New York with her daughter.

To Tame a Highland Earl by Tarah Scott
My Highland Lord
A Knight of Passion
Lord Keeper

Connect with Tarah
tscott@tarahscott.com
https://www.facebook.com/groups/TarahScott/
www.tarahscott.com

Printed in Great Britain
by Amazon